The Necklace M

Bailie Lawson

Chapter 1

Why is there a photo of me in a foreign newspaper?

Oriana stared in shock. "It is me!"

Rob said, "what is it?" and turned his head to see where she was staring. He only saw a man sitting at the next table, a newspaper open, hiding his face. He looked back at Oriana and repeated, "What is it? What is the matter?"

"Don't you see?" Oriana gasped. "That photo in the paper! It is me!"

Rob turned to look again. Luckily, the man reading the paper was conveniently hidden behind it so they could both stare openly, unobserved by him.

"It is a photo of a little girl," Rob said, puzzled.

"Yes, but it is me as a child!" Oriana exclaimed. "It is exactly like photos of me as a child. Except for the hair. It's longer in the photo."

"But it couldn't be you," Rob pointed out reasonably. "Maybe it's a child who looks very like you used to look."

"Don't you see the resemblance?"

Rob's blank expression told her he hadn't.

The waiter approached unbidden and poured more coffee for them.

Oriana gestured towards the paper. "Is there a place to get that paper?" Oriana asked, mixing the few words of Portuguese she knew with English.

"We just want to see the photo of the child," Rob explained.

"There is a copy in the restaurant if you just want to see the picture. I will get it, yes?" the waiter responded in excellent English.

He returned in a moment with the paper folded so that the girl's photo was prominently displayed.

"Do you know about this case?" he asked. "Such a terrible thing! A little girl was kidnapped outside her home and never found."

3

But Oriana was staring at the photo, transfixed. Up close, the resemblance was even more striking. This was her as a child!

The waiter appeared not to have noticed the resemblance between Oriana and the child in the paper and was responding to Rob's question.

"I can't read Portuguese," Rob was explaining. "Could you tell us what the article says?"

The waiter translated. *On June 29, 1999, five-year-old Maria Alfonso Taglia disappeared from outside her family's restaurant where she had been playing with her young cousin. Extensive searches and questioning revealed no clues about where she had gone. It was suspected at the time that she had been abducted. The family, owners of the popular Carbonara Seafood Restaurant, never gave up hope and continue to believe that Maria is alive. As the twentieth anniversary of Maria's kidnapping approached, the family appealed to the police and to the Lisbon newspapers. And so, today, on the twentieth anniversary of Maria's disappearance, we are republishing the story. The case has been reopened by detective Diego Garcia, who declines to say if they have new leads.*

The waiter put the paper down on the table, looking solemn. "It is so sad, but twenty years have passed. It happened exactly twenty years ago today. What can they find now? I know the family. They are nice people. It is still so difficult for them. They say they will never give up."

Several people had taken seats at the surrounding tables, and the waiter went to attend to them, leaving the newspaper on the table where Oriana continued to stare at the picture with a mixture of shock and fascination. Her own eyes stared back at her. She knew it with a certainty that was disturbing.

Rob said mildly, "it couldn't be you, but I can see a resemblance."

Oriana suspected Rob was being agreeable and didn't really see the resemblance.

"Do you remember those photos of me from childhood?" Oriana asked. "I wish I had them with me."

"I remember you showed me photos, but it was so long ago. This picture doesn't look familiar, but then I haven't seen your photos for a while," Rob admitted.

"Look at the eyes, Rob," Oriana entreated. "Now look at my eyes."

Rob dutifully complied, but clearly did not see in the photo what Oriana saw. It was frustrating.

"This picture looks familiar. I've seen it before," she said.

"They say everyone has a double," Rob said. "It must be unsettling to find your double is a missing child."

"I want to get a copy of the paper to take home with me," Oriana said. "I want you to see this photo next to the photos I have from childhood. Then you will see what I see. I know my face has changed its shape over the years. It was rounder when I was a child. I understand why you don't see the resemblance to this photo when you look at me."

Rob nodded. "Yes, maybe I'll see the similarity then." Clearly, he thought she was overreacting.

Oriana continued. "This child is five or went missing when she was five. The photo might have been taken when she was even younger. I don't remember any photos of me from when I was five or younger. The photos I have were all taken after we arrived in New Falls. I was seven then. I wonder if my mother has any photos from when I was younger."

"She must have, surely," Rob said. "You are her only child. People take countless photos of first babies."

"Why did I never see them? She never wants to talk about those years before New Falls. I don't even know where we lived. I know nothing about her life before New Falls."

"You're not seriously suggesting you are this missing child?" Rob asked, a smile on his face but something like concern or worry in his eyes.

"No. That would be crazy. But why is this photo in this paper? And why does she refuse to tell me about my father?"

Rob had heard this before. Now he said what he had said in the past, and what he believed. "You have a right to know about your father. You don't know if he is alive or dead. Even if she thinks he is a horrible person, you have a right to know the details."

"Well, you know I have tried. She just clams up, retreats into some private world. When I was in my early teens, she promised to tell me when I was eighteen."

"But she never did."

"By then I was away at college, caught up in my new life. I didn't bring it up. I hadn't lost interest exactly. It was more that I didn't want her to clam up on my visits home. She would become distant then. I didn't want that."

"But now we are married. And we plan to have children in the future. Maybe you can convince her you need to know about him, if only for medical reasons."

"I'll try again when we get home."

Oriana and Rob had been sipping coffee at the small outdoor restaurant around the corner from their hotel when she became startled by the newspaper with the picture of the little girl. It was a warm late June morning in Lisbon and early, only seven am, but they were still on Eastern Standard Time, still a little jet-lagged and had been awake since five. They had arrived in Lisbon only two days before to start their European vacation.

They were married a year and hadn't had a real honeymoon, just a long weekend in Bermuda after the wedding. This was their long-awaited honeymoon now and, so far, it was interesting, romantic, exciting - everything Oriana could have wished.

Last night, they had had a romantic dinner followed by passionate lovemaking in their hotel room. Life was good. They had been sipping the excellent strong coffee, Oriana smiling happily at Rob over her coffee mug, while he raised his eyebrows mischievously at her.

Oriana had glanced idly toward the only other occupant of the small patio, wondering if he was a tourist or perhaps a European business executive visiting Lisbon for a day or two. That was when the man opened the paper wide, and Oriana's composure was shaken by her photo on the front page of the paper.

Chapter 2

Now, as she held the paper the waiter had brought, and studied the picture, Oriana admitted to herself she no longer bore a strong resemblance to her childhood self. It was understandable that Rob was confused. In fact, she was a little confused herself. Her shock of recognition had worn off.

The child in the picture had long hair. The photos her mother had taken of her as a child always showed her with short hair. Of course, this couldn't be a photo of her. It was ridiculous to think it was. Yet this photo stirred up something in her, some faint memory. Maybe she'd had long hair at one time. She would look through the old photos when she returned home, even ask her mother if she'd ever had long hair.

They finished their omelets and croissants, had more coffee, returned the paper with thanks to the waiter and left a generous tip. On the street, the newsagents displayed the paper prominently and Oriana hurriedly bought a copy.

She focused on the name of the little girl and the restaurant from which she had been abducted.

"I would like to go to that restaurant, the Carbonara," she said. "Maybe we could have dinner there tonight."

Rob nodded in agreement.

They had planned to spend the morning sight-seeing and Oriana tried to shake the image of the little girl from her mind and become immersed in her surroundings. They had been so looking forward to this trip. She wanted to enjoy it. She had overreacted to that picture, probably because it stirred up old anxieties related to never having had a father and not remembering anything about the first few years of her life. Now it was time to forget about the picture in the paper and her childhood and her life with her mother.

They visited the National Museum of Ancient Art, which Rob had been eager to see. It contained an extensive collection dating back to the Middle Ages in Portugal, and Oriana was soon lost in exploring the exhibitions, her love of history and art ignited as they moved from one room to the next in the museum.

Oriana's love of romance languages, art and history had been nurtured at college when she studied those subjects, finally settling on art history as her major, but taking many courses in Spanish literature. She had interned one summer at the Museum of Fine Arts, in Boston in their Latin American Art section. This led to an opportunity to volunteer, which she continued to do throughout the rest of her time at Boston College. After graduating, she felt lucky to be hired at the Peabody in a junior position and had been there for the past three years.

She had met Rob in her sophomore year. He had shared similar interests but had focused on history and had become interested in historic preservation, setting as his goal a career as a historic preservation specialist, where he would be involved in preserving and maintaining historical buildings, structures, and landmarks.

Rob now worked with the preservation team of a Boston nonprofit agency, which specialized in maintaining and restoring historic properties. Rob's practical mindset was well suited to assessing structural needs, implementing preservation strategies, and coordinating with architects, engineers, and construction teams.

For a couple of hours, Oriana forgot about the girl in the picture, but her image still lurked at the back of her mind and came flooding back when she spotted a small girl holding onto her parent's hand. The girl had black wavy hair rippling down her back. Was the child about five?

Afterwards, they stopped to rest on a small bench outside the museum and Rob said out of nowhere. "You know nothing about your father. He could be Portuguese. You blend in well here. You could be part Portuguese."

Oriana nodded, startled. "Yes, that could account for the resemblance. I always assumed I looked like my father, since I definitely don't resemble my mother. We don't even look like we are related. And I really need to know about my father, now that we are hoping to have a child, I need to know about his health history. It is ridiculous that my mother won't talk about him, just because she doesn't want to see him."

"You could get a DNA test done," Rob suggested. "It wouldn't tell you who your father is, but you would know more about his ethnicity."

Oriana nodded in agreement. It was farfetched, but she liked Rob's suggestion that she might have Portuguese heritage, which would account for her resemblance to the girl in the paper and her sense of comfort and pleasure here in Lisbon.

She had no siblings. It was appealing to imagine she might discover long-lost cousins here in Portugal—or ancestors, at least. She already loved Lisbon. How magical it would be to discover she had ancestors from here.

She hadn't thought about her father in a few years. Marrying Rob had fulfilled her and taken away the loneliness Oriana had often felt when it was just her and her mother. Then, her mother's detachment made her lack of a father more prominent. In the past Oriana had wondered if her mother had wanted her, if her birth was an unfortunate accident, a grim reminder of a man her mother wanted to forget?

Oriana had yet to discover a way to get her mother to reveal her secrets. For as long as she could remember, her mother had talked only about their life in New Falls. She could talk a lot about that, sometimes describing in excruciating detail the minutia of her neighbor's lives. At such times, Oriana would block out the repetitive details.

But now that Oriana had become interested in her lineage, she wanted to know about her mother's family, too. Rhea would only say she had not been close to her family who lived "out west". She added once, "believe me, you don't want to know them." Once, when Oriana had been unusually persistent, she said in exasperation her mother's name was Martha, but she was dead. There were no other living relatives.

Chapter 3

"The Carbonara might be crowded because of the newspaper article," Rob warned. "People can be voyeuristic and drawn to the scene of the kidnapping,"

"I still want to go," Oriana said. "Maybe that makes me voyeuristic too, but I feel so drawn to that picture of the missing girl. The guidebook describes it as a popular seafood restaurant, and we don't know any restaurants in Lisbon."

But her primary motivation was her fascination with the child in the paper. She was drawn to that face.

They returned to the hotel in late afternoon, showered and rested for a couple of hours, and then headed out to the Carbonara for dinner. Rob had made reservations and got directions while Oriana was showering. He said it was not far away.

The old cobblestoned streets near the coastline housed a variety of seafood restaurants, and it was busy, as tourists and locals thronged the streets. Oriana was fascinated, gazing through the windows of shops and restaurants. The area reminded her of some place, but she couldn't think of where.

Rob had taken to using a navigator on his phone, a type of google maps, but not that. Oriana kept forgetting the name. Now he exclaimed, "it is around the next corner," and as they turned, Oriana saw a sign in green and yellow, hanging on an old black wrought-iron hook, a sign that swayed slightly in the breeze, a sign that looked familiar somehow.

"I've been here before," she muttered, but Rob didn't hear her as he had already walked ahead and was opening the door of the restaurant.

Oriana stared at the old dark wood door with its ornate metal hinges and knew it would creak as it opened, and then it did.

Something was happening, something she didn't quite understand, but she knew this place, just as she knew the picture of the child in the paper.

A young man appeared from behind the large counter inside the door and, after Rob gave their name, led them to a table at the back of the room. He kept glancing at Oriana, eyes wide. It was busy, almost all the tables occupied. But the tables were far enough apart to allow for some privacy.

Oriana glanced around carefully, but nothing in here seemed familiar. She hesitated about telling Rob about her premonition about the creaking door and the feeling she had seen the restaurant sign before. He was a kind and patient man, and had tried all day to be understanding, but he clearly thought that she was imagining the resemblance of the girl in the paper to her childhood pictures, and he would think she was now imagining the familiarity of the entrance to the restaurant. She knew he would point out that it probably reminded her of a place in Mexico, or even California, a place she had visited but didn't recall right now.

She had resolved to say nothing and then the waitress arrived at the table. Oriana was studying the menu and didn't look up until she heard Rob's gasp. She looked at his astonished face. Rob was staring at the woman's uncomprehending face—the brown eyes, heart-shaped face, brown wavy hair. The woman could have been her twin! She was even about the same height and general shape as Oriana.

The waitress had been focused on Rob. Oriana's face had been half-hidden behind the menu. Now she looked at Oriana and her eyes widened. Oriana stared back. The resemblance was uncanny. The two women looked at each other for a long moment, and then the waitress spoke in Portuguese.

Rob interrupted, saying, "I don't understand. I only speak English."

The woman stopped and said in English. "I was asking if you are a cousin, maybe. Should I know you?" She was addressing Oriana.

Oriana found her voice. "I don't think so. I have never been to Lisbon before and I know of no relatives from here. But I know nothing about my father's family.

"Your father is from here?" the waitress asked. "What is his name?"

She didn't quite understand, and Oriana realized the woman's English was basic. Oriana switched to Spanish. She knew a little Portuguese, but her Spanish was quite fluent.

"I don't know his name and I know nothing about him," Oriana answered. "My mother wouldn't talk about him. But I never met anyone before who looks so much like me."

"I am Carmela Taglia," the waitress said. "The restaurant owner is my father. I help here on weekends. We have cousins in Lisbon and also in the countryside. Maybe you know them?"

Oriana said, "no, I don't know anyone here." She realized Carmela still thought they might be related.

Somehow Rob had given Carmela their orders for dinner, and she departed with a puzzled nod.

"That is astonishing," Rob said, staring after her retreating back. "She even walks like you".

Oriana just stared silently. There was something very disturbing happening, something she didn't fully understand. Maybe she *had* been here before. Carmela must be the sister of the missing child, Maria Taglia. And Carmela looked astonishingly like her. Would a grownup Maria Taglia also look like her? Maria's picture looked like her as a child.

It was a crazy notion. Of course, it was too far-fetched to be true, reminding her of fantasies she'd had about her father when she was a child. Because her mother refused to discuss her father, Oriana had retreated into wild imaginings about him. At one point, she had been convinced her father was a famous actor. Another time she thought he was a prince in some far-off kingdom, which would mean she was a princess. Her father would appear one day and whisk her away to a magical castle.

Oriana remembered nothing much from before the age of seven when she and her mother first moved to New Falls, New York. Her mother would occasionally talk about the time "before we settled down" and vaguely indicate that they had travelled to different places when Oriana was too young to remember.

Her mother, a self-proclaimed hippie, had lived "an alternate lifestyle", but had never mentioned being in Europe. As an adult, Oriana had become more cynical, believing her mother didn't know who her father was. Now she wondered if maybe she had brought Oriana here to Lisbon when she was very young. Maybe the father who was never mentioned was a cousin of the Taglias.

Oriana was quite silent during dinner and Rob seemed to understand. Carmela came back to the table once and asked for Oriana's last name, saying she would ask her parents if they had any relatives of that name, or anyone who went to live in the United States.

"My name before I married was Oriana Stone, and my mother's name is Rhea Stone," Oriana said hopefully. "Maybe they will recognize our names."

Oriana saw Carmela talking to the young man who had shown them to their tables and saw him glance curiously in her direction.

When they were leaving, Rob gave Carmela a card with Oriana's email written on the back and Carmela wrote her email on the back of the restaurant's card and gave it with a flourish to Oriana, saying "maybe we will find that we are cousins."

Oriana and Rob promised to come to the restaurant again before leaving Lisbon.

Chapter 4

On the street, Oriana realized they were to leave tomorrow for Madrid. There wouldn't be time to come back to the Carbonara. She wanted to come back, even though she had felt overwhelmed in the restaurant and hardly remembered what she ate, though Rob pronounced the meal excellent. She felt anxious, fearful, but there was something hauntingly familiar about the place. There was the smell of the place, its mixture of garlic, spices, and fish, which calmed her, comforted her. But there was also Carmela, whose similarity to her was disturbing.

She, once again, stared at the restaurant sign swinging over the door on its metal hooks, and finally confessed to Rob that it had looked familiar when they arrived first. Then she told him about the door, about how she had expected it to creak before he had opened it.

"It's like I've been here before, but I don't remember being here. It's familiar, but I don't know why."

Rob listened gravely. He didn't say that it probably reminded her of some other similar place. She breathed a sigh of relief. He was taking her seriously.

He led her to a small table in a patio outside a bar and ordered them drinks. It was quiet and secluded here and they could talk.

"It is possible that I was here before the age of seven and don't remember, isn't it?" Oriana said. "It's not such a wild idea if you think of my mother's lifestyle back then. Or what I imagine her lifestyle might have been. She hinted at having no roots, drifting from place to place. She never talked about being in Europe, but then she never talked about the past."

"I remember being seven and moving into the house in New Falls with my mother. But I remember nothing from before then. Maybe she took me here to Lisbon as a child. Or maybe she took me from here. Maybe my father is from here and she didn't want him to find us. I often thought he must have been a bad guy, and that was why she never wanted to tell me anything about him. She didn't want us to find each other. She could have been trying to protect me. Only now, I really need to know, even if the truth is disturbing."

"She really has to tell you about your father—and about her side of the family, too," Rob said firmly.

Oriana looked at the ornate clock visible on the wall of the bar. "It's still daytime in New York. I could call her now."

"And say what?" Rob asked. "Since she has refused to talk about it, I think you need to confront her in person. Then you can watch how she reacts when you tell her about the Taglias. If you take her by surprise, you might learn more."

Oriana nodded. "That makes sense. But I wish there was something more I could do."

"You could try to find out what this detective knows about the missing girl," Rob said.

"DNA tests," Oriana said suddenly. "I could get a DNA test done, maybe compare Carmela's DNA with mine. Would that be strange? I mean, to ask her for a DNA sample?"

"Why not?" Rob answered. "She was the one to first say you could be related, and you said you knew nothing about your father."

"But the missing child," Oriana said hesitantly. "What if asking for a DNA sample raises their hopes, and she thinks I am her missing sister? It would be cruel."

They stared at each other, and she was sure they were both thinking the same thing. What if she *was* the missing child?

As if Rob had spoken, Oriana answered, "that would mean my mother kidnapped me here outside that restaurant, that she isn't really my mother. That would be bizarre."

"The child was taken twenty years ago when she was five. You are twenty-five, the same age as this girl would be now."

They stared at each other. "And I look exactly like her sister," Oriana said slowly. "And that photo in the paper ... when I saw it first, I thought it was me in the photo. The photo is familiar, as if I've seen it before."

"But my mother, would she have done that? She is nutty and has her own moral code, but would she have kidnapped a five-year-old child and kept it a secret all these years?"

Rob didn't answer. Instead, after a minute, he said, "we could see this detective Garcia, the one who is investigating the case of the missing child. We could probably get a DNA test done here instead of waiting until we go back to Boston. We could try to see Garcia tomorrow before we leave Lisbon."

Rob was taking this seriously. That was both comforting and disturbing. Rob was logical, practical, not given to flights of fancy.

"It does seem crazy," Oriana admitted, "but if I am related to the family, then a DNA test would reveal that—if I am a cousin or ...." She didn't finish the sentence because it was such a bizarre possibility.

In the end, they decided they would call the number listed in the newspaper for Detective Garcia that night and leave a message. He might respond early in the morning, and they might see him before leaving for Madrid.

Oriana dialed tentatively, mentally rehearsing the message she would leave. To her surprise, the phone was answered by Garcia himself. She spoke slowly, realizing the man might not speak English.

"Hello, Detective Garcia. I am calling about the child in the paper."

"Yes!" The voice was alert, tense. "You have information?"

"I don't know," Oriana said. "The photo looks very like photos of me as a child, but it might be because I am related—that is, I don't know if I am...."

She knew she wasn't making sense. He might think she was a crank, or even a prank caller.

She continued, "you see, we just arrived here for the first time a few days ago and we are leaving Lisbon tomorrow afternoon, but I was hoping to see you in the morning."

"Are you available now?" Garcia asked.

"Why yes," Oriana answered, surprised.

Garcia said he would be at their hotel in twenty minutes. They would meet in the lobby. Oriana hung up, feeling startled. The phone conversation and Garcia's eagerness to talk to her made this strange story seem more real, not some wild imagining. He was taking her seriously.

Rob held her hand silently as they sat in the lobby waiting for Garcia.

Chapter 5

He entered quickly, a slight man with watchful eyes, and stood for a moment inside the main doors, his eyes searching. He immediately identified them. As he approached, his eyes widened in surprise as he looked at Oriana.

He sees the resemblance to Carmela, too.

He shook hands with them and took a seat opposite them, glancing at the three people sitting a short distance away who were engaged in a loud conversation. No one else was within earshot.

Garcia studied Oriana's face. He said nothing, but she saw the question in his eyes. He couldn't seem to take his eyes from her face.

She hadn't intended to start this way, but she volunteered, "we were at the Carbonara tonight and Carmela was there. All of us were startled at the resemblance. She asked if I was related, maybe a cousin. She promised to ask her parents if they had any relatives in America."

"But the reason we went to the restaurant is that I saw the picture of the missing child in the paper this morning. The picture looked just like me when I was a child. I don't think Rob saw the resemblance, but I did."

"But you say you have never been in Lisbon before and have no relatives here," Garcia said.

"Yes, that's true. But after we left the Carbonara, Rob and I talked about how I never knew my father. I know nothing about him. I don't know who he was or where he came from. The thought occurred to me that maybe I could be related to the Taglias through my father–a cousin. Maybe he is Portuguese. That is what we said to Carmela."

Oriana broke off in confusion. "This must sound very flimsy. I have no proof of anything. I don't want the family to hope they have found their daughter and be disappointed. The last thing I want to do is cause more pain to that family. I don't have any information that would make me think I am their daughter. It was just the resemblance and the photo in the paper..." she tailed off.

Garcia said, "I appreciate your contacting me. I am glad to follow up on any leads. Let me get some details first." He took out a notebook. "I asked a colleague to join us. His English is better than mine. He will be here shortly. Perhaps then you can provide us with some background information."

Oriana nodded. She thought Garcia's English was excellent, but she didn't comment, concentrating instead on answering his questions about her full name and address and where she had grown up. He then moved on to questions about her parents.

He looked sharply up from his pad when Oriana said she didn't know her father's name and that her mother refused to provide any details about him.

"So, you see, it is possible he is related to the Taglias," Oriana said. "Or if he is not related, he is possibly Portuguese."

Garcia's face was impassive. She imagined he only wanted to deal with facts. He was on a mission to find the kidnapped child.

He continued methodically recording details of Oriana's life. She dutifully reported she had no siblings, did not know any relatives on her mother's side, either. There had always been just Oriana and her mother.

"Do you remember your life before you were five?" He asked.

"I have a few hazy memories, but I only know they are from before I was seven," Oriana answered. "At seven, we moved to a small town in New York state, New Falls, where we settled down. I thought we hadn't stayed anyplace for long before then and just have vague memories of places and people."

A young, dark-haired man wearing a gray suit had entered the lobby and was approaching them. He introduced himself as Detective Molina. He spoke English with an American accent. He looked at Oriana with great interest, but not with the shock of recognition that Garcia had shown.

Garcia spoke to him rapidly in Portuguese and then switched to English. He said, "I was asking about any memories Oriana might have since childhood. She remembers nothing much before the age of seven."

Rob, who had sat silently while Oriana answered Garcia's questions, now intervened. Turning to Oriana he said, "I think you should tell them about your feelings when we approached the restaurant tonight".

Rob, the practical one, had taken her feelings of déjà vu seriously.

"Yes," Oriana answered. "First, I have no memory of ever being in Portugal before, but when we approached the Carbonara tonight, the sign hanging outside the restaurant seemed familiar. I thought I had seen it before. Also, when Rob opened the door of the restaurant, it creaked—but I expected it to creak—I knew just before it happened that it would creak. And even the street outside the restaurant-it seemed familiar somehow."

"When we saw Carmela in the restaurant and saw how alike we looked, that was when I started to wonder about my father, how I didn't even know his nationality. I knew my mother had drifted a bit before we settled in New Falls. I wondered if I had been in Lisbon as a child, played outside the restaurant. Maybe I even knew Maria."

Oriana hesitated, her expression troubled. "I am just guessing at all of this, trying to make sense of it. I somehow gave Carmela the impression that we might be related—cousins. She suggested it and I agreed. I knew it was far-fetched, but not as far-fetched as suggesting I was the kidnapped child. Even then, in the middle of my confusion, I didn't want to raise the family's hopes. I let her think my father might be related to their family. She was going to check with her parents to see if they had relatives in America."

Garcia listened alertly, nodding from time to time.

Rob broke in, "is it possible for you to do a DNA test, maybe get a sample from Carmela and test for a match? Wouldn't that provide some answers?"

Garcia nodded, his expression brightening. "In fact, we have a DNA sample from Maria Alfonso Taglia. When she was first missing, we got a DNA sample from a hairbrush. That is on file still."

He nodded again. "That would be the best next step. If you are willing, we could compare your DNA to that of the missing girl. You would have to come to our forensics lab. I could arrange for a test sample to be taken tomorrow morning."

Rob said, "we are to leave for Madrid tomorrow afternoon. We were planning to stay there for two days before going on to Seville." He paused, then continued, "When would we know the results of the DNA test?"

Garcia said, "I will ask them to give it priority, but it could still take two days." He stopped and looked at them. "I think you should continue with your vacation. I will call as soon as I have results, and then we can take it from there."

Rob, ever practical, said, "it will be a complete match, a partial match or no match at all."

There was a pause as they all pondered the implications if it was a match.

Oriana burst out impulsively, "I wish I didn't have to wait two days. I will not be able to think of anything else."

Garcia said, "maybe it is better if you are in Madrid. It will be a distraction."

He and Molina left shortly afterwards. It was only then that Oriana realized that there had been no discussion about contacting her mother and trying to get information from her. But Garcia had carefully recorded her mother's name, address, and phone number. Surely, she would be arrested if indeed she had kidnapped Oriana.

Oriana didn't know what she thought about that. It was too wild an idea to entertain. She was not allowing herself to believe she really was the kidnapped child, though she quite liked the idea of being a long-lost cousin of the Taglias. That would be the best outcome.

Chapter 6

The rest of the evening felt like an anti-climax. After the two detectives left, Rob and Oriana silently made their way upstairs to their hotel room. They talked no more about the strange events of the day. As if by mutual agreement, they were going to withhold judgment until they had more information.

Oriana was tired, exhausted in fact, and went to sleep almost immediately, leaving Rob sitting in bed reading.

It was dark when she woke up. She was breathing hard and frightened. She was cold and had dreamt she was on a train that made repetitive chugging sounds.

As Oriana struggled awake, the chugging noises still reverberated in her head and the fear remained. It was just a dream, she reminded herself. A dream that had gone on for ages. Gradually, her breathing slowed, and she was aware it was quite warm in the room, not cold at all. Rob was breathing quietly next to her, in a sound sleep.

She tried to remember the details of the dream, but she could only recall the feeling of anxiety, the cold, the constant motion, and the sound of the train. She thought it had been a train, but could recall no visual imagery, just the sensations.

Well, they had been travelling, though not by train, and the events of yesterday were enough to make her anxious. She lay awake quietly for a while, reassured by Rob's warm presence and his calm breathing, and eventually, she drifted back to sleep.

Next morning, they were up early, had some instant coffee in the hotel room before making their way to the police forensic lab where a sample would be taken of Oriana's DNA. They saw on a map the lab wasn't far from the hotel, but they called a cab, not wanting to risk getting lost and missing their appointment.

It was all very efficient and clinical, just a medical test. It didn't take long. Oriana signed a form which allowed police access to the results. They were told by the calm and competent medical personnel that Detective Garcia would be in touch with the results.

Oriana was rapidly accumulating vocabulary in Portuguese. She had studied Spanish and was quite fluent. Portuguese was easy to learn. A few more days here and she would be much more proficient.

They left the police lab and found an outdoor café to have breakfast. By then Oriana needed the strong black coffee they were served.

"I'm glad to have done it," Oriana said. "I want the results immediately, which I know is impossible."

"You have done everything you can. We should take Garcia's advice and just enjoy our vacation now," Rob said.

They hadn't planned activities for their last morning in Lisbon. After breakfast, they needed to return to the hotel to pack and check out. They could leave their luggage there until about four pm, when they would pick it up and leave for the airport. After checking out, they would have a few hours free for more sightseeing.

"We actually don't have that much time," Oriana said, "but we could explore the Torre de Belem. It's fairly central."

"Good idea. It's a beautiful city. I could spend longer here. Who knows, we might spend a lot of time here in the future," Rob said. "Imagine if you really are Portuguese!"

"I really want to know about my father," Oriana said. "I always did, but now more than ever. My mother really must tell me. Even if he was someone awful, it is still better to know everything."

"I don't think today's DNA test would show if you were Portuguese, only if you were related to Maria Taglia," Rob said. "If you have your DNA tested by one of those ancestry sites, that's when you might find out if you have Portuguese ancestry."

"But the police test will show if I am related to Maria Taglia. Or if I am, in fact, Maria Taglia," Oriana said wonderingly. "Wouldn't that be amazing?"

"It would be astonishing, but let's take one step at a time."

"I don't know what I want the results to show. All my life, I longed to be part of a big family. The Taglias still care so much for the little girl they lost. Even after twenty years, they are still searching. I would have an instant big family. I would like that."

"If you really are Maria, what would that mean about your mother?" Rob said.

Oriana stared at him in horror. "I can't believe I didn't think of her part in this before now. I did a little, but not really. It would make her a kidnapper, not my mother at all. She would be a criminal. What would they do to her?"

Rob shrugged. "It has been twenty years. You are now an adult. I don't know if she could still be prosecuted. But I know nothing about the law here in Portugal, or how much cooperation there is with U.S. authorities. Let's take things one step at a time. Let's see first what the DNA test results tell us. Then we can deal with the rest of it."

"If only I could remember what happened before I was five," Oriana sighed. "There are such hazy memories of lots of unfamiliar people around, then being just with my mother in our new house in New Falls. I remember those first years in the new house very well, but nothing really before that."

"Don't force it. Take Garcia's advice and enjoy the vacation until we hear from him," Rob said.

They returned to the hotel and, after checking out, they proceeded with their sightseeing plans. Oriana became lost in wonder as they explored the Torre de Belem, the tower of Lisbon, built in 1520, and the main entering and exiting point for the city for centuries. They climbed to the top and gazed out over the city.

"This is wonderful," Rob said.

Oriana nodded happily. She loved this city.

They then continued to the Jeronimos Monastery, which was close by. Rob was fascinated by the building, erected in 1502 to memorialize the exploration voyage of Vasco de Gama. They visited his tomb in the church there.

As they strolled back to the hotel, Oriana sighed, "I'm not ready to leave. I love it here."

"We'll come back, no matter what happens," Rob promised. "And to think we might not have come to Lisbon at all."

"Yes, it's all so strange. Like fate stepped in and brought us here," Oriana said.

Chapter 7

Madrid was hot, but exciting. The hotel room was large and luxurious. The city was lively, and the buildings were beautiful, the architecture ornate.

Garcia was right. It provided an ideal distraction. Oriana was thrilled to be here and delighted that she could easily understand the language being spoken all around her.

They went for a stroll in the evening and had a late dinner of paella at a restaurant near the hotel. Afterwards they walked along some streets in the city center, which were filled with people seemingly in a party mood. They turned onto Calle Huertas, which Oriana knew from the guidebooks she had read, was commonly just called Huertas. There they found small bars, restaurants, ice cream parlors and loud music bars. On the street was a mixture of people, old, young, tourists and those who appeared to be locals.

Tomorrow they would visit the Prada and see the Royal Palace. Oriana had decided that they should enjoy Madrid and forget about Garcia and the DNA test for now. She was happy to see this would not be a challenging task. They both were looking forward to the Prada, and she was determined to not let the events in Lisbon distract her or prevent Rob from enjoying Madrid. Besides, being in a different country, a city with a very different tempo, made her suspicion that she was a kidnapped child seem dreamlike—an engrossing and strange story she had read, far removed from the reality of her life.

It was late when they got to sleep and late when they woke up, in keeping with the rhythm of Spain. They had breakfast in the hotel dining-room and lingered leisurely, enjoying the ambiance. They had booked tickets for the Prada to see a special El Greco exhibition at noon. Rob, with his usual efficiency, had done that from New York weeks ago.

The exhibition was crowded enough, but engrossing. Afterwards, other parts of the museum were not as populated, and they spent an agreeable two hours there. Later, Oriana couldn't resist some ornate jewelry in the museum shop, supposedly replicated from old renaissance pieces. She chose a pair of pearl drop earrings and an unusual gold necklace.

They visited a tapas bar for a late lunch, where they combined many delicious tapas of various types for a filling lunch. They tried croquettes, delicious fried balls made from a variety of vegetable fillings, fish, and meat. Oriana wanted to try gilda, which she discovered comprised anchovy, olives, and chili peppers on a skewer, so they had that too.

Oriana enjoyed ordering in Spanish and particularly enjoyed having the server understand her. She cheerfully ordered Vino Tinto to accompany their tapas.

"That's red wine," she laughed.

"That much I could understand," Rob laughed.

They were in a festive, holiday mood.

Afterwards, they visited the Royal Palace, where Rob was enthralled with the tour and carefully examined the architecture. He was less enthralled when they visited some upscale clothing stores later. They were a little too pricey in Oriana's opinion.

"Far too pricey," Rob commented.

The beautiful leather shoes and bags were way out of her price range, but she enjoyed looking at them. She hadn't intended shopping anyway, just looking, she assured Rob.

It was close to six pm before she checked her phone for messages again. She had done so before twelve and turned her phone off when entering the museum. She had enjoyed the day's distractions. In fact, the events in Lisbon now seemed unreal, the DNA test an excessive reaction. There was no message yet from Garcia, but he had said it would take a few days, so she wasn't surprised.

"Does your mother know we were planning to visit Portugal?" Rob asked, as they walked hand in hand along Paseo del Prado. The area was known as "The Golden Triangle of Art".

"We have to visit there," Rob had said earlier.

Now they gazed around them in fascination. Other than the prominent Prado, the boulevard stretched past Museo Thyssen Bornemisza. Notable highlights along the way included the vertical garden at the Caixa Forum, the Royal Botanical Garden, and the Fountain of Neptune.

"Tomorrow, perhaps we can visit the Caixa Forum and the Botanical Garden, if you like," Oriana said. "I am overwhelmed today with everything we've seen."

"Yes, time to sit at an outdoor café and people-watch," Rob said.

Once they had settled at a table and ordered sangria, Rob asked again, "what was your mother's reaction when you told her we would be in Lisbon?"

So much for allowing Rob to enjoy Spain without a reminder of the mystery they had stumbled into in Lisbon. He was mulling over the problem, anyway.

"She knows about our European trip, of course," Oriana answered. "I told her about it when we first planned it. She wasn't very enthusiastic and suggested going to Hawaii instead. I remember telling you that when it happened. I was insistent that we wanted to visit Paris and Madrid. We had quite an argument about it. So, yes, she knew we would visit Madrid and Seville, but ... remember our original plan was to fly into Paris? I think I never told her we had changed plans and were instead flying into Lisbon. I didn't want another argument, so I stayed off the topic of our European trip. So, no, she didn't—doesn't — know of our plans to fly into Lisbon."

The airline had changed the time for the flight to Paris, and when notifying them had indicated they could switch to a different flight with no penalty. Rob had found a cheaper and more convenient flight to Lisbon and so they changed their plans a few weeks earlier. They had decided Lisbon would be interesting to visit and promised themselves they would "do" Paris another time.

"How odd it is," Oriana now said. "We hadn't planned to be in Lisbon. And to have been there the morning that picture was printed in the paper."

"The anniversary of the kidnapping," Rob said.

Oriana knew he thought that if she really was Maria Taglia, it was indeed a strange twist of fate that brought them to Lisbon on the anniversary of the kidnapping twenty years earlier.

"Why was she so opposed to you visiting Europe?" Rob asked.

"She said it was too far away and we would need passports. I pointed out we already had passports, and that Hawaii was just as far away, maybe even further. It made no sense to me. Now, given what happened in Lisbon, it seems even more peculiar."

Once again, Oriana thought of her mother and how little she knew of the life Rhea had lived before their arrival in New Falls.

Chapter 8

Oriana dutifully went to visit her mother in New Falls every two to three weeks and called regularly in between. Rob accompanied her on her visits only occasionally. He disapproved of her mother, Oriana knew, even though he didn't express it. Oriana knew Rob thought her mother made too many demands on her. And he knew how much Oriana wanted to know about her father and that Rhea had always refused to talk about him or his family, or even Rhea's own family, meaning Oriana was deprived of knowing her relatives.

The change in flight plans had happened after the last visit to New Falls and Oriana had decided not to mention it in her phone conversation with her mother before they left for Europe. She had been preoccupied, but she hadn't had the opportunity either. There had been some saga concerning the neighbor's dog digging up her mother's vegetable garden, and her mother trying to decide what to do about it. It hadn't been the first time. They had spent most of the time on the phone discussing that.

Oriana tried to be a good daughter, but she found it hard work relating to her mother. They had little in common. But more difficult for Oriana was her mother didn't really share her thoughts and didn't talk about her life before Oriana, or her family, and of course wouldn't mention Oriana's father. Oriana had grown used to her mother's refusal to answer questions about family or about her past.

In her teens Oriana had sought the company of friends she could confide in and realized when she saw them with their parents that she really wasn't "close" to her mother in the way people always assumed because "there is just the two of you" as they often commented.

Oddly enough, her absent father was not a topic of interest among her friends. They were used to their generation living in single-parent families and seemed to assume that her parents were divorced.

Now Oriana thought about Rob's question. "I didn't mention Lisbon when I called my mother before we left for the airport. You know my mother. She doesn't really ask questions. She was more interested in talking about the neighbor's dog than about our big trip. It was as if she had lost interest in it."

"Oh, just wondering if she had any reaction to us going to Lisbon," Rob said.

"Oh, my God! What if it's true!" Oriana exclaimed worriedly. "My mother is eccentric, but it couldn't be that she has anything to hide."

Rob didn't answer. He rarely said much about Oriana's mother. She knew he tried to be sociable on the occasions they all met, but she also knew that he didn't really like her mother. He never had said so, but it was his lack of comment at times like this that told her she was right. Rob would have no trouble believing that Oriana's mother was capable of questionable behavior.

It was Rob's comment when they were still in college that had made Oriana first realize Rhea never paid taxes. She had commented about her mother not owning a credit card and reluctantly owning a checking account. Rob had said, "she probably doesn't pay takes either. I bet that shop pays her in cash for her necklaces and her work in the shop."

Oriana had protested. "Of course, she pays taxes."

Only she wasn't so sure. It was possible Rob was right.

That night in bed, long after Rob had fallen into a deep and peaceful sleep, Oriana lay awake. She tried very hard to remember her early childhood, the time before they went to live in New Falls.

Those first days in New Falls were very clear. They always had been. The new house was exciting and seemed spacious. She loved having her own room and having a backyard to play in. She was cautious at first about going to school, but soon felt comfortable there too and made friends with several other small girls.

But she couldn't remember where they had lived before New Falls. Why was that? Why was it such a blur? Of course, when asked, her mother was vague and said, "we lived with my friends, don't you remember?" but gave no details.

Oriana vaguely remembered the name Kim but didn't remember if they had lived with someone called Kim before New Falls, or if Kim had simply been a friend of her mothers.

But now lying in the warm darkness of the Madrid night, Oriana remembered her delight at having her own room in New Falls, and her delight at the backyard, where there was even a swing.

So, I didn't have that before. That was a treat, having my own room. It was new to me. We lived in a smaller place and there was no backyard.

But she couldn't remember anything about the smaller place or a shared room, could conjure up no image.

Her mother worked in a small shop that sold incense, candles, pottery, handmade jewelry and "alternative books". The owner, Mallory Johnson, was a friend of hers, perhaps her only friend. Mallory made pottery in a room at the back of the shop and the pottery was sold in the shop.

Oriana used to do her homework at a desk in a quiet corner of the shop in those first years, while her mother worked at the counter, stringing together beads to make necklaces when there were no customers. Her mother strung the beads together in unusual patterns to make necklaces and bangles, sometimes even earrings. These she sold in the shop. There was a surprisingly large stream of customers for a small town off the beaten track, but never a crowd all at one time.

Oriana remembered how fascinating the shop was to her when they first arrived in New Falls. There was the shop to explore, as well as the swing in their garden. In those early days, she was still very shy and hadn't made friends with children at school yet.

Then, as she lay in the dark, Oriana suddenly remembered something that now seemed much more meaningful. It happened shortly after they first moved to New Falls. She was sitting at the small desk at the back of the shop, drawing a picture with a vivid blue crayon. She remembered the blue crayon very well. Her drawing engrossed her, and she was not paying attention to the customers in the shop.

Someone asked, "where is the bus station?" Then they asked the same question again. Oriana's mother said, "I don't understand. I don't speak your language."

Oriana looked up, surprised her mother didn't understand the question or had forgotten where the bus station was. There was a young couple standing in front of the counter. Without thinking, Oriana responded, "It is only around the corner, not far." She stood up and pointed.

The young couple beamed in relief and thanked her, and then said something surprising. "Where are you from? Portugal?"

Oriana knew nothing about Portugal. She was about to answer, "I am from here, New Falls, of course", but didn't get a chance. Her mother, with a shocked face, had grabbed her and was almost lifting her into the stockroom, almost pushing her into the room and locking her in. Oriana remembered protesting that she didn't have her crayons or her picture.

She was at first more upset about that, but shortly after, became puzzled about what she had done wrong. She didn't understand, as she had just tried to be helpful. Her mother had never been so harsh with her before. She had only tried to help the strangers who had quickly exited the shop.

As Oriana now thought about it, it seemed she had understood that young couple who were speaking in Spanish and had answered automatically in Spanish! But she hadn't realized that they spoke Spanish, or that she had answered in Spanish. That is what she believed years ago—that she had answered in Spanish and her mother didn't like it for some reason.

But Oriana hadn't studied Spanish until she started Junior High School years later. Then she had learned it remarkably quickly. The teacher, Mrs. Ramone, said she had "a remarkable facility" for languages. Oriana had imagined that she must have known children who spoke Spanish and picked up some words and phrases that she already knew at age seven.

Now, as she lay thinking in the warm Madrid night, she remembered that response from the friendly man in the shop who had asked about the bus depot. He had asked, "Where are you from? Portugal?"

He had said Portugal, not Spain. Had she spoken to him in Portuguese? The languages were similar. Obviously, she had understood their question and responded. But what if she had responded, not in Spanish, but in Portuguese?

How would she have learned to speak Portuguese at age seven? There was no one they knew in New Falls who spoke Portuguese. So where had she learned it? And why had her mother never mentioned it?

And now, in Portugal, the language had seemed so familiar. She was quickly becoming familiar with it. When they first arrived in Lisbon, Oriana thought that was because she was now fluent in Spanish. But was that the only reason?

It was her mother's shock and reaction that long ago day in the shop that Oriana now thought about.

Oh, God! Could it be true?

Why would her mother have panicked that day when Oriana had spoken in Spanish to the couple? Or had she spoken in Portuguese? Why hadn't her mother been pleased that her young daughter had such a facility for learning languages? That would have been a normal reaction. Had her mother been terrified that Oriana's identity would be discovered? What other explanation could there be?

She lay awake, struggling to remember more, until eventually she drifted off to sleep. When she awoke, it was morning and Rob was already in the shower. The memory of the incident in the shop was still vivid, as well as was her mother's panicked face.

By the time Garcia called, she was no longer surprised at what he had discovered.

Rhea

Chapter 9

Rhea stared at the phone, listening to the voicemail from her daughter. Her vision blurred for a second. She was aware her hand was shaking.

Waiting for our flight to Lisbon, then on to Madrid and Seville. So excited!

Lisbon! Why were they going there? Her mind raced. What had happened? They were supposed to go to Paris, then Madrid and Seville. When had they changed their plans? Why?

She was still standing in the hallway, staring at the phone. She forced herself to walk into the living room and sank down into the faded maroon armchair.

A few months ago, she had been startled when Oriana announced Rob wanted to take her on a European trip to celebrate her 25th birthday. It was also a belated honeymoon. Now her heart thrummed in her chest as she realized her daughter would be in Lisbon on June 29th, exactly 20 years after it happened.

Rhea had settled into a complacent cocoon over the years. Now she was angry with herself. How could she have become so relaxed?

But her daughter was an adult with a husband and with a mind of his own. What could she have done to stop them? She could no longer control Oriana's movements, and she had no influence whatsoever over Rob's.

She knew Rob didn't like her and thought she was too controlling with Oriana. Rhea didn't believe she was controlling. She had an exaggerated sense of responsibility, maybe. It was time to relinquish that and to remind herself Oriana was no longer her responsibility. She had fulfilled her duty even if she hadn't quite appeased her conscience. She had kept Oriana safe all these years.

Rhea forced herself to sit and breathe deeply before returning to the hall to pick up the phone. Even then, she hung up several times before finally leaving her message, finally deciding on just a few words.

Why Lisbon? What happened to Paris?

She hung up, but continued staring at the phone, waiting for a response. After ten minutes, she decided they had boarded the flight and Oriana had turned off her cell phone. It would be hours before she would call, days even. It was unbearable not knowing, but there was nothing more she could do.

Rhea had refused to own a cell phone herself, refused to use email or to own a computer. She knew it made her a dinosaur, but she felt safer not having her name show up in too many places.

Besides, she liked living in a cocoon, sheltered from the outside world, without the intrusion of television, internet, news. She understood Oriana was very connected. "Connected" was one of the words Oriana used when she periodically urged Rhea to get a cellphone or a computer. "It is so much easier to connect to people," is what Oriana said. As if that was a good thing.

Rhea's life had slipped by uneventfully in the past eighteen years, years of quiet routine, that lulled her gradually into security. She still found the quiet uneventful life she lived comforting.

In the last five years especially, she dwelt less on the turmoil of the years before New Falls. Those years were fading into the past, as if they had happened to someone else. She had a new life now, a new name even. She had reinvented herself.

At first, she had been so anxious, startled if a stranger stared at her too long, if an official-looking piece of mail appeared in her mailbox, if she heard people speaking Spanish or French.

She had chosen the small town of New Falls because it was isolated, far from the tourist track. It had its share of tourists in the summer, frequenting the gift shops and restaurants, keeping them in business. But they were tourists who came by car from Ohio and Pennsylvania and New York City, occasionally from Canada, rarely from Europe. She still remembered how terrified she had been when the Spanish couple had come into the store and when Oriana had answered them, seemingly unaware that she was speaking in Portuguese.

Later, after her shock had subsided, she thought of how Oriana had responded so naturally, so easily. Oriana, who now spoke English perfectly and appeared to have forgotten everything that happened before they arrived in New Falls. What other parts of her former life were there, ready to reappear at any time given the right cue?

The episode with the Spanish couple had happened shortly after they first arrived in New Falls. Rhea had been shaken for a while after that, watchful, afraid of her own shadow. It had gradually become easier as Oriana turned into a little American schoolgirl and a proud native of New Falls.

There was a bohemian community in the area that welcomed the woman and girl and encouraged Rhea's New Age views. She found a market for her wooden jewelry and artwork and could make a living for the two of them.

Oriana's facility with languages was alarming to her at first, but it led to a scholarship to Boston University. Rhea could not have afforded to pay for college tuition, so the scholarship was very welcome. Oriana met Rob during her second year and shyly mentioned she had a boyfriend. She came home less often after that.

In fact, after Oriana left for college, she had never lived in New Falls again. She dutifully came to visit and sometimes stayed overnight, but Rhea soon became aware that Oriana no longer regarded New Falls as her home.

She had been surprised then at her feeling of relief—not pangs of loneliness or loss—just relief. It was over! She had done everything she could. Oriana was an adult now.

Now she could live her own life. Only she didn't know what she wanted any more. What *was* her own life? Her life before she was Rhea? She couldn't go back there. Or could she? She thought of it at times. She could resurface as her old self—her real self. But that was the self that Gregory knew. Was he still looking for her? Had he ever been looking for her? The threat had seemed so real. Now, twenty years later, she wasn't sure of anything.

After Oriana had left for college, Rhea had seen a newspaper article in the New York Times with a baby picture of Oriana. The headline screamed **KIDNAPPED GIRL'S FAMILY SAY THEY WILL NEVER GIVE UP LOOKING.**

That was when Rhea first learned that Oriana had been born Maria Alfonse Taglia, that she had been born into a loving family in Lisbon, that the family owned a well-known seafood restaurant, that the little girl had not been a homeless, destitute child. That, all these years, a family had grieved.

Rhea read the article with a growing sense of dread, then reread it. The paper had been left behind in the shop and she had idly picked it up. She didn't read papers and hadn't owned a television since moving to New Falls.

She had some sleepless nights then, thinking of the family who had been looking for their daughter all those years while Oriana had been growing up. She almost told Oriana then, but when she came to visit, she was loving and happy to be home, threw her arms around Rhea when she arrived, saying, "I missed you Mom".

Oriana was already seeing Rob then. She was twenty. Rhea had learned from the newspaper article that Maria Taglia's birthday was April 19th. Of course, Rhea had always known Oriana's birthday was not June 29th, though that was the date on her official documents, and it was the day they had celebrated every year.

Rhea couldn't tell her. Oriana loved New Falls, she told herself. This is her home, her family. She is happy at college with her friends and her boyfriend. These people in Lisbon are strangers to her. They are no longer her family. I am her mother now. It is too late.

Oriana

Chapter 10

"Are you okay?" Rob reached out across the table and put his hand on Oriana's, his eyes concerned.

"I don't know what I am—or who I am, more to the point," Oriana answered.

Garcia's call had been brief, his voice barely suppressing his excitement.

"It is a 99.8% match," he said. "You are Maria Alfonse Taglia."

Oriana had been silent.

Garcia asked, "are you there?"

Oriana answered, "Yes. Are you certain?"

Garcia said, "yes. And you are a 50% match with Carmela."

Oriana spoke slowly, trying to take it in. "50% means...."

Garcia interrupted, "you and Carmela have 50% of your DNA in common. That is seen in full siblings."

"So, I couldn't be a cousin?" Oriana asked, though she already knew the answer.

"No. It is quite conclusive. Of course, we could gather DNA samples from other members of the family, from the parents, but I had them run a second test on the samples we had."

"What will happen now?" Oriana asked, her mind reeling. "I still remember nothing. I don't know what to do next."

Garcia answered gently. "I understand Mrs. Chalmers. You must be so shocked. I must report to the family, but of course you are no longer a minor, so you can decide when and if to contact them. I am sure they will want to see you."

"What about my mother?" Oriana asked.

As she spoke, she realized that, of course, this meant Rhea was not her mother, but Garcia understood what she was asking.

"There will be charges filed by our police department—by me - and sent to the authorities in New York where she lives. There could be a request for extradition to Portugal. The American authorities may decide to take no action because it all happened so long ago, and because you are an adult. But in Portugal it is a serious crime. If the family wants to sue, then Mrs. Stone could face some serious legal problems for that too."

Rob had come out of the bathroom and was standing silently, looking at her.

"I need to talk about this to my husband before deciding on anything."

"Yes, of course," Garcia agreed. "I will let the Taglias know the joyful news. I will call you again later today, and we can discuss the next steps we need to take."

Oriana didn't need to say anything. Rob could read her face. He held her, and she buried her face in his shoulder.

"I am Maria. I am that little girl."

They stood like that for a while until Rob eventually led her downstairs to the hotel restaurant, where they attempted to eat breakfast.

"You are in shock," he said. "You need to let it sink in. Let's have some coffee and food. You don't have to decide yet. You don't have to do anything."

Oriana sat with a dazed look on her face, gazing unseeingly at the food on her plate.

She looked helplessly at Rob. "What should I do?" she asked. "Should I call Mom? Maybe there is an explanation? The police—what will they do?"

Rob had no answers.

Oriana stood up resolutely. "I have to call Mom. She is my mother after all—or she's not, of course. But I should talk to her." She walked away.

Rob called after her. "I'll wait here".

Oriana made her way to their hotel room. She needed privacy and quiet for this call. In the elevator, she thought of what she would say: *Mom—Rhea—This is Maria Alfonse Taglia. Why did you kidnap me?*

That's not what she would say, but it's what she wanted to say. She thought of the name, so foreign to her ears, and realized in disbelief *that is my name. I am Maria Alfonse Taglia.* She knew she couldn't start the conversation with her mother like that.

As she dialed, she congratulated herself for having paid for an international calling plan despite Rob's objections that "we won't need to call the United States." Then she chastised herself for thinking of her cell phone costs—this was inconsequential when her entire identity was in question.

"Mom!"

"Oriana!" Her voice was surprised, pleased, then a cautious, anxious tone crept in.

"Where are you? Is everything okay?"

"I'm in Madrid." Oriana answered automatically.

"Oh, that's good."

"Something did happen, though. Well, it happened yesterday—no, the day before - while we were in Lisbon." She wondered why she was struggling to be precise about the time and place.

"Something happened in Lisbon?" Rhea asked.

Was there a tense note in her voice? Did she know what Oriana was about to say?

Oriana plunged on. "There was a picture in the local paper here that looked like one of my baby pictures."

There was no sound from the other end.

"Mom! Are you there?"

"Yes, I'm listening,"

"The photo was of a kidnapped child—kidnapped twenty years ago — on my birthday. Her name is Maria Alfonse Taglia."

There was a noise, a moan, or a choking sound, but Rhea said nothing.

"It is me, isn't it, Mom? I am Maria?"

Just one word. "Yes" was all Rhea said.

"You knew! You always knew!" Oriana said in disbelief.

Rhea had found her voice. "I didn't always know. It was only when you were in college that I discovered your identity. I thought it would be too disruptive to your life to tell you then."

"Disruptive!" Oriana burst out. "You kidnapped me! That was disruptive!" She became aware that she was shouting.

"No! No! I didn't kidnap you!" Rhea was shouting now too. "I saved you. I rescued you from that evil man. But he was looking for us. We had to escape. I had to keep you safe."

Oriana became quiet. Was her mother—Rhea—unhinged? Escaping from an evil man?

Growing up, she had known her mother was eccentric, not like other mothers, but she had never seriously thought she was mentally unstable. It would explain why she had kidnapped her—Rhea thought she was saving her. But she'd had a lot of time to think up a convincing story.

Rhea was continuing. "He could still be looking for us."

Was Rhea delusional? Or just concocting a story?

Oriana spoke calmly and slowly. "I am an adult now. He can't harm me."

"If he thinks you remember him and what he did, he could still be dangerous."

Oriana repeated, "I am an adult now."

Even as she spoke, she remembered what Garcia had said - that Rhea would be in legal trouble. Garcia had said it was a serious crime. Rhea deserved to know.

She continued, "the Portuguese police know now. They know my identity. They did a DNA test, which proves I am the kidnapped child."

She couldn't bring herself to say *that I am Maria Alfonse Taglia.*

"And they will inform the police in New Falls. They might have done so already. You could be arrested, extradited to Portugal even. I don't know what they will do. You should find a good lawyer, get some legal advice. It's important."

Rhea didn't answer and again Oriana asked, "Are you still there?"

"Yes," Rhea answered, almost in a whisper. "I think you should go to see them—your family. They never gave up hope. They deserve to see you. Goodbye, my love."

And she was gone. The line went dead.

Oriana stared at the phone for a moment. Those words, "my love," brought back memories from when she was a child. Rhea would tuck her in at night in the new house in New Falls. "We are safe now, my love," she would say. Rhea used to call her *my love* then, but not since she had grown up. When had she stopped? And now Oriana was calling her *Rhea,* no longer calling her *mom*, even in her own thoughts.

We are safe now! That is what she used to say. And Oriana had never questioned it, never wondered why her mother used that word safe.

Chapter 11

Carmela sent her a text. Her phone on the restaurant table beeped as Oriana sat across from Rob and told him about the conversation with Rhea.

Rob had been saying, "but she knew you were Maria and yet she says she didn't kidnap you, that she saved you. She did it. Of course, she did even if she has some excuse now. But she is or was your mother for as long as you can remember."

For once, his practical nature faced a dilemma. This woman was the only mother Oriana remembered, but she was also her kidnapper. Oriana could see he was horrified at the crime, but he understood Oriana's wish to protect Rhea, her need to urge her to consult a lawyer.

Oriana was saying, "but will she consult a lawyer? You know my mother. It's anyone's guess ...," when she saw the text come in on her phone.

"Maria!" It said, "minha irmã é você"

Oriana held up the phone so that Rob could see the message and translated for him. "It says, *Maria, my sister, it is you.* "

She stared at the message. This made it real. This stranger, Carmela, was her sister.

"Garcia told them already?"

"Of course. He would have told them as soon as possible," Rob said.

Oriana translated the rest of the text. "We are overjoyed. Please come to see us as soon as you can. It is a miracle."

"We have to go back to Lisbon," Rob said. "How do you feel about that?"

"Overwhelmed. I don't know who I am anymore. What do I say to these people—strangers who are my family?"

She looked helplessly at Rob. "I feel guilty almost. They are so overjoyed to be getting their daughter back, but I don't know them. The Taglias are strangers, after all. And yet that feeling of familiarity when I was at the restaurant, and when you opened the door. It makes sense now."

"Maybe you will remember more when you see the family. They are probably living in the same house where you lived as a young child. It might stir up some memories when you go to see them."

"Why don't I remember anything? My earliest memories are from the age of seven. I don't remember any of my life with the Taglias and there were two years after I was kidnapped that I don't remember either. People remember things that happened when they were four or five years old."

"Not everyone does, but many people do. I think trauma can block out memories," Rob said gently. "The shock of being snatched away from your family, your life, could have caused some memory loss."

"Why did she do it?" Oriana moaned. "She was loving, a good mother in her own way. Even though she was eccentric, she never treated me badly. She struggled financially so that I would have everything I needed. I am worried about my—about Rhea. She is the only mother, the only family, I remember. It's all so confusing. Aren't you supposed to hate your kidnapper?"

Rob, for once, had no solution to offer. He sat silently, frowning, looking down at his hands, which were clasped together, a frown on his face.

"And my name isn't even Oriana. Everything in my life has changed."

"Not everything. You are Oriana Chalmers, my wife. That is real. That doesn't change," Rob said, reaching for her hand.

"But if I've lived under a false identity, married you using a false name, are we really married? Maybe even that has changed. My passport, birth certificate are all fake." Oriana's voice had risen.

"We will straighten it out," Rob said firmly. "I am not going anywhere. We will see a lawyer when we get home, and it will be fixed. I'm sure of it. None of this is your fault. There will be ways to fix it."

Oriana chose to believe him. The legal ramifications were beyond her grasp.

"You are the victim in all of this. You shouldn't be subjected to any legal trouble because of your mother's—Rhea's — actions."

Oriana's thoughts were chaotic. "Do I have to change my name? Will everyone call me Maria now?"

"The Taglias will call you Maria, but you are still Oriana to me and to your friends. This is all too new. You need time to absorb it. We don't have to go back to Lisbon immediately. We could spend another day in Madrid as we planned and tomorrow, instead of going on to Seville, we could go back to Lisbon. The extra day here will give you a little more time to get used to things."

Oriana nodded mutely. She was incapable of deciding anything.

"I'll change our reservations," Rob said. "Then we can go for some walks—maybe go to the botanical garden. Just have a relaxed day. But please eat something."

Oriana absentmindedly picked up the croissant and took a bite.

"And only yesterday we were thinking how wonderful it would be if you had cousins in Portugal. Now you have more than that. You have a mother and father, a sister. Maybe you have a brother."

"I have a father," Oriana said, wonder in her eyes. "All my life, I wanted a father. Will I recognize him? And my mother? Will I recognize her? Maybe I look like them."

"The chances are you do. You and Carmela could be twins. You'll see. It will be exciting. This is a good thing."

Oriana munched hungrily on the croissant. "Yes, I'll focus on what I have gained, not on what I have lost."

Rhea

Chapter 12

Rhea knew what she had to do. She had dreaded and yet prepared for this day for many years. Only she thought it would be him, she would be escaping. Instead, it was the police.

Oriana hadn't understood that she had been saving her, that she had rescued her. She knew Oriana so well, knew by her pauses, by what she hadn't said, that Oriana thought she was delusional. But she had been so shocked she hadn't explained properly. She had stumbled over her words. Now there was no more time. The chance to explain to Oriana had slipped out of her grasp. And there was no time for regrets. She had to go. She had to save herself.

A calm had set in where before she had been anxious, terrified even. Now she was organized, resigned. She moved quickly and quietly.

Upstairs in her bedroom, she opened the closet door and pushed the clothes aside to pull out the locked suitcase at the back—a large, dark brown suitcase. It was quite heavy. She had to drag it to the bed where she heaved it on top and opened it with the small key on her keyring.

Laying on top was a wig of red hair. It was a dark auburn, styled in a long bob with bangs. She quickly placed it on her head, tucking her own grey hair underneath, and glanced in the mirror. The transformation was astounding. She knew that, of course. She had prepared for this day.

There was another wig, a blond wig, which she pulled out of the suitcase. That had been for Oriana. She didn't need it now, but she couldn't leave it behind to prompt them to think of disguises.

She grabbed the black pants and beige cotton jacket from the suitcase, placed them on the bed. The jacket was slightly wrinkled, but that couldn't be helped. The outfit was in marked contrast to the gauzy, multicolored dresses she usually wore. She was wearing one in purple and pink, which she removed quickly and put in the closet. She found a white tee shirt. That would have to do under the jacket. It would be hot on this early July day, but that couldn't be helped. She added some pink lipstick from the suitcase and grimaced. She hadn't worn lipstick in years. Finally, she added plain black pumps.

She removed the black leather purse from the suitcase, glanced inside. Her documents were all safe there. Then she removed a large black nylon tote-bag with a zippered top. She stuffed the blond wig into the tote-bag and several rolled-up pieces of clothing from the suitcase and a few other items. The suitcase was empty now, but she checked carefully in the outer pockets before closing the suitcase and putting it back in the closet.

In the hallway she hesitated, then left by the back door. She would still have to walk towards the front of the house to get to the street, but she would have a good view of anyone passing by before they could see her. The last thing she wanted was for a red-haired, conservatively dressed woman to be seen leaving Rhea Stone's house.

The house was close to the corner so, once on the street, she just needed to walk past the next house. John and Margie Lewis should be out at work. She would turn onto Charles Street, a broad street with several shops and more people. There she could disappear.

She put on dark glasses, also retrieved from the suitcase. It was important not to wear anything that would look familiar and that would be associated with Rhea Stone.

She had thought all of this through carefully in the past, planned meticulously. But in recent years, she had really believed she wouldn't need the suitcase after all. She had become complacent.

It was lucky she hadn't put on weight. The clothes fit her perfectly. She had bought them at the large shopping mall close to Syracuse twelve years ago, handpicking classic styles she hoped would not go out of fashion. It had been a big expenditure given her limited budget, but one she needed to make and for which she was grateful.

It had been more difficult to find outfits for Oriana without her knowledge. Oriana had been thirteen then and growing fast. In the end, she had settled for the blond wig and decided they could take plain jeans and tee shirts from Oriana's own clothes if the time ever came when they had to leave in a hurry.

She should have removed the blond wig from the suitcase after Oriana turned eighteen and went away to college, but by then she had become complacent, had not even checked on the contents of the suitcase for a few years now.

At least Oriana was safe. Later she would think of Oriana being reunited with her family. But not now. Now she had to move quickly.

How long before Gregory heard about this? How long before Rhea Stone's picture was everywhere, and he recognized her? In twenty years, she had aged, and her hair was now grey. But he could still recognize her. The chances were, they would use an old photo of her. It would be easier for him to recognize her. He would come looking for her. She had been careful to not accumulate photos, but Oriana probably had some. Would Oriana hate her now and help the police track her down?

And would Oriana be safe? Rhea was sure she didn't remember Gregory. But Gregory didn't know that. Oriana had been so young. Rhea knew she was the one Gregory would come after. She is the one who could identify him. And Oriana had the police and Rob to protect her.

There was no-one on the street. She was lucky it was early afternoon on a weekday. People were still at work and children were in school. Or maybe their summer vacation from school had already started. It was already July.

She kept her head down as she walked to the end of the street and breathed a sigh of relief when she turned the corner and saw several people on Charles Street—people she did not recognize. None of them looked in her direction.

Further down on Charles Street, there were more tourists browsing the various gift shops, eating outside the ice-cream shop, eating lunch outside. She could blend in. Of course, there would be locals who knew her as well. She had to hope her disguise was good enough.

The walk to the bus station wouldn't take long. It was too risky to call a cab, to be scrutinized, to have to engage in friendly chatter, to have one of the local cab drivers recognize her voice. It was three long blocks to the bus station, but at the end of Charles Street she could turn onto a quieter, more residential street.

There was a bus that went to Cleveland at 3:30—that used to leave at 3:30, she corrected herself. She had been lax, she realized. She hadn't checked the bus schedule in two or three years. The schedule could have changed, probably had.

She decided she would just get whatever bus was leaving first. It wouldn't make sense to wait around at the bus station. It made more sense to get out of New Falls as early as possible.

She was almost at the end of Charles Street when Mitzi Holland appeared out of nowhere—well, she came out of Dickinson's Deli, but she was suddenly there on the street and was walking in Rhea's direction. Mitzi always stopped to chat to Rhea when they ran into each other. Rhea had to force herself to keep walking, to look straight ahead, not look in Mitzi's direction.

Mitzi walked by her without a second glance, eyes and attention focused on her phone. Phew! The wig and sunglasses worked! Or maybe she was saved by Mitzi's preoccupation with her phone.

She was glad to get off Charles Street. Now she was closer to the bus depot and walked quickly, more purposefully. She even nodded hello to an elderly man emerging from his garden gate.

At the bus depot, she eagerly scanned departures. The Cleveland bus was scheduled for 3:45, but a bus for Rochester was leaving in fifteen minutes. She quickly bought a ticket, paying in cash, and made her way to where the bus was already waiting.

Rochester was perfect—not far from the Canadian border. But she would think of that after she got to Rochester. She would stay in Rochester overnight and then move on tomorrow.

Oriana

Chapter 13

Rob canceled their flight to Seville and hotel reservations there and booked them on an early afternoon flight back to Lisbon to leave the next day.

"It's all planned. I got us a room at the Asuncion—not the same room as before, of course," Rob said. "So we can take the day here to get used to things."

Oriana nodded mutely. He was such a rock. He didn't talk about it, as they wandered around Madrid, visiting the botanical garden first, where the calms natural beauty surrounding them had a soothing effect on her. Rob held her hand and pointed out interesting and unusual plants.

Again, Oriana had turned off her phone, and it was only at lunchtime when they stopped at a tapas bar she glanced at it.

In several impassioned texts, Carmela pleaded with her to come and see them tomorrow night, no matter how late it was when they got in. Garcia must have told her when they were returning to Lisbon. Carmela wrote that her parents—their parents — were so excited they couldn't sleep without seeing their long-lost daughter.

Oriana shrugged helplessly as she showed the text to Rob.

"We could check into the hotel and then go to see them immediately," he said. He studied her face and added, "Only if you feel ready."

"When am I going to be ready?" Oriana exclaimed. "I am so... in shock, I suppose. I don't have words to describe my feelings. Shouldn't I be overjoyed? But I'm not. These people—my family — can't wait to see me. But I am—terrified. And confused. I am not the same person I was a few days ago."

"But you are the same person," Rob protested. "You have discovered something you didn't know about your childhood. You are adding that to your identity, but everything you have experienced is part of you still — your childhood, college, our marriage — it's all still there."

"And Rhea. She is real. She was my mother. What is she now? My kidnapper? It's just hard to wrap my head around it."

"It will take time to process."

"I want to call her again. Maybe she will tell me more. And I want to see if she found a lawyer."

After lunch, they found a quiet corner in a nearby park and Oriana made the call to New Falls. Rhea didn't pick up. Oriana left a brief message. "Hope you are making arrangements to take care of yourself. I'll call again." After a brief pause, she added, "love you."

Turning to Rob she said, "she's not answering. She should be home. Normally she would be home, but nothing is normal anymore."

"Maybe she is meeting with a lawyer," Rob said.

"It's early morning there, only eight am," Oriana reminded him.

"She might have gone to Syracuse, or another city, and have left early. She might not want to hire a local lawyer. Rhea would not want people in New Falls knowing her business."

"I should have helped her find a lawyer."

"There's not much you can do from here. She can take care of herself," Rob said.

There was an edge to his voice. He had been restrained about criticizing Rhea's actions, allowing Oriana time to come to terms with what Rhea had done. But Oriana could sense from his tone, from what he was not saying, that he was unforgiving and felt Rhea deserved no help.

Garcia phoned in the evening as promised. He would see them in his office the morning after they returned to Lisbon.

"I visited the Taglias last night to report the news officially in person. They were overjoyed, as you can imagine. I provided some details about where you had been living and the woman you believed was your mother. But they have many questions I couldn't answer. They are very excited to see you."

"Carmela texted me several times and I will go to see them tomorrow as soon as I get back."

"Good. I can keep it from the reporters for another day, but not much longer," Garcia said. "It is good if you see the Taglias before it becomes public knowledge."

Oriana gazed at Rob, her eyes wide and troubled. "Reporters! I hadn't even thought of that. This will be big news! International news!"

She shuddered.

"You don't have to talk to reporters," Rob reassured her after she hung up.

"One thing at a time, right?"

Reporters were not at the top of her list of things to worry about, but maybe they should be. What would they discover about her life in Boston? And how easily would they discover Rhea's identity? She should have asked Garcia for more details about what information they would release to the press.

She tried calling Rhea again in the evening, knowing it was after midnight in New Falls. There was no answer again, just the voice mail asking her to leave a message. The voice wasn't even Rhea's, but a generic male voice that had come pre-programmed into the voice mail. Rhea had never recorded her own greeting. In fact, Oriana remembered her reluctance to install voicemail, only agreeing because Oriana had pointed out that it came with the phone package Rhea was already paying for.

****

"I have been trying to remember," Oriana said after they were seated on the plane waiting for takeoff. "Shouldn't I remember something about the kidnapping? I was five years old, yet I remember nothing."

"But the family restaurant felt familiar. Maybe you will remember the family when you see them, or it will jog your memory and you will remember more."

"Oh, that makes me more anxious! They will expect me to remember them. I don't want to hurt them."

"It's a good idea to see them as soon as possible. Then the first meeting will be over with. It will be easier after that," Rob responded.

Oriana didn't know if that was true or if Rob really believed it, but she chose to accept it.

After checking into the Asuncion, the hotel they had stayed in before, Oriana chose a pink cotton dress to wear. She shook it out, relieved it had survived her suitcase and was relatively wrinkle-free. The earrings she had bought in Madrid would be a dressy addition. Rob assured her they looked perfect.

She knew she was being unusually fussy about her outfit and her appearance. She knew she wanted to fit in, not look too "foreign", too American.

Finally, Rob took her hand and said, "you look fine—let's go".

In the hotel lobby, she texted Carmela to say they were on their way.

Carmela responded immediately. *We are all here waiting*.

Carmela repeated what she had said in previous texts. The family would be waiting in their living quarters above the restaurant. Oriana was to ring the doorbell of the green door next to the entrance to the restaurant, which was closed for the evening, a very unusual occurrence.

Once again, as they turned onto the cobblestoned street near the Carbonara, Oriana felt that rush of familiarity she had had the first day. Her hand tightened on Rob's, but she didn't speak. She looked around curiously at the other restaurants on the street, brightly lit and buzzing with activity. The Carbonara alone was dark, its doors closed. This was where she had been playing when she was kidnapped. It was full of people. Had it been this way twenty years ago? How could a little girl have been taken while so many people looked on?

Chapter 14

The green door was open when they arrived, and Carmela was standing in the hallway just inside, peering out, the excitement palpable on her face. She threw her arms around Oriana.

"Oh, it is a miracle! I am so excited!" She spoke in Portuguese, but then glanced at Rob and switched to English. "I am sorry, but I am so excited."

A young man was standing behind Carmela. He was staring at Oriana's face with fascination.

"Oh, this is Manuel—your brother," Carmela said, pulling him forward. "He was just a baby when ...... he doesn't remember you."

Manuel hugged her shyly. Oriana could see that he felt just as awkward as she did and was grateful that he was restrained. Carmela's comment had made her wonder if Carmela had memories of Maria from childhood. She thought Carmela was younger, but didn't know how much younger she was.

There were voices from the top of the stairs and Oriana could see a figure. "Bring her up. Why are you delaying at the door?" He spoke in Portuguese, but she understood. The language was coming back more quickly now.

The deep male voice stirred something in her — was it a memory? There was something about it—not quite a memory, but a sense of the familiar. This was a voice she used to know well.

She was guided forward. The stairs were steep and narrow but brightly lit. The railings were black wrought-iron, intricately carved. Again, there was a faint stirring of something familiar from long ago. Her hand idly traced the filigree.

She led the way, with Carmela close behind as if to prop her up, then Manuel and finally Rob. The others were following her slow progression, *as if I am royalty.*

The woman at the top of the stairs had tears in her eyes—eyes that searched Oriana's face with a look of longing as she ascended the last steps of the stairs. She stood unmoving until Oriana had reached the top of the stairs.

"My Maria—It is really you!" Her voice was trembling as she continued to stare in wonder.

It was Oriana who made the first move forward and went to her and hugged her. She smelled of lily-of-the-valley and vanilla, a smell from long ago, familiar, comforting. Her arms felt like home. Feelings were surfacing, feelings Oriana had no words to express. She only knew she wanted to stay here in this cocoon. They held each other wordlessly for a long time and when they broke away, tears were streaming down Oriana's face.

Her mother touched her face tenderly, lovingly, but uncertainly, as if afraid she would disappear. She brushed the tears away gently, her fingers feeling like the lightest feathery touch.

"Still the same face, the same eyes. I would know you anywhere, my Maria."

Then she was enveloped in a bear hug by the burly, deep-voiced man who was her father. He was more vocal, murmuring words of love, "my little pet, my darling child."

Oriana understood everything they said and was responding to them in Portuguese. She realized she had switched effortlessly to Portuguese. There was a feeling of safety, of familiarity. She knew them, but she still couldn't remember any specifics. She couldn't put anything into words. Memories hadn't come surging back as she'd hoped. But feelings had been stirred up, feelings of warmth, comfort, safety — home.

They had all been crowded into a small hallway. She was led into a sitting room and guided to a sofa. Nothing was familiar about the room. Her mother sat beside her on the sofa, her arm around

Oriana's shoulder as if afraid to stop touching her. She looked into Oriana's face again, wonderingly.

"I always believed you would come back. I knew I would see you again. But twenty years is a long time."

Oriana nodded, at a loss for words.

Her father sat opposite her in an armchair, sitting on the edge, leaning forward. Manuel ushered Rob to a chair and took one next to him. They made a little circle, all staring at Oriana's face in fascination.

Carmela alone remained standing, moving restlessly. "Garcia said you remember nothing. It was the photo in the paper you recognized."

Oriana found her voice. "That is true. I have no memories from before I was seven." She glanced with concern at the faces of her parents. "But there is a familiar feeling now that I see you. I don't remember details."

Then, looking at the fixed smile on Rob's face and the glazed look in his eyes, she was reminded he understood nothing and said, "this is my husband, Rob. He understands no Portuguese." She repeated the words in English.

Her father said, "welcome Rob," in English, and Carmela said, "Rob, our apologies, but we are so excited, and our parents understand very little English."

Rob said, "I understand. Please don't be concerned about me."

The exchange caused Oriana's mother, also named Maria, to half stand, saying, "of course, we have prepared dinner. We will eat."

"We can wait a little," Carmela said. "Let Maria tell us what she remembers." Turning to Oriana, she asked, "what is it that brought you here to Lisbon on the twentieth anniversary of your disappearance?"

"I didn't know. I believed I was the daughter of Rhea Stone, who refused to tell me who my father was."

At the mention of Rhea, Oriana's mother shook her head, grabbed her hand, and asked, "did she hurt you? Treat you badly?"

"No. She took good care of me. I thought she was my mother. I never questioned that. But the photo in the paper looked so like photos of me as a child—all taken after I was seven years old. I was startled. I was convinced it was my photo in the paper. But it seemed so unlikely. I thought maybe my father was Portuguese. When I saw Carmela, I thought my father might be a cousin. The door of the restaurant when it opened stirred up a memory and the sign outside."

"You used to play on the street outside with your friend Anna. Do you remember?" her mother asked. "We thought it was safe. It was always so busy, with our neighbors out there."

Oriana shook her head. "Maybe I will start to remember now. I remember nothing about being taken or who took me or the time after. I only remember moving to the house in New Falls.—that's a small town in New York where I grew up."

They nodded, trying to understand.

Finally, her father said, "let us eat."

The table was set in the adjoining dining room. Oriana welcomed the delicious aroma wafting from the kitchen as they seated themselves around the large table with its intricate legs of some dark wood. Her father had disappeared with Carmela, and they reemerged with large platters of some delicious seafood concoction. She was surprised to realize she was ravenous. She had eaten little during the day as she anxiously prepared for the momentous reconciliation.

Her father was pleased with her appetite. He made some attempt to include Rob in the conversation, speaking in heavily accented English. Oriana told them of how she and Rob had met in college and had married last year.

"This trip was the honeymoon we didn't have then," she said.

"And you came home. Something brought you back," her mother said with conviction.

Oriana didn't explain that they hadn't originally intended coming to Lisbon and had changed their minds with the flight to Paris had been rescheduled. But, doubtless, her mother would say fate caused her to choose Lisbon rather than another flight to Paris. Who was she to argue?

Chapter 15

Back at the hotel that night, Oriana clung to Rob. "I feel as if I stepped into a dream or was playing a part in a play. I don't know what is real anymore. Only you. You are real."

"It is all so astonishing, and it happened so fast," Rob murmured as he held her. "It is going to take time to get adjusted."

"They are so loving, so accepting, but they are strangers to me. Yet there is something so familiar about them. I wish I could remember."

"They don't want to rush you. They are happy you are alive and safe. You can take all the time you need," Rob said. "They know you have a life in the United States."

"It's astonishing how quickly I remembered words in Portuguese. That room felt familiar after a while, and my mother – how she felt, how she smelled – it stirred up memories. No, not memories, but sensations. And something similar happened when I first heard my father's voice."

They would spend the rest of their vacation here in Lisbon, but after five days they had to return to Boston to their jobs. They were invited to stay with the Taglias. They declined but Oriana promised to visit every day. Rob insisted that she go alone some of the time. He assured her he had plenty to keep him busy. He would enjoy exploring Lisbon and the surrounding area.

There were long conversations between Oriana and her long-lost mother, with Carmela and her father often joining in. Her father and Manuel did much of the cooking in the restaurant, with Carmela as the hostess, sometimes doubling was a waitress. While they worked, Oriana and her mother were left alone together.

"I look like you," Oriana said one day with wonder, gazing at her mother's face. "It is wonderful to look like I belong in this family. I looked nothing like the woman I thought was my mother. As I got older, I thought I must look like my father. But she refused to talk about him. I spent so much time wondering who my father was."

"The evil woman. You are sure she didn't hurt you, my little Maria? You must have been so frightened."

"I don't remember being taken. I have tried so hard to remember. The first thing I remember is being seven and going to live in New Falls. I liked the house and the garden. And I liked school. I made friends there."

"And you spoke English then?"

"Yes. But once I spoke in Portuguese to people who were lost. They spoke in Spanish, and I wasn't even aware I answered in Portuguese. My – Rhea was shocked and pulled me away. I didn't understand what I had done then. Much later I thought I had spoken in Spanish but didn't know why."

Her father took her to the kitchen at the back of the restaurant one day and she helped prepare food. She did no more than chop vegetables, which Manuel was glad to demonstrate. He had become more talkative, asking her many questions about Boston.

"You must come to visit," Oriana said, and he beamed with pleasure.

Her father was pleased she wanted to learn how to cook his specialties and said she showed some talent.

There were sighs of regret and tears on the night before Oriana and Rob were to return to the United States.

"But we will talk on the phone all the time," Oriana promised. "And I will visit again soon, and you will visit me."

There were murmurs of assent and many hugs and promises of phone calls every week. Carmela and Manuel promised to visit Boston. Her mother said she would prefer her little Maria come back home for visits instead, that it was difficult to leave the restaurant. Oriana thought her parents did not want to see her new life and wanted instead to get to know her here in Lisbon where they thought she belonged.

Oriana had asked Garcia to keep her informed about the search for Rhea. She had learned that the local authorities in New Falls had attempted to contact Rhea but had found no one home on several occasions. She had called several times herself, always leaving messages but never getting a call back.

"Do you think she went on a trip?" Garcia asked.

"It is possible," Oriana said cautiously. "But I don't know where. She didn't mention any plans to me."

Of course, Rhea never went on trips anywhere. Oriana knew that. She had hoped Rhea would find a good lawyer. That was why Oriana had called to warn her and to encourage her to get good legal representation. But Rhea might have chosen to disappear instead. That was looking increasingly more likely.

Rhea hadn't answered when Oriana called the phone at the house and she hadn't returned the calls. Rhea didn't have a cell phone as far as Oriana knew. But then Rhea had lied to her all her life. Oriana didn't know what she should believe anymore.

At times Oriana even wished she could feel more animosity towards Rhea. She deserved to be punished, didn't she? But Oriana also knew she didn't want Rhea dragged through a trial and imprisoned. Rhea had cared for her all her life and was the only mother she had known. Things had become more strained between them after Oriana left for college, but she had been happy and well-cared-for as a child. Rhea had been a good enough mother. Oriana didn't want her punished.

She didn't say that to Garcia or to the Taglias. She didn't need to say it to Rob. He understood even if he didn't agree.

Now he asked Garcia, "is there a warrant for her arrest?"

"No. She is described as a person of interest, someone who is being asked to cooperate with the local authorities. If a lawsuit is filed, then a warrant could be issued."

"But no one has filed a lawsuit," Oriana said.

"It would be up to the Taglias – or you. You could file a lawsuit," Garcia said.

Rob glanced quickly at Oriana's shocked face and then back again at Garcia and answered, "it is too soon to decide. I can't answer for the Taglias, of course, but I think Oriana needs time to absorb all of this."

"I would like to talk to Rhea when I get back," Oriana said. "I want to hear her version of what happened."

Garcia nodded. "But remember, in Portugal she is accused of a crime. Charges can be pressed, and a request can be made to extradite her."

"How likely is it that the request would be granted?" Rob asked.

Garcia shrugged. "It is hard to say. Since the kidnapped child is now an adult and has suffered no abuse that you remember, and has been reconciled with her family, the U.S. authorities would not regard it as a high priority. But it is outside my area of expertise. I just don't know. I had hoped she would talk to the authorities in her town, and we would receive answers in that way."

Garcia shook their hands formally and promised to be in touch if there were updates. To her relief, he didn't ask Oriana to keep him updated. She fully intended confronting Rhea and demanding answers from her.

Chapter 16

As Oriana stepped into the house that had been home to her for so many years, memories flooded her mind, evoking a mixture of nostalgia and sadness. The place felt frozen in time. Rhea had vanished without a trace, leaving behind a perfectly preserved home.

Oriana had called repeatedly since they had returned from Lisbon. The phone was never picked up. Now she had driven alone to New Falls, assuring Rob he didn't need to accompany her. She was convinced Rhea had disappeared and didn't share with him the tiny doubt that Rhea had fallen ill, and she would discover her body. That fear had increased as she drew closer to New Falls.

Rhea didn't own a car, so a missing car didn't provide a clue as Rhea pulled into the driveway. She used her key to let herself in through the front door, not bothering to ring the doorbell. She was sure there would be no response.

There had been mail in the mailbox outside, which she retrieved and glanced at briefly. Bills mostly. On the floor, pushed under the front door, was an envelope with a return address listed for the New Falls Police Department. Oriana placed the envelopes on the hall table.

The place felt still and empty. She walked through each room quickly, finally ending in Rhea's bedroom. Rhea, of course, wasn't here. She wasn't anywhere in the house. Oriana breathed a sigh of relief. At least she hadn't found Rhea's dead body.

Her relief was quickly followed by a sharp pang of loss. If Rhea had disappeared, did that mean she would never see her again? Rhea had been her mother all of her life, at least for the part she remembered. How could she just disappear and abandon her?

Oriana walked through the empty house again, this time slowly, her gaze lingering on familiar objects and photographs that told the story of their life together. It was eerie, the stillness and untouched nature of everything. It felt as though her mother could return at any moment. And she would still be her mother.

Yet, as Oriana continued her exploration, she began to notice subtle signs that hinted at Rhea's departure being unplanned. There was a book left open on the bedside table, a half-drunk cup of coffee still in the sink, and an unfinished string of wooden beads on the table in the living-room. These small details suggested Rhea had left abruptly, perhaps in haste or with a sense of urgency. Perhaps she had left immediately after Oriana had called to tell her about Garcia and the DNA test.

Where had she gone? Rhea never travelled, never talked about friends in other places, never talked about family. Oriana sank down on the living-room couch and forced herself to concentrate. Occasionally, they would go on the bus to Syracuse where they would shop. There was that cabin they had visited for weekends when she was a child. Had it belonged to a friend? Oriana didn't recall.

There had to be some clue in this house, either a clue to where Rhea had gone or an answer to why Rhea had kidnapped a child in Lisbon twenty years ago.

With a mix of apprehension and determination, Oriana began to search. She meticulously combed through every room, examining photographs, looking at the backs for dates or labels.

There was a framed photo of her and Rhea in the living room. It had been taken at school when Oriana had been awarded a prize. Her hair was short and curly. She was about nine then. Rhea was smiling, looking proud. Her hair was still brown then. It was grey now. Oriana stared at the photo, remembering how she had liked school, had readily made friends. She hadn't been a troubled child. Not then nine years old. Had she blocked out the trauma of the kidnapping? She had heard of such things. Not remembering something painful or terrifying.

Rhea kept the bill receipts and documents in the desk in her bedroom. There might be something useful tucked away there. Oriana rifled through old bill receipts for electricity, phone, heating.

There must be documents. Rhea must have somehow faked Oriana's birth record. Her birth certificate had looked authentic, but then Oriana hadn't had a reason to scrutinize it. Now she knew her birthday was not June 29th, the day she had celebrated as her birthday all her life. That was the day she had been abducted. The day Rhea had celebrated as her birthday. She had discovered in Lisbon her actual birthday was in April.

Hidden away, at the back of a drawer, was a stack of old notebooks. Oriana recognized Rhea's handwriting and saw that the oldest one was dated eighteen years ago. The entries contained a mixture of to-do lists, ideas for designing jewelry with illustrations, and comments on her anxieties and concerns. As she leafed through the pages, she discovered a series of entries that hinted at Rhea's growing fear of being discovered by him. No name was mentioned, just fears that *he might find us.*

At first Oriana thought sadly the writings revealed the depth of Rhea's paranoia, guilt, and her constant vigilance in protecting her secret.

Then one comment caught her attention. Rhea had written, *he is an evil man, and my Mimi is still so young and must be protected. My job is far from done.*

Mimi. The name resonated. There was something—a memory she couldn't quite reach, somewhere in the shadows. Had there been another child, a child called Mimi?

As if Rhea was on a noble mission to protect Mimi from evil, rather than a kidnapper who had stolen her from her loving family. Oriana felt a chill as the thought struck her that Rhea might have done this before. She might not be the only victim. But what had happened to Mimi? If Rhea had abducted another child, then

Oriana had a responsibility to do what she could to help find Rhea and to learn the truth.

Oriana remembered what Rhea had said on the phone when Oriana had confronted her. She had said something about an evil man. Oriana had thought then Rhea was deranged and, after meeting her father, she was sure he couldn't be the evil man Rhea talked about.

But who then was the evil man? If Rhea was not paranoid, then it was possible there had been another evil man. This journal entry was from eighteen years ago. It was possible Rhea had a paranoid delusion for all these years, but although eccentric, Oriana had never thought she was paranoid.

Was it possible there was another man, a man who truly was evil, that Rhea was running from? Had Rhea been married? Had Rhea's husband been the kidnapper? Her mind racing, Oriana searched through the journals for more clues. Had Rhea run away with Oriana to protect her? Or was she just looking for a way to make Rhea's behavior more acceptable?

Within the pages, written over ten years later, Oriana found references to a small box, one that Rhea had entrusted with valuable information should anything ever happen to her.

Rhea had written, *when she is older, I will tell Oriana where it is. But not yet.*

Oriana's heart raced with anticipation as she searched the bedroom. There was no box. Finally, she made her way to the attic. She had rarely been up here. She looked around at the dusty cartons and discarded knickknacks. The cartons mainly contained old toys and books from Oriana's childhood. Rhea had difficulty throwing out things.

Finally, hidden in a corner behind a box of toys, Oriana uncovered a smaller box taped shut with duct tape. The other boxes were all untaped and easy to open. She tore the box open to discover a collection of photographs, a few newspaper clippings, and handwritten notes.

There was the newspaper clipping with the picture of Maria Taglia from the Boston Post, stating it had been fifteen years since the disappearance of the little girl. Oriana had been twenty then, away at college. Was this truly the first time Rhea had known she was Maria Taglia?

For the first time, Oriana wondered why Rhea had kidnapped her. It hadn't been for ransom, obviously. It could have been the act of a desperate woman who couldn't have a child of her own. Maybe it was. Maybe the evil man Rhea described wasn't evil at all, but someone who wanted to return Maria to her parents. Or the evil man was a pedophile and Rhea had rescued her. Oriana shuddered. Rhea had mentioned in the journal that Oriana was still too young and still needed protection from him.

She knew she had to find answers. She wanted Rhea to vindicate herself. Why hadn't she stayed to explain things?

Chapter 17

Buried at the bottom of the box was an envelope, battered and discolored with age. Inside was a photograph of a young laughing, carefree woman and a handsome young man. The woman was Rhea. But Rhea as Oriana had never known her. It wasn't just that she was younger in the photo. It was the life and energy, the glow of happiness that emanated from the photo that was unfamiliar.

Who was the man? Could this be the evil man Rhea had referred to? He looked so wholesome. And he looked happy too. They looked happy. In love. Oriana flipped the photo over. On the back was written *Lulu and Simon, August 1997*

Lulu? Was that a nickname? The photo was dated two years before Oriana's abduction.

She almost missed the driver's license, which had been tucked into the corner of the envelope. Rhea's youthful face stared out at her, this time looking solemn, but clearly taken around the same time as the other photo.

But the name under the photo! It said Lulu Ackerly. Date of birth was listed as October 1, 1977.

Rhea's real name was Lulu Ackerly.

Of course. It made sense. Rhea had needed to disappear without a trace after the kidnapping. She had given herself, as well as Oriana, a new name.

And now? Had Rhea become Lulu Ackerly again. Or had she adopted yet another alias? And how had she done it? Who had helped her? She would need help from someone who could forge documents that looked authentic. But at least Oriana could now search for Lulu Ackerly when she could get to a computer. Rhea, of course, didn't have one.

That could wait. While she was here at the house, Oriana wanted to see what else she could find. As she delved deeper into the contents of the box, she found more photos. These were of another man. This man was serious, with a brooding expression. He was handsome in a way that disturbed Oriana. His face scared her.

There were three photos. One had the ocean in the background. The photo had captured the man's profile as he stared at something. Another showed a small house and a glimpse of an ocean in the background. The third was a closeup of the man's face. That was the one Oriana reacted to viscerally. She flipped the photo over and caught her breath at the inscription on the back. *Gregory, June/July 1999, Portugal.*

June 1999, in Portugal, was when she was kidnapped. And her reaction to this man's photo was fear. Was she staring into the face of her kidnapper? Was the fear tied to a memory which was struggling to surface? Forcing herself to breathe normally, Oriana searched the box frantically, but found nothing else about Gregory.

Her agitation was increasing. She wanted to stop, to get out of this small, confined attic with its stifling heat. She wanted to run from this house. But she forced herself to stay.

Just a little while more. Then I won't have to come back up here again.

Her perseverance paid off. She found something else. A picture of an old cabin hidden deep in the woods, a place they had visited together when she was a child. It was a secluded retreat, known only to the two of them. She thought it had belonged to a friend, but she had been young when they had gone there. By the time she was in her teens, they didn't go anymore. Oriana had forgotten about it until now.

Oriana's heart raced with a newfound hope that Rhea might have sought refuge there. She might be there even now. That might mean that the friend who owned the cabin could be trusted. But who had that been? Could it be Mallory Johnson, the owner of Bits and Pieces, the shop Rhea worked in for years?

Should she pay a visit to the shop? Maybe not ask outright, but see if Mallory would volunteer any information?

She didn't think she could remember how to get to the cabin, though she remembered Rhea had made her memorize the route. They had gone on the bus to a small town called Lakeview. They had bought supplies at a poky little general store and had trekked quite a distance into the woods. She probably could no longer find it after all these years.

Before trying, she should first see if Mallory knew anything.

Oriana carefully put everything from the box back in place, first taking photos with her phone of Lulu's driver's license and the photos of Gregory.

After leaving the attic and downstairs in the familiar living-room she felt less anxious. She doubted Rhea would return anytime soon but wrote a note anyway, which she stuck to the outside of the fridge with a magnet.

Please call me as soon as you return.

In the hall, she picked up the mail and stuffed it in her bag. She would pay the bills. What would happen to the house if Rhea didn't return? Would she be assumed dead after enough time had passed? Would Oriana be responsible for any outstanding bills?

Uncertainly, she examined the sealed envelope from the police department, which had been pushed under the door. It was addressed to Rhea. She shouldn't open it. She left it propped up on the hall table and let herself out of the house, carefully locking up.

The letter from the police raised another question. Should she file a missing person's report? That would be the normal thing to do. But not just yet. She would talk to Rob first, see what he thought. It would seem normal to have come to the house and checked when Rhea didn't return her calls.

If the circumstances were normal, that is. But when the police knew Rhea had kidnapped her in another country, how would they regard her visit to the house and her silence? It was too much to grapple with right now. She would wait and talk to Rob.

Mallory's store was just around the corner on Charles Street. As she walked there, Oriana thought of what she would say and by the time she arrived, she was prepared.

There were customers in the store. Mallory looked a little frazzled but smiled in welcome when she saw Oriana, her wide blue eyes looking curious.

"I thought my mom might be working," Oriana said when Mallory walked over to her, leaving the two customers examining pieces of pottery. "But it doesn't look like it."

"I haven't seen her in a week," Mallory said. "I was hoping you were bringing me news about her. She said nothing, just didn't show up. Don't you know where she is?"

Mallory's tone was accusing, her normally calm demeanor ruffled. She created pottery and did a decent business selling her creations in the shop, but didn't like to be confined to working here. Rhea wasn't the most sociable person in the world, but she had run this shop for close to twenty years. Mallory's frustration was understandable.

"I was away on vacation and just got back. She didn't answer the phone, so I came down to check on her, but she's not at home," Oriana said, injecting a tone of worry into her response. She *was* worried, but if Mallory knew nothing about Rhea's double life, Oriana wouldn't tell her.

"She disappeared and didn't tell you where she was going?" Mallory said, her tone now critical.

"Well, I was away—in Europe."

Oriana did her best to look mystified.

Mallory now seemed worried, as if she had suddenly realized that something might be wrong.

"Do you have any idea about where she could have gone? Did she mention anything, or anyplace she had to go?" Oriana asked.

"No. Everything was very routine the last time I saw her. She was working on some beads she was going to bring in to sell." Mallory shrugged helplessly. "Did everything seem normal at the house?"

"Yes. Everything was orderly. There was mail in the box."

"Look, I wouldn't worry too much. She will show up any day now. Maybe she just went on a trip somewhere. But if you hear anything, let me know."

Mallory didn't sound convinced, but Oriana nodded in agreement.

They exchanged numbers, promising to stay in touch, and Oriana left the store wondering how long she should wait before reporting Rhea missing.

Would it look odd if she didn't file a missing person's report? She didn't know what the local police had been told. Her last conversation with Garcia had suggested the police in New Falls would ask Rhea to contact them regarding a case under investigation in Portugal.

Would that, and the unanswered letter from them, raise their suspicions about Rhea's disappearance? If Oriana lied, and said she knew where Rhea had gone, the police might come looking for answers about Rhea's whereabouts so that she should be questioned about the kidnapping.

Oriana realized how ridiculous it was that she was protecting her kidnapper. But if Rhea really had been coerced and had been protecting her all those years ago, she deserved Oriana's loyalty now. The least Oriana could do was cover for her.

Chapter 18

"After visiting the cabin—if we can find it — you could file a missing person's report with the New Falls police," Rob said. "If we don't find her at the cabin, then we should check back at the house, and then go to the police station."

It was obvious Rob didn't expect to find Rhea at the cabin. He agreed reluctantly that Oriana didn't need to offer the police the information about her kidnapping.

"They might question you about her state of mind the last time you talked," Rob pointed out.

"The last time was when I phoned her from Madrid. When she admitted I was Maria Taglia. She said she was saving me from an evil man. I thought then she was making excuses. Or that she believed my father was an evil man. Now I wonder if that evil man was the man in the photo—Gregory. Were we both running from him?"

"Don't you think you should tell Garcia about that photo? Send it to him? They might identify Gregory. And at this point, you can honestly report that Rhea has disappeared without a trace."

"Yes, I could do that," Oriana said. "I would not be revealing Rhea's whereabouts because I truly don't know. I don't have to mention the cabin. That is just a hunch."

"You know how I feel about that. I think Rhea should be found and should be questioned, but it's your decision."

"Thank you for being there for me through all this turmoil," Oriana said softly. "You are my rock through all of this."

"Always," Rob said.

"There is something else. I don't want to make you even more anxious, but if the New Falls police can't find Rhea and suspect there was foul play, they will look for a motive. If they then learn about the kidnapping and that you were the victim, it would give you a motive to ...."

"To kill her? Is that what you are suggesting?" Oriana recoiled in horror. "You are saying I would be a suspect in Rhea's disappearance?"

"Well, look at it from their point of view," Rob said. "Rhea disappears without a trace after you discover she kidnapped you twenty years ago."

"But we were in Europe. She left the house days before we got back. There was unopened mail in the house."

"I agree. The most likely explanation is that she knew she was guilty of a crime and chose to disappear."

"So, should I not report her missing? She is not technically missing. I believe she is trying to save herself from imprisonment. She doesn't want to be found."

"Let's postpone the decision for now," Rob said uncertainly.

Rob insisted on accompanying Oriana on her mission to find the cabin. But it would have to wait until Saturday. He couldn't take time off work after just returning from vacation. It wasn't the best time for Oriana to take off from work, either.

She called Garcia, and he returned the call a few hours later.

"Rhea seems to have disappeared about a week ago. I found an envelope from the police department at her house and other unopened mail. Her employer says she didn't show up for work about a week ago and sent no explanation."

"It is up to the local authorities to find her," Garcia said, his tone resigned.

"I have told no one here about the kidnapping. I don't want to answer their questions," Oriana said.

"It is better that way," Garcia said. "If the news isn't public in New Falls, there is a better chance she will return. But it is all over the newspapers here in Portugal."

"There were some news articles here too, with that photo of me which appeared in the Lisbon paper, but Rhea's name isn't mentioned."

"We didn't release it, or your present name, stating the investigation is ongoing."

"Thank you for that. I am not ready yet to explain to friends and employers," Oriana said, feeling a surge of gratitude towards this very kind and discerning man. She owed him something in return.

"I searched through Rhea's belongings, and I found old photos in the attic. There were some of a man and a house by the ocean. On the back was written *Gregory, Portugal, June/July 1999.*"

"Can you send me copies?" Garcia's tone was alert. Oriana could hear the interest in his voice.

"Yes. I made copies on my phone. I also felt something like fear when I looked at that man's face. I can't claim to recognize him, more a feeling of fear. It made me wonder if he was the one who kidnapped me and if Rhea thought she was saving me from him."

"I can run his picture through our files. And we can try to find the house. This helps. Of course, it is too early to know about Rhea's involvement, but it is possible this man enlisted her help to kidnap you."

He promised to let Oriana know of any updates.

Oriana hung up. Rob had been listening to her end of the conversation. "I might have reported something useful. He is going to search for the house in the photo and to see if Gregory shows up in any police files. The rest—that Rhea is or was Lulu Ackerly—I don't want to share for now."

Rob nodded. "Do what feels right. I think it would also be easily explained if you wanted nothing to do with Rhea after this. If you had no more involvement."

"Do you mean if I didn't file a missing person's report it wouldn't look odd?" Oriana asked.

"Yes. You tried to reach her for an explanation after you returned home. She had disappeared. You are traumatized. You moved on and forget about her. Besides, you reported her disappearance to Garcia."

Oriana nodded. "It sounds reasonable. In the meantime, I can search for information about Lulu Ackerly. Who was Rhea before she was Rhea?"

The search had to wait until evenings. Even if she found time to search while at work, Oriana didn't want to take the chance that someone there would stumble on her search and wonder who Lulu was.

She would be home before Rob, who had to work late several evenings in a row this week, as he caught up on projects that had fallen behind schedule while they were on vacation.

The evening after her return from New Falls, Oriana made herself a quick sandwich in the kitchen and settled down at her computer to start her search to uncover Rhea's past.

Excitement surged through her as she discovered information about Lulu Ackerly, born October 1977. Finally, she might have some tangible leads that could shed light on the missing pieces of Rhea's and her own past. She quickly jotted down the key information—Lulu's birthplace, high school, college, and her move to Seattle with Simon.

Determined to dig deeper, Oriana focused her search on Rogersville, Idaho, listed as Lulu's birthplace, and matching the address on the driver's license Oriana had found in the attic. This was Rhea, without a doubt.

The yearbook for Rogersville High School revealed the smiling youthful faces of Lulu Ackerly and Simon Lovell and it was clear they were a couple.

Intrigued, Oriana searched next for information about Simon Lovell and found references to a tragic accident and a link to an obituary. Oriana read through the articles, now filled with sadness for the smiling young man in the photos and for the young carefree Lulu.

According to newspaper clippings and local reports, Simon had been involved in a fatal car crash while driving alone one fateful night in 1997. The details surrounding the accident were murky, but Oriana could only imagine that Simon's passing had been sudden and devastating for Lulu.

Losing someone she was so deeply in love with must have deeply affected Lulu, perhaps leading her down a path of darkness and self-destruction. Was this why she had kidnapped an innocent child?

Chapter 19

As Oriana continued reading the news reports of Simon's accident, her empathy for the young Rhea, then Lulu, increased. A picture was forming of Lulu's young life. She and Simon had been inseparable throughout high school, had traveled to Seattle together. They had probably planned to marry. The pieces of the puzzle were coming together, revealing a story of profound loss and shattered dreams.

And Rhea had never had a boyfriend all the time Oriana was growing up. Indeed, she had never mentioned a boyfriend or husband. Oriana had assumed, of course, that there had been a husband—her father—but now she knew there hadn't been. Had Rhea continued to mourn for Simon over all these years? What had happened during those two years between Simon's death and the abduction of Maria Taglia?

Oriana returned to the high school yearbook, searching for clues about friends of Lulu's. But she already knew Lulu/Rhea had not kept in contact with any of them. She hadn't kept in contact with her family. The Rogersville phone directory listed John and Martha Ackerly living at the address listed on Lulu's driver's license. Her parents might still be alive and living at the same address where Lulu had grown up. She had told Oriana her parents were dead. It was clear Lulu had made herself disappear. She had cut all ties with her life in Idaho.

Had Rhea wanted to keep her, the young Maria, so badly she was willing to cut all other ties? Oriana felt a mixture of guilt and despair. Rhea had sacrificed her whole life for her. But it hadn't been necessary. She had a grieving family in Lisbon all that time. It was bewildering.

She badly needed to understand Rhea's motives. Had Simon's death pushed her over the edge, so that she had been temporarily deranged and then had decided to live with the consequences of the kidnapping rather than return the young Oriana to her family?

In the yearbook, both Lulu and Simon had written a warm tribute to their teacher, Mrs. Johnson. Here was one person who must have known the young Lulu well. Mrs. Johnson might have kept in touch with Lulu after high school. Oriana formulated a plan that might be risky.

Rob was tired when he got home, though he listened patiently as Oriana updated him on what she had found. He had little to say about it and Oriana changed the subject, asking about his progress on his work project. They talked about that a little before Rob announced he needed to sleep.

Next morning, with Lulu, Simon, and their connection to Mrs. Johnson still on her mind, Oriana impulsively called Rogersville High School.

"I am trying to reach Mrs. Johnson, one of your teachers."

"Oh, Mrs. Johnson is now retired, but you could leave her a message," the friendly voice informed her. "She does some volunteer work for us, so she is here frequently."

Oriana thanked her and left her name and cell phone number. The friendly voice didn't ask for a reason for the call, and Oriana didn't offer one, so she didn't expect a call back.

To her surprise, Mrs. Johnson called a day later. Oriana was in the park where she had brought her lunch. The timing was perfect as Lisa, who usually joined her for lunch, was busy that day and Oriana was alone, sitting on a bench in a quiet part of the park.

Startled, she answered the call, realizing she should have thought about how she would explain her interest in Lulu and Simon. She did the best she could.

"Mrs. Johnson, thank you for returning my call. I am the daughter of a close friend of Lulu Ackerly and I am helping to put together a tribute to Lulu to surprise her at an upcoming celebration."

Mrs. Johnson expressed surprise at Oriana's inquiry about a former student from decades ago, but said, "I remember Lulu well. She was an excellent student and then, of course, the tragedy makes her stand out in my mind even more."

"It is understandable that she wouldn't want to talk about her time with Simon, but it means we know nothing about her high school years."

"I hope she is doing well. No one has seen her in Rogersville for years. She hasn't been back," Mrs. Rogers said, her voice tinged with sadness.

"She doesn't mention it, or any relatives, but Rogersville was obviously a large part of her life. I would be grateful for any information you can give me," Oriana said.

"I can only say positive things about the years I knew Lulu in high school," Mrs. Johnson replied. "But I know nothing about her family or why she hasn't been back."

"Whatever you can tell me would be helpful, as we know nothing," Oriana said.

This sounded promising. She ignored the twinge of conscience she felt at lying to this nice lady.

Oriana listened intently as Mrs. Johnson reminisced about Lulu Ackerly. She described her as a spirited and independent young woman with a penchant for challenging the status quo. Lulu's countercultural interests and her desire for adventure had made her stand out among her peers.

Mrs. Johnson recalled Lulu's love for art and literature, often doodling in the margins of her notebooks and engaging in deep conversations about philosophy and societal norms. Oriana learned Lulu had been an active and ambitious student. She was involved in various extracurricular activities, from student council to sports teams. Lulu had shown great promise and had even been recognized for her academic achievements.

"She was part of a close-knit group of friends who shared her interests and aspirations for a different life. Most of them left Rogersville for more exciting places. I don't know if they kept in touch."

"Oh, do you recall any names?" Oriana asked.

"I remember Lulu and Kim Lee were best friends. There was another girl too. I can't recall her name. It might have been Amy or Annie. And then, of course, there was Simon. Poor Simon."

As their conversation progressed, Mrs. Johnson talked more about Lulu's relationship with Simon Lovell, her high school sweetheart. "The couple had been inseparable, exploring their shared fascination with counterculture movements and unconventional lifestyles. However, tragedy struck their young love, leaving Lulu shattered and lost. Simon Lovell, Lulu's high school sweetheart and partner in their pursuit of counterculture ideals, met with a tragic accident which ended his life."

Oriana listened, mesmerized by Mrs. Johnson's flowery prose. She told Lulu's story as if it was a story written in a romance novel. Oriana wondered how much time Mrs. Johnson spent reading romances.

"I saw Lulu at the funeral. She was numb with grief. Lost. I believe she returned to Seattle after that. I didn't hear from her again, but there were rumors she was drifting. Overwhelmed by grief, she sought refuge in the numbing embrace of addiction, desperately trying to escape the pain that consumed her."

Mrs. Johnson hesitated. "Oh dear, you don't want to hear about this. You are looking for uplifting memories to celebrate Lulu's life."

"I welcome any information," Oriana said hastily. "We care about her, and she doesn't talk about those times. Knowing about them helps us understand her better, so please tell me everything you know."

"I don't know this for sure. It is speculation based on how close Lulu and Simon were for years. I believe the absence of Simon created a void in Lulu's life, leaving her adrift and uncertain of her own identity. The tragedy had shattered their shared dreams and aspirations, leaving Lulu with a profound sense of loss and an overwhelming desire to fill that loss with distractions. Counterculture movements and alternative lifestyles became an escape—a way for Lulu to cope with her inner turmoil and find solace in a world that deviated from the conventional."

"There were reports about drug addiction. She disappeared into that world and friends and family heard no more from her."

Chapter 20

Oriana was excited as she filled Rob in on the information she had gathered.

"This is how I understand Lulu's story. After completing two years at a local college in Idaho, Lulu moved to Seattle with her longtime boyfriend, Simon Lovell. When she first arrived in Seattle, she wrote to Mrs. Johnson about her exciting new life. She gradually lost touch with the people she had known in Rogersville. But then, in Seattle, in 1997, when Simon tragically died in a car crash, Lulu became even more estranged from her life in Rogersville. They heard nothing much about her after that. There were occasional reports that Lulu was devastated and lost herself in drugs and presumably found new, but more self-destructive, friends."

"What I still haven't learned is what happened between 1997 and 1999, when she kidnapped me. What led her to that action? And the two years after I was kidnapped are a blank for me. I only remember first arriving at our house in New Falls in 2001. If I can find out what happened during those five years, I could really start getting answers."

"So, your search has produced nothing for those years? And social media wasn't around yet then," Rob said.

"I'll persist. I'm not giving up yet."

However, despite Oriana's determination, the trail was cold after Simon's death in 1997. An address and phone number were listed for Lulu Ackerly and Simon Lovell in Seattle for that time, but Oriana couldn't pin down how long Lulu had lived in Seattle after Simon's death. Oriana scoured online databases, public records. She even looked for information about Kim Lee, Lulu's best friend in high school, with no success.

Frustrated, Oriana had to admit there seemed to be no further information available on Lulu Ackerly. She had vanished from the public record by late 1997. Some time after that, she had become Rhea Stone. But when? Had Lulu become Rhea as early as 1997? Oriana had assumed Rhea changed her identity after the kidnapping. It made the most sense. But it could have happened earlier.

Why didn't I think of that? I need to search for Rhea Stone. I need to find the earliest record for Rhea.

Rhea's address in New Falls and her phone number were listed. Nothing else emerged, no matter how Oriana tried. There was no previous address or phone number.

Rhea had kept a low profile over the years. Oriana now saw Rhea's New Age lifestyle in a different light. It was not simply a rejection of mainstream culture based on her philosophical beliefs. It was designed to leave no public record, to make her hard to track down.

Oriana thought back over her childhood. Rhea owned no credit cards, paying in cash when she could and reluctantly using her checking account to pay bills when paying cash would have drawn unwelcome attention. There were only a few regular bills, electricity, phone, and rent. Their house had been rented for twenty years from the same private landlord, Tom Mansfield, who lived two blocks away. The house had belonged to his mother.

Oriana, when she was old enough to think about it, assumed Rhea hadn't had enough money to buy a house. When she was older still and working herself, she realized Mallory paid Rhea in cash for her work in the bookstore where Rhea also displayed the jewelry she made and received payment from customers. Rhea probably didn't pay taxes. Oriana didn't remember ever hearing Rhea mention paying taxes. She hadn't thought of it before now. She didn't have a car, and Oriana assumed she didn't have a driver's license issued to Rhea Stone.

But she had a driver's license when she was eighteen, when her name was Lulu Ackerly. The driver's license Oriana had found in the attic had probably never been renewed. As Rhea, she had been careful to stay off the grid. And the only friends she had were residents of New Falls. No old friends visited, no family.

Rhea had said she was an orphan when Oriana had asked about grandparents. She had lied, of course. Her parents were still alive and living in Rogersville. Oriana had briefly considered trying to contact them, but it was unlikely they knew anything. And she couldn't bear to meet people she longed to meet as a child—people she thought were her grandparents.

Hadn't Rhea missed her friends in Idaho? Hadn't she wanted to go back there to live? Saving the old driver's license had been uncharacteristically reckless. With its photo and address, it had allowed Oriana to discover who Rhea really was. Or who she had been before. Anyone who discovered it could have done that.

Why had Rhea, so careful to hide her identity, kept that driver's license and the photo of her and Simon? Keeping the photo of her and Simon made more sense than keeping the driver's license. Oriana could only imagine Rhea had wanted to hang on to a symbol of her real self, a reminder of who she had been.

She felt an uneasy pang of guilt. Rhea had given up her life to keep her safe. The woman had loved her, sacrificed for her. She didn't doubt that. She had to find out the truth about Rhea and about the circumstances that led to her kidnapping. And she had to make sure Rhea was now safe. But that seemed increasingly challenging.

Finally, it was Saturday, the day she and Rob would try to find the cabin in the photo, the cabin Oriana remembered visiting as a child. They started out early for the drive to Lakeview. Oriana had carefully written down what she remembered about the cabin and how to get there. She remembered the bus route well. They rarely took trips when she was a child, and Rhea had made her memorize the directions so that if she had to, she could go there alone. That was odd, though Oriana didn't remember thinking it odd when she was a child.

Rhea had used those words. "If you had to, you could go there alone. Repeat the directions back to me." Oriana had dutifully repeated back the directions but had protested, "you will always come with me, won't you?"

"Of course, that is what I want. But if you needed a place to hide—if I told you to hide — you could get there on your own."

For a while Oriana had been intrigued to be in the cabin alone, but then had decided she didn't want to be there alone at night. She thought the last time they had gone there was the summer she was thirteen.

Lakeview comprised one street, with two or three short streets of houses veering off from the main street. The bus stop was in the same place as Oriana remembered. And there was the old wooden general store still standing and unchanged, surprisingly spacious and air-conditioned inside and with a variety of unusual merchandise. Besides food, there was camping gear, lanterns, candles, greeting cards.

They parked in a small empty parking lot near the store, which had an old sign outside that said Camden General Store. They bought bottles of water and granola bars inside.

"We have to walk from here. There is a pathway through the woods. There is no road."

Rob nodded. She had already explained. Excited now that nothing had changed so far, Oriana led them past the Camden General Store to the end of the street. There was a small side street to the right, with several houses in a row along one side. On the other side, there were no houses, but a row of trees. A small clearing among the trees revealed a narrow dirt pathway.

"Through here," Oriana directed.

The pathway meandered for about five minutes. A small worn sign said Pines Bluffs.

"It's this way," Oriana said, turning towards the even narrower pathway that forked off to the left. This track was overgrown in places and barely navigable.

"This isn't used much," Rob commented.

"It opens up further down," Oriana said. "At least, it used to."

Finally, she stopped and turned sharply to the right. "It's in here."

Rob peered uncertainly. "I see nothing."

"The trees are hiding it," Oriana said, almost running now.

They walked past the large oak tree, and finally, the cabin came into view, its weathered exterior standing as a testament to the passage of time.

"Let's be cautious," Rob said. "We don't want to startle her if she's here. There could even be other occupants. We don't know who owns it, and we don't have a key."

He approached the old wooden door and knocked. There was no doorbell, only an old-fashioned knocker.

Oriana called out, "it's Oriana. Is anyone home?"

But there was only silence from within.

"It looks unoccupied," she said.

She bent and rolled aside a large boulder to the side of the pathway and stooped to pick up the key that had been buried underneath.

"It's still here."

"Hold on," Rob said. "Let's walk around to the back. Let's make sure there is no sign of a forced entry."

Oriana followed him. The windows at the back were intact.

"She hasn't come here," Oriana said with disappointment. "I didn't really expect she would, but it was worth trying."

"Now that we are here, we should go inside. Maybe we will find something useful," Rob said.

Chapter 21

With cautious steps, Oriana turned the key and entered the cabin, her eyes scanning every corner, searching for any sign of Rhea's presence. It was smaller than she remembered, and musty, comprising one large room, with a door leading to a small bathroom. The kitchen in the corner was old, with a sink and two burners on a counter. There was no fridge.

There was a sleeping loft with a rickety staircase leading up to it. Rob carefully climbed up and shouted back, "it's empty. There's no sign anyone was here."

As Oriana visually explored the space, her gaze fell upon an old wooden chest tucked away in a corner. She didn't remember that.

"What's this?" Oriana opened it, astonished to find it contained a collection of photographs, letters, and newspaper clippings. Heart pounding, Oriana stared at what looked like a collection of memories meticulously preserved by Rhea.

"Why would she have kept such precious records here? This cabin is hardly secure. Anyone could have broken in at any time," Rob said.

"I'm sure she didn't even own the cabin," Oriana said. "She owned very little, not even our house which we rented. Why did she feel so secure in this cabin? Who owns it, and why has it never been broken into?"

"It's not as secluded as you remember. It's barely a ten-minute walk from the village street. As a child, you probably found the walk longer."

"Yes, I thought it was a much longer walk. Still, it's isolated enough, and it looks like no one has been here in a while."

"Your mother—Rhea, that is — might have come here alone in the years after you left home. She obviously felt it was secure enough to leave her personal information here."

"I feel I'm prying. But she has disappeared, and I need answers," Oriana said.

Her mind raced with questions as she sifted through the contents of the old wooden chest. The photographs depicted moments from Lulu's childhood, her graduation from high school, and college, moments Oriana had never got Rhea to talk about and had eventually believed had no meaning for Rhea. But they had been important enough for Rhea to save the photos.

"I'm not sure why she would have hidden them here," Oriana murmured, her forehead wrinkling as she tried to understand. "But there must be a reason, a secret behind it all."

"She felt it was safer to keep them here instead of at your house," Rob answered. "And she couldn't bear to destroy them."

Rob joined Oriana by the chest and studied the items in the box. "Perhaps your mother had a connection to the cabin or its owners," he suggested. "Maybe it was a place of significance for her, a sanctuary of sorts."

Oriana's brows furrowed as she considered Rob's words. "She was happy when we came here. She was more relaxed than usual."

"I remember her mentioning a friend who owned a cabin in the woods," Oriana recalled, her eyes fixed on a faded photograph of her mother with an unknown man by a lake. "I thought she meant in the past before I was born. Could it be that she had a deeper relationship with the cabin's owner? Maybe they allowed her to use it as a haven, a place to keep these mementos away from prying eyes."

Rob nodded thoughtfully. "It's possible. But there is no sign of a man's presence here. Whoever it was didn't come here."

As Oriana continued to explore the contents of the chest, she noticed a worn notebook tucked away beneath the photographs. It contained a jumbled collection of notes. Some were dated, others were not.

Oriana gasped. "Rob, come here. Look at this. Some of these notes are dated 2000, the year after I was abducted."

Many of the notes revealed the emotions and aspirations of the young girl, who was Lulu. She wrote of experiences and goals she shared with Simon. She wrote of her journey into despair after Simon's death. There was a recurring theme of loss and grief and references to a significant event which had redeemed her.

Oriana read on, but the significant event was not clarified. Rhea wrote that she now had clarity as to the purpose of her life. Oriana's heart sank as she read the poignant words, realizing that Rhea had suffered from a deep sorrow, one she had kept hidden from the world and from her. It was as if the cabin and its hidden chest had become a vessel for her mother's pain, a place where she could tuck away her memories and shield herself from the weight of her past.

"I think you are right, and this cabin served as her sanctuary, her refuge from the outside world," Oriana said. "It was her way of preserving these mementos and protecting them. And perhaps she left them here for me to find when she disappeared, to help me understand the depths of her experiences."

Rob placed a comforting hand around Oriana's shoulder. "It looks like your mother wanted you to know her and to understand her journey. She was careful to leave nothing incriminating at the house, and only you knew about this cabin. Of course, her driving license and that photo in the attic—she must have forgotten them. Maybe all this," nodding at the contents of the chest, "was in the attic at the house at one point."

"Or maybe she came here and wrote her memories while here," Oriana said. "But now, it's up to me to uncover the truth behind these hidden memories."

"There must be a record of ownership of the cabin in the village tax office, or more likely in the county Lakeview belongs to," Rob said. "But we need the address to look up the information."

"There is no number on the door, no name," Oriana said. "We don't have an address."

"There may be a map in the village office," Rob said. She could hear the doubt in his voice.

"If Rhea has been using the cabin without permission, I don't want to alert the authorities," Oriana said.

"She felt safe enough to leave her personal memories here," Rob said. "That means she didn't fear losing the use of the cabin."

"But so far her writing hasn't revealed her identity," Oriana said. "I haven't read everything, but she doesn't mention her name, only Simon's. And she doesn't mention his last name. I know she wrote it because I recognize her writing, but if a stranger found this, they couldn't trace it to Rhea unless they, too, recognized her handwriting. There are no identifying marks."

"And I know what she wrote must be true only because I found the driving license for Lulu Ackerly and investigated her and learned about the tragedy of Simon's death. So, we know a bit about who Rhea was in the past, before she kidnapped me. What we don't know is what led to the kidnapping. Why and how she carried it out?"

Lulu

Chapter 22

I'm lost since Simon died. I feel I should die too. Our lives were so interwoven, our hopes, our goals. I don't know who I am without him.

It's been two years. I'm still lost. Maybe I always will be. They have drifted by in a haze. I know I have been self-medicating. I don't really care. But today is Simon's anniversary. I was dreading it, but something odd happened. Something unexpected.

I woke up this morning feeling ashamed. Simon would think me a coward. He would say, "don't waste your life, Lulu. Live your dreams. Pull yourself together."

So, somehow, I have found the courage to start my life over. I need to make changes, drastic changes. I need to clear my head, stay away from alcohol and drugs. Stay from people who make it easy to drift into that world.

Yesterday, a woman came into the bookstore and asked for the section on holistic medicine. I pointed her towards the shelf that contained that stuff. I rarely look at it. She was there a while, engrossed. Finally, she came back with a book, *Healing Your Life*.

"Is it possible?" I asked sarcastically.

She had an open, friendly face. There was no animosity. She regarded my question seriously and then said, "I really believe it is. I think nutrition is a first step. What you put into your body makes a difference. The wrong foods can make your mind foggy, make you apathetic."

I must have looked skeptical because she quickly added, "I don't mean to sound preachy. It's just what I have discovered is true for me."

I nodded and refrained from any other negative comments. Today, somehow, I thought of that woman, and wondered what would happen if I stopped putting alcohol and drugs into my body and started eating healthy foods? Maybe I would fall apart. But wasn't I falling apart, anyway? I had been falling apart for two years. Going nowhere, with no real friends.

What if I started over? Made a fresh start, maybe in a different city. Seattle has too many memories of Simon. I couldn't go back to Rogersville. My whole life there had centered on Simon. I would never forget him, but I need to build a life without him.

I will move, but one thing at a time.

*****

Funny, but that woman came into the bookshop again, and we had a nice, long conversation. I have been true to my promise to Simon, made to him on his anniversary. I have ingested no substances for the past two weeks. My head is clearer. I feel calmer. It's not what I expected. People had warned me I would have withdrawal symptoms, but I didn't. Maybe that will still happen.

The woman's name is Alice, and she is from a small town in New York State near the finger lakes. We got to talking and her life growing up sounded remarkably like my childhood in Idaho.

I suppose my mood is better now that I am not drinking. I was more pleasant. We went for coffee, and I ended up telling her I was trying to start over, cutting out alcohol, etc. She was encouraging.

We are going to jog together. I warned her I was out of shape but used to be a student athlete. "You'll be back in shape in no time," she assured me. I'm not so sure, but I like her optimism.

Now that I might have found a friend, I am less sure about leaving Seattle. Alice said maybe I need a vacation first before I decide where I want to move.

"Go somewhere new and different, somewhere you've always wanted to go," she said. "Then, when you come back, you can decide if you want to leave Seattle."

"I have no money to travel, but I have some vacation time coming up," I said.

"So, start saving, and start daydreaming," Alice said.

She believed in me, believed I could accomplish things. It helped enormously.

I might go to Europe. I always wanted to see Paris and Rome and Madrid. Simon and I talked about going someday. I will go for him.

*****

I am saving money and jogging with Alice. We have become good friends. I even told her about Simon, a first, since I have avoided talking about him with everyone. It helped a lot to unburden myself to Alice. She totally understood why I wanted to escape the pain. Alice said I owed it to Simon to live the best life I could and to work on my dreams. She even knows someone who is living in Paris and will give me her name so I can see her when I go there.

I am feeling more energized and optimistic. I think Alice is right, eating well and exercising makes a huge difference. Sleeping well too. And of course, having a friend to talk to.

*****

I made it here. Yesterday I arrived in Paris. It's exciting, glamorous. Also, a little scary. I'm thinking of Simon more here than in Seattle. He would have loved it. We did everything together. It is strange to be sightseeing on my own. And of course, Alice isn't here. That would have helped so much if she had come.

A few weeks ago, I said, "why don't you come with me?"

Alice smiled and shook her head. "You know I can't come. I am saving my money to study acupuncture in the fall. And besides, I wouldn't get a cheap flight this late. It will be good for you to go alone. And you can tell me everything when you get back."

Alice gave me the name of a friend to contact. The friend is nothing like Alice, who is so open and friendly. Stephanie is blasé, looked hungover when I met her last night. She is someone I would avoid in Seattle now that I want to remove myself from that lifestyle. Still, I was entranced to be sitting sipping wine at an outdoor café. Yes, of course I had to have a glass of wine. An occasional glass is okay. No drugs, though.

But here I am alone. I'm not used to that. Stephanie wants to introduce me to people. I'll do that. Oh, I'll sightsee. I have a list of things to see. I can do that alone. And I'll only be in Paris a few days before I get the train to Madrid. There, I will know no one either.

It might be a struggle, spending all this time alone. I think of Simon and how we would enjoy being in Paris together. I didn't tell Stephanie about Simon. She didn't ask about my life in Seattle, and I volunteered nothing.

Instead, I asked how long she'd been here and what she did. She's been here eight months now and is a musician. She plays the guitar and works in a bar to make money. She likes the scene here.

Chapter 23

I'm glad I met Stephanie and her friends last night. The bar was in a seedy-looking area, but inside it was so bohemian. The friends were a collection of Europeans from all over Europe. One guy was very intriguing—handsome, too. We talked a lot, and he said he was driving to Spain in a few days, and he could give me a ride if I wanted.

I happily accepted. I will save on train fare. Besides, I think he's interested. There have been other guys who seemed interested in getting to know me. But he is the first person I felt drawn to since Simon. I'm not sure though. I have the uneasy feeling I would be unfaithful to Simon. But there is something exciting about him. He is part French and part something else. I couldn't hear properly in the din. His English is quite good. His name is Gregory.

***

Gregory asked to meet the next day, and we had coffee at an outdoor café. It felt very Parisian. We talked for ages. He offered to take me to Giverny to see where Monet painted in his beautiful garden. He drove like a maniac through the Parisian streets but expertly, and after we got a little outside Paris, the traffic was less frantic.

He is ready to go south to Spain whenever I am ready to leave Paris. I told him it was my first time in Europe and that I was not used to being alone. I didn't say much about Simon, only that my boyfriend of several years had died in a car crash. He was kind, and said he was a good driver, but would be careful and take no risks.

He told me his mother was French and his father was a part Turkish, part Rumanian and was a diplomat. He works for an international child welfare agency.

Giverny was magical, and I enjoyed Gregory's company. It dawned on me I had been so lonely for most of the past two years.

I had withdrawn, isolated myself after Simon's death. Alice's friendship had been comforting, and I had become used to it. I had missed it in Paris in those first couple of days. Gregory filled that gap in my life, and besides, he was so handsome.

A couple of days later, we set off on our journey early in the morning. We drove south, stopped for lunch at a small town, then drove for a few hours again, finally arriving in Bordeaux in the evening where we had dinner and found a small inn to stay the night. I felt apologetic that Gregory was doing all the driving, but he said he was used to it. I didn't have an international license, and he said he didn't want to risk me getting a traffic violation ticket.

The inn wasn't cheap. Gregory insisted on paying. We shared a room with two beds but ended up in the same bed. I was a little apprehensive, but I needed to take chances, to live my life, as Alice would say. I went along with it.

He is so handsome. And mysterious. I still don't know much about his life. He says he is twenty-eight, five years older than me. His father had a Turkish name, and I can't pronounce it. I didn't like to ask how he spelled it. It sounds like Kreganz. Something like that.

I'm going to think of this as a vacation fling and have no expectations. This is time out, an escape from my everyday life.

Next day we continued our journey early in the morning, crossed into Spain and had lunch in San Sebastian. I was fascinated with the town, and we wandered around for an hour before getting back in the car to continue our drive through Valladolid and then Salamanca. I was enchanted with everything we saw and confessed I had simply picked Madrid because I knew so little of Spain, but these cities were fascinating.

He asked me if I'd like to take a detour to Portugal before continuing to Spain. I agreed. Everything is new to me. He might have friends in Lisbon where we could stay. He said Lisbon is an interesting city, and he thinks I would like it. As long as I'm back in Paris for my return flight, I don't care. When we stopped at Salamanca for the night I called and cancelled my hotel reservation in Madrid. From now on, I will just flow with things, live in the moment.

*****

Gregory was just as fascinated as me by the small towns we passed through in Spain on our way to Portugal. He stopped several times in places that seemed to me to be in the middle of nowhere. I could see from the map we were not far from the Portuguese border, and I could see nothing of great interest.

But everything is new to me, so I'm open to all experiences. He takes a surprising interest in the local children, stops to talk to them and encourages me to do so, even teaching me a few words of Spanish. Of course, I can't speak the language. But the children are beautiful, open, and trusting. I glanced around for their parents.

"They are unsupervised, probably from poor families, maybe even street urchins," Gregory said.

I was surprised. I thought of street urchins being found in large cities. Gregory said there is a tendency to abandon children in this area. I was shocked.

He said, "it makes you want to rescue these children and find a good home for them with parents who really want them. It troubles me to see them like this."

I didn't comment. I didn't see things the same way. The children didn't look miserable to me, though they might have been poor. Growing up in rural Idaho, it wasn't unusual for children to be left alone to play without an adult in sight. It was safe to do so. It's probably different in large cities. Maybe the attitude is different in Europe. I imagine growing up in Paris, as Gregory did, was a vastly different experience from mine. It might make him feel it wasn't safe to leave children unsupervised.

Chapter 24

Close to Lisbon, Gregory said, "there is a house by the ocean a few miles on the other side of the city where we can stay."

"Does it have a beach?" I asked happily.

"I believe so," he answered, smiling.

It sounded perfect to me. He said his friends wouldn't be home, but he had permission to stay. This vacation was working out so well.

Curious about his work, I finally asked him, "do you have to get back to work soon?"

He paused before answering, his eyes on the road. "My employers are quite flexible," he said.

"What is it you do exactly?"

"I work for a charitable organization. We place children in foster homes. We find suitable homes for children who have been abandoned."

"Oh, that is why you were so interested in the children we passed on the road," I said, thinking I understood now.

"Yes. They still lie heavy on my mind. I don't want to pass by any others. I want to help them."

"That is kind," I said uncertainly. Was he proposing whipping them up and carrying them off to another home? I didn't believe he would do that, but unfortunately, I discovered before long it was closer to the truth than I could imagine, even in my wildest nightmare. The romantic adventure took a more sinister turn not long after.

We drove into Lisbon as the sun was about to set. I was enchanted by the colors in the sky, the colors of the buildings, the old cobble-stoned streets.

"We can stop and have dinner at a seafood restaurant," Gregory said as he reached for my hand.

Only we never entered the restaurant. I can see the sign still in my mind as it swung in the light breeze. It said "Carbonara."

The little girl was playing outside on the cobblestone street. The child waved. She had sparkling eyes and beautiful, long curls. I waved back, said something in Portuguese. I was proud of having learned a few words. She laughed as if I said something funny. Her eyes were bright and mischievous. She was about five with a glorious smile and big, trusting brown eyes. She was holding a toy puppet.

Gregory stopped, stooped down and said, "It is Bobbsie. I have one too. Would you like to see my Bobbsie?" His voice was friendly, warm.

The child nodded yes.

It was that simple. I can still see it so clearly in my mind.

She walked with us willingly around the block to the parked car. He opened the door. The Bobbsie was in the back seat. I had noticed it before but hadn't commented. The child climbed in, reaching for it to examine it.

He swiftly moved to get into the driver's seat, saying to me, "get in."

I still don't know why I climbed into the back seat next to the child. Maybe I was startled by the urgency in his voice. Or maybe I thought we were all going to admire the Bobbsie together, before taking the little girl back to where we had found her.

He worked in a job taking care of vulnerable children. I told myself he was to be trusted. He wouldn't do anything to hurt her. It didn't even enter my head, though I remembered warnings from my own childhood about not going anywhere with strangers, certainly not getting into a stranger's car. As a child, I would have known better than to get in a car with a stranger. But at what age had I known that?

He revved up the engine and took off quickly, picking up speed and leaving the cobblestoned streets behind with astonishing speed.

We were in a newer part of the city and heading out into the countryside.

I must have pulled the rear door shut. I don't remember when I did that. I was startled. Something was terribly wrong.

The child had now become frightened. She started to cry, repeating something over and over in Portuguese. I didn't know what it was, but it was probably "I want to go home." Once she wailed, "Mama." My heart went out to her.

"What are you doing?" I demanded urgently. "She is frightened. We need to take her back now."

He didn't answer.

"You need to stop. This is wrong. We need to bring her home."

He still didn't answer. He kept driving, eyes straight ahead. I couldn't see his face, just that his jaw was clenched.

I did my best to comfort the child. As I held her, her sobs subsided, and she stuck her thumb in her mouth, looking at me trustingly with those big brown eyes, before closing them.

There was a sharp anxiety in the pit of my stomach. I was clinging to her, trying to fight off the growing terror. Who is this man? I know nothing about him, only what he has told me. I can't even spell his last name. What is he planning to do next?

I remain silent now, no longer protest. I don't want to disturb the little girl who might be sleeping. But I am also too shocked to formulate any questions.

Eventually, as the road became quieter, emptier, he spoke. "I explained to you what I do. I will find her a better home with people who have money. She will have a better life with a better family. People who have money. And they will pay me. If you take care of her, you will be compensated too."

I made no response. When he mentioned being paid, I understood this was not about the child's welfare. The last vestige of hope left me. Of course, he didn't work for a children's charity. Or, if he did, it was a cover. This was about money. He was kidnapping the child. And he had used me to help him. How foolish I had been.

There was no point in arguing. But I didn't know what to do. We were trapped here in the car.

Perhaps appearing to accept the situation was my best bet until I could come up with a way to escape. Besides, the little girl was now quiet, snuggled up to me, and I didn't want to upset her even more.

The drive seemed interminable. It grew darker, and the traffic thinned out more and more as we drove. Finally, he turned down a narrow road and then down an even smaller road, no more than a track. I could hear the ocean.

The car came to a stop outside a small, secluded house. It was in darkness and appeared deserted. I could see no neighboring houses.

As soon as the car stopped, I thought of running, but to where? There was no one who could help us. And how far could I run with a protesting child in my arms? I couldn't leave her behind. I already knew that.

He opened the rear door, saw she was sleeping, and said, "carry her inside."

I picked up the child and carried her into the house. It was small inside, but clean and quite bare. The little girl had fallen asleep and was heavier than I expected. She didn't wake as I carried her inside.

"Let's put her in this room," he said, opening the door to a small room with a single bed furnished for a child. There was a rag doll on a chair, a toy truck on the floor in the corner.

I looked around and shuddered. He had done this before. How many terrified children had slept in this room? Or not slept, but lay awake sobbing for their parents, asking to go home.

I laid her down on the bed, covered her gently with a quilt, and followed him out to the small kitchen. What would happen next?

"Let's have some dinner, finally. We earned it," he said, as if they had done something laudable. He opened the refrigerator, which appeared to be stocked with basics. "There is some pasta and bread. Not the seafood dinner I promised, but we will have that another time."

He boiled water for the pasta and heated some sauce he retrieved from the refrigerator. I laid plates on the table. Part of me observed my automatic movements and noted I was acting as if everything was normal. It was because I didn't know what else to do. I was playing for time, hoping that I would come up with a way out. I was still stunned.

He took my silence as evidence that I saw things from his point of view. I pushed food around my plate, unable to eat, as he explained in a calm conversational tone that he had customers lined up who would pay him well, that the child was a street child, poor with only a miserable life ahead, that everyone would benefit.

"It's a win-win situation," he said.

The child looked well cared for. She didn't look like a child living on the streets. He was lying. He had kidnapped her for money. It was a cold-blooded kidnapping. I was numb with shock.

He looked pleased, confident. He thought he had convinced me. That now I saw it all as he presented it. He didn't fear me, didn't think I was a threat. To him, I was a silly love-struck girl, easily manipulated.

I fought back the anger, the indignation. I had been so willing to fall in with his travel plans, the last-minute changes. He had used my infatuation and my lack of experience against me. My presence had helped lure the little girl into coming with us and would have made the interaction seem more innocent to any bystanders.

A frightened wailing from the child's room tore at my heart.

I stood up. "I'll go to her, get her some food." Before he had a chance to respond, I walked to the child's room.

At first, she wouldn't eat. Her cries for Mama were pathetic. I could only say, "soon. I will take care of you," knowing that she didn't understand. I wished I had learned more words in Portuguese.

Finally, I got her to eat a little of the pasta left over from our meal. When she was finished, I said, "let's sleep now." When she didn't understand, I mimed lying down and sleeping. She put her arms around me.

"Yes, I will go with you. I won't leave you."

Without another glance at Gregory, I went into the little room with her, and we curled up on the small bed. She clung to me all night, whimpering occasionally.

Chapter 25

I lay awake long after the little girl, whose name I still didn't know, slept. I heard movement from the kitchen, the clink of dishes and running water. He was washing up, putting things away.

The bedroom door opened. I kept my eyes closed and my breathing steady. The door closed again and shortly after, there was a faint noise through the wall. He had gone to sleep in the room next door. I listened for more sounds and when I heard nothing, I allowed myself to breathe normally.

I couldn't imagine sharing a bed with him again. I fought down the panic. I had to think.

Could I escape with the little girl while Gregory was sleeping? If we were silent and could make it to the car, we could drive to the nearest police station.

I eased myself gently from the bed and tiptoed over to the window, careful to make no sound. If I had heard him moving about in the next room, he could hear me. I couldn't see the road from here, but I could hear the waves breaking on the beach. It was very dark.

There had been a long stretch of dark road before we arrived at the house. There were no other houses. We hadn't passed through a village. That could mean there was no police station for miles. I didn't know how long a drive I would have. But once in the car, we would have an advantage.

But where were the keys? I didn't remember if he had taken them when we got out of the car, but he probably had. That was a reflex action for most people. Might he have left them in the living room or the kitchen? They could be on the kitchen table. Or had he taken them with him to the bedroom?

I padded silently to the door and inched it open. It hadn't creaked when he opened it earlier and thankfully, it didn't creak now. My eyes had accustomed themselves to the dark and I could make out dark shapes, but I needed more light. I didn't dare to switch on a lamp. I edged over to the kitchen counter and felt along its expanse. There was nothing. Now I moved towards the table where we had sat to eat. It was empty too.

I froze as I heard a slight creaking noise. Was it the wind? Or was he awake? Even watching me? I crept closer to the bathroom door. That would be my excuse if he found me, that I needed to use the bathroom. As I got used to the dark, I could make out the shape of the door next to the child's bedroom. It must lead to the other bedroom, where he slept. It remained closed. I took a deep breath but remained unmoving a little longer.

After what seemed an age, I crept back to the child's bedroom and closed the door with a sigh of relief. I crawled into bed beside the child who, mercifully, was still sound asleep, and again lay awake thinking.

I had to be ready to make a sudden move. Whenever the opportunity arose, I would only have a few minutes to act. That was almost certain. Even more difficult, I had to make sure the child would be cooperative and silent and would do what I asked without a fuss. She seemed to trust me, clung to me, and was comforted by my presence, but I needed to be sure. I needed to convince her I would take her home. That would be difficult since she understood no English and I couldn't speak her language.

And it was important that Gregory be relaxed, unsuspicious. I now saw that my shock had benefited me. He had interpreted my lack of protest as compliance. His ego had caused him to believe I was so infatuated with him I would go along with his plans. I needed him to continue believing that. I needed him to be unguarded, leave his car keys lying around, not expect me to flee.

At the same time, I would become closer to the little girl, try to engage her trust. She would be less tearful, easier to handle. He would be pleased, thinking I was helping him. He wouldn't expect me to escape with her. To him, I was an American tourist with little money, unfamiliar with the country or its language. I had told him too much about my life. He knew I could drive, though. That might make him more guarded about the car keys. The hardest thing would be biding my time until the right moment.

We remained in the house for several days. At first it was difficult, but then became oddly normal. I made breakfast in the morning and then took the little girl to play on the beach. I tried to stay down there as long as possible before coming back and having lunch, which he often prepared.

On the second day, he took the car, saying he would go to buy some food. He would get more of the cereal we liked and some bread and other things.

I tried to get information. "How far do you have to drive? Maybe you could take us with you, just to do a little sightseeing."

"It is better if you stay here. We don't want to attract attention. I'll bring back some presents." He smiled at the little girl, who smiled back.

She liked the beach. We walked along, picking up seashells. She prattled along in Portuguese, and I nodded, not understanding anything.

Once I pointed to myself and said "Lulu."

She giggled and pointed at me, saying, "Lu-Lu."

I pointed at her. She laughed and said "Me-Me."

And so, I called her Mimi. Later, of course, I realized my mistake. Her name wasn't Mimi.

On the beach too, I pointed to things and tried to learn the Portuguese word. She was clever and caught onto the game quickly and named the sea, the sand, the sky.

I even took my camera and took photos of the house from a distance, trying to get as much of the surrounding countryside into the shot as possible. Once I even got a shot of Gregory in profile. He didn't see me. I didn't know if the photos would be useful, but if I escaped and had to explain where he'd kept us, they could help. I was pleased I had got a photo of him. I hadn't expected that. Of course, I didn't know how clear it would be. I wouldn't know that until it was developed.

I tried to keep track of the dates. We had arrived at the house on the night of June 29th. It was July 1st when he made the trip to buy groceries. Then another couple of days passed. He was becoming restless. Maybe that meant his deal to sell Mimi wasn't going smoothly. Because that's what he was doing—selling her.

Then, after breakfast, I think on July 3rd, he announced he had to drive to town.

"We have enough food," I said. I had a sinking feeling in my stomach. If he was shopping for food again, it meant we would be here even longer. He said, "I wasn't planning on shopping for food, but if there is anything you want, let me know."

He was treating me courteously and had not commented on the fact that I continued sleeping in Mimi's room. It was possible he believed I was doing what was necessary to keep her happy.

I tried again to get him to take us with him. "It would be nice to have a change of scene," I said, attempting to pout and play the part of a sulky girlfriend.

"It will only be for a short time more. Then we will go out on the town and celebrate. Be patient, Cher. It will be worth it."

He gazed into my eyes, and his fingers lightly stroked the side of my face. I forced myself to return his gaze and to not flinch at his touch.

He continued, "you have been excellent with the child. I will not forget your help. Just another few days. Be patient, my love."

Chapter 26

He wouldn't say how long he would be gone, saying only he had to contact customers. He needed to find a phone to do so. There was no phone in the house. I was well aware of that. If there had been, it would have been easy to place an emergency call. I shivered as I realized that was why there was no phone. The house had been used for the same purpose before. How many times? And had he always enlisted the help of a gullible, infatuated girl?

He said it would only be a few days more. Last time, when he'd gone for groceries, he had been away for almost two hours. That might be all the time we had. If we started walking, we might escape on foot. We might find another house. I had to try.

I said to Mimi, "would you like to go on a long walk?"

She nodded. Even with Gregory watching, I had ventured out of sight of the house frequently, always returning shortly afterwards. It had been a test. He had made no comment. That might mean he knew there was nowhere to escape to. Or he might have become complacent.

Now there was a chance. I put my wallet in the pocket of my shorts, my passport in the other pocket, quickly put some cheese between slices of bread and stuffed the sandwiches into a small tote bag and stuffed my camera in there, too. If he was here when we got back, it would all look innocent. He would think I was getting restless and decided to explore a little.

I took Mimi's hand and walked along the expanse of beach, urging her to walk quickly. I didn't know how long he would be gone. We might have little time.

The beach ended not far from where the house stood. We had walked to the end one day, and I had seen a small dirt road that veered to the right and then turned to run along by the ocean. That's where we were headed.

The road seemed endless. It climbed gradually but steadily. I could see Mimi was getting tired. I told her stories to distract her. Then, when I thought we could climb no further, I saw we had reached a lookout point and down below on the other side was a small harbor with fishing boats.

My heart soared. A boat. I hadn't thought of that. A boat could take us far away, out of Gregory's reach. I grabbed Mimi's hand. "Now we go downhill," I said. "Can you run?"

She grabbed my hand, and we ran. The road started to wind, and the boats which had seemed so close were taking longer to reach. I was impatient, out of breath. But even though it was mid-morning, there were boats moored. They hadn't all left yet. That was hopeful.

I had money still in my wallet, thanks to Gregory paying for everything since we started our travels together. I could pay a fisherman to take us somewhere, as far as he was willing to go. Even if Gregory found him and learned where we had been taken, we would have a head start.

It would help if I knew where we were now. The drive from Lisbon had taken over an hour. I didn't know if we had driven north or south, but we were still along the coast.

My heart sank as I got closer to the boats. Two of them looked too battered to be seaworthy. And there were no people around.

I had gestured to Mimi to be silent as we approached before I saw it was deserted. I didn't know who we would encounter, and I wanted to leave no clues for Gregory.

Just as I was about to give up hope, a young man emerged from behind one of the boats and waved at us, looking curious. He was thin, with questioning eyes.

"Allo?"

"Hi," I answered. I doubted he would understand English, but I had no choice. "We want to go out in a boat," I said, gesturing towards the decrepit boat.

"Ah, non," he answered, "It is not mine."

He spoke in French. And I understood a little French. What a relief.

I tried again in a mixture of English and French to convey to him that I wanted to go on a boat away from here.

He said to follow him and around a small bend was a small boat, looking much more seaworthy.

"It's mine," he said in French.

"Can you take us?"

"When I fix it, I will go to Sainte Marie. It is in France. I can take you there."

"Excellent. Please. It would help us greatly."

He hadn't asked why, hadn't asked for money. Could it be this easy?

"I can pay you," I said.

He shrugged. "You are here without possessions and are ready to go anywhere I go. You are in trouble, no?"

I hesitated. "There is someone we need to escape. He can't know where to find us."

"I will take you,"

He gestured that he needed to continue his repairs. I took Mimi to sit on a rock and we watched. She was tired after our long walk. I took out the sandwiches I had made earlier. She was thirsty, but there was nothing I could do about that. I would not budge from this spot and there was no drinkable water in sight.

I watched impatiently as the man worked on the boat. The repair was taking longer than I wanted. Now that there was a real chance of getting away, I wanted it to happen immediately. I kept glancing up at the path we had come from, afraid to see Gregory appear suddenly. If he returned to the house and got suspicious, he could drive around looking for us. It wouldn't take that long to find us.

After what seemed like an age, the man, who had told us his name was Etienne, announced the boat was ready. He pushed it towards the slip. I grabbed Mimi's hand and hurried over.

Chapter 27

On the boat I was filled with exhilaration and as we pulled out into the ocean and the land vanished over the horizon, I was tempted to share my excitement and tell Etienne that we had escaped a kidnapper. I restrained myself and settled for squeezing Mimi tightly and joining her as she gazed over the rails. She was enthralled as she watched the waves.

Etienne had asked no questions. I wondered why. We had communicated well enough in our mixture of French and English. Maybe he didn't want to know. But he wasn't doing it for money. He had asked for none and shrugged it away when I attempted to pay him. Should I offer him some again, anyway? Maybe when we reached our destination.

Would there be coastguards or other authorities waiting when we arrived ashore in France? I had assumed since Etienne had come ashore in the quiet Portuguese cove with no authorities in sight that it would be the same once we reached France. But maybe it would be more formal there. Well, then I would deal with it. I had my passport. I would not be breaking any laws by entering. It would be a matter of explaining to the authorities what Gregory had done.

I could hand over Mimi to them, and she would be returned home. Yes, it would all work out. I would make it back to Paris. There, I would avoid Stephanie and her friends. Gregory would not find me. I would return to Seattle on my return flight as planned.

Gregory knew my name. He had seen my passport. And my driver's license. He had studied it carefully when I had offered to drive one day. Had he memorized all the details? Would he come to find me? How dangerous was he?

Lost in thought, I didn't answer at first when Etienne spoke. He repeated his question. "How long will you stay in France?"

"A few days, I think. I have friends."

"Where?"

"They are in Lyon." It was the first city I could think of which I knew was in the south of France. It probably was far away from where we were landing.

"It is far."

"We can get a train."

He shrugged. "A bus, maybe."

He pointed to a small compartment tucked under the seat. "Ici, une carte."

"Merci."

I bent to pull out the creased map. Circled in ink were the words *Ste. Marie.* The closest town was Biarritz. I recognized the name.

"A bus to Biarritz, then a train to Lyon?" I asked.

Etienne nodded. "You have no luggage. Are you in trouble?"

"We are running from a dangerous man. He must not find us," I said.

"You have papers?"

"Yes." I hesitated. "For me, but not for Mimi. There was no time."

There. I'd said it. I had lied, giving the impression she was legitimately with me.

"It is a small place, quiet, where we will come. No one to check passports. Then you must go. I want to help but I want no trouble. When I go to fish I am in Espana, Portugal. They don't question. But if I bring people back, then they will question. It will be bad for me."

"I will make no trouble for you," I said. "You have helped us so much."

"I will take you to bus stop when we reach Ste. Marie, but you may wait long."

"It is no problem."

He gestured for me to open a box securely pushed in a corner. It was a small cooler. It contained bread, some cheese and water.

"Eat."

I sliced some cheese and placed it on a chunk of bread. I offered it to him. He accepted, eating with one hand while the other stayed on the rudder. The water was choppier now. Had the man given up a day's fishing to carry us back? It was better not to ask. I gave some bread and cheese to Mimi. She was looking a little sleepy. It was hot. We had been on the boat for hours. That's how it felt, anyway.

"You don't fish today?" I asked Etienne.

"No. It is better early morning. My engine broke. It is why I was in Portugal. I need more parts." He glanced at me. "It is safe to go back."

I nodded.

He looked at Mimi, who had brought her Bobbsie, and was talking to it in a whisper. "I have small girl. And wife. I feel bad for you."

"Thank you again. We will be safe now."

I still felt giddy with relief that we had escaped, but now I realized I was escaping to another country, probably about to enter it unlawfully, with a child not my own. Startled, I realized I could be the one now accused of kidnapping. I had no proof Gregory was the one who had kidnapped Mimi, and that I had rescued her. How could I prove Gregory even existed?

I knew I couldn't go to the police when we landed at Sainte Marie. They would have questions about how I got there, which could cause trouble for Etienne. If I said we had come on a boat from Portugal, it would be easy for them to track down who had taken a boat out that day. I would wait until we reached another town before bringing Mimi to the police station and explaining what happened.

After what seemed liked hours, Etienne pointed into the distance. "Voila!"

I could see a speck, which gradually grew bigger. The French coast was drawing closer.

Mimi had curled up on a tarpaulin on the floor sleeping sweetly, clutching her Bobbsie.

"I will stop at small place near Sainte Marie," Etienne explained. "There will be no-one there. You will get out and wait for me. I will return in my car and take you to bus station."

"Perhaps we can walk to the bus station."

"It is far. I will take you."

The little cove was isolated. There were no other boats in sight. I woke a sleepy Mimi, and we got off the boat. I was lightheaded and hungry, but we had succeeded. We were in France, far away from Gregory. Pride in my accomplishment energized me.

Mimi gaily waved goodbye to her new friend. He understood no Portuguese, so I had stopped trying to get her to be quiet. He probably thought I spoke Portuguese, that my husband was Portuguese, and I was struggling to communicate with him in French.

Did he know I was American? Probably I had given that away in some unconscious ways. But he would tell no one. He had already admitted helping us could bring him unwanted attention.

Mimi was hungry, which she mimed dramatically, making me laugh. She had already learned a few words in English and seemed to understand when I said, "soon."

It was a half-hour later when a red truck came chugging along the dusty small road. Etienne had come as promised. As he made several dizzying turns and drove along the deserted small roads, I was grateful again for his help. I would have been hopelessly lost if we'd had to walk to the bus stop. And it did seem a long way.

Finally, he stopped suddenly a short distance from where the little road joined a larger road. "It is down here. You will see it. You can walk from here."

I understood he didn't want us to be seen getting out of his distinctive red truck. I nodded gratefully and produced my wallet. He shook his head.

"Please take something," I said.

He finally accepted ten francs. I knew it was very little, but he refused to take more, saying, "you need money for bus and train."

Mimi and I got out, and she waved merrily as he drove away.

Chapter 28

When we emerged from the narrow dirt road, I saw the bus stop immediately. There was a bench nearby to sit on and a sign listing the schedule. It would be two hours before the next bus arrived. It could be worse. While I was impatient to continue our journey, I was heady with success. We had put a big distance between us and Gregory. Soon, this ordeal would be over.

The schedule posted at the bus stop said we would arrive in Biarritz at 19:50. That would be at 7:50 pm. There were stops several stops along the way at places I'd never heard of. In fact, I knew nothing about Biarritz except it was a seaside resort. I imagined it would be big with lots of visitors. It would be easy to get lost in the crowd. There, I could find a police station and safely report the kidnapping without causing trouble for Etienne. I could claim to not know even his first name. He had never told me his last.

Mimi was holding my hand, gazing up at me with trust. She had done everything I'd asked and not complained. I realized with a pang I would miss her.

"Are you hungry?" I asked, rubbing my belly and putting my hand to my mouth. She copied me and said "Hungry."

I nodded. "Si." She was a bright little thing and had already learned several English words.

There was a shop across from the bus stop. I pointed to it and took Mimi across the road. I bought some mini-quiches, orange juice, and chocolate bars. It was the best I could do. That would have to be our supper.

We returned to the bench by the bus stop, and both of us ate hungrily, ignoring the curious glances from occasional motorists driving by. There might be other places to buy food nearby, even a restaurant, but I didn't want to push our luck. We would stay here and try not to draw attention to ourselves. We were far from

Portugal, but Mimi's picture could be in the papers. She was a missing child.

About twenty minutes before the bus was to arrive, people started to show up. We scooted over to make room on the bench. An elderly woman with an ornate shawl around her shoulders walked slowly towards us, accompanied by a young teenage girl with a pierced nose. Two boys appeared next and stood chatting at a little distance from us, eyeing the girl and exchanging shy smiles.

I gestured to Mimi to be silent, holding my finger to my lips. I had made it into a game, this "shhh." Luckily, she was playing along. I didn't want her giddy prattling in Portuguese or practicing English words to draw further attention to us. She was still preoccupied eating chocolate but nodded to show she understood. The other people waiting for the bus must know we were strangers. I assumed they lived locally, and we obviously did not. I didn't want to advertise anything about us that would help further identify us.

I was glad we didn't have luggage, though on the boat I had regretted not packing a small bag with a change of clothes. This way, we could be on our way home on the bus after a day's visit to see friends or relatives.

I watched carefully as the other people got on the bus ahead of us and was relieved when they offered money and received change. The sign at the stop had given no indication if we needed a bus ticket, but I imagined Etienne would have warned me if that was necessary. This was a rural route, so people wouldn't have access to a bus depot to buy tickets. I was relieved as we settled into our seats. Another hurdle over.

I had chosen seats at a distance from the other people who had gotten on at Sainte Marie. There were some people already on the bus. The seat closest to us was occupied by a teenage couple who were absorbed in each other and paid little attention to us. Still, I continued to gesture for Mimi to be quiet. She enjoyed looking out of the window for a while and then the motion of the bus made her sleepy and she slept with her head on my lap. She was such a sweet little girl. I had grown so fond of her.

The sun was going down by the time the bus pulled into the depot in Biarritz. Soon it would be nighttime. The events of the day were catching up with me. I was exhausted and starving.

Mimi had woken up and was irritable. She was overtired, I could tell. It had been a long day for a five-year-old. The bus had grown crowded and people were talking loudly. That, and my exhaustion, caused me to be less vigilant about Mimi's ongoing chatter. She was asking me something. That much I could tell. It was frustrating not to understand.

We emerged from the bus station into a crowded, busy street. There was a place that sold pizza nearby, a fast-food joint. We badly needed food.

We joined the noisy crowd in beach attire surging into the place, and I bought a pizza and some soft drinks, and we found an unoccupied table. The pizza tasted delicious. We munched silently. I decided to find a place to sleep for the night and go to the police station in the morning.

Looking back, I see it was the first of many acts of procrastination. That night in Biarritz was the first time I could have brought Mimi to the authorities and told my story about rescuing her from a kidnapper. It was the first place I could safely do that without risking drawing attention to Etienne's help and explaining the boat ride from Portugal.

All I can say is that I was tired, too tired to be careful about what I would tell the police. I needed to sleep and to have time to think so that I wouldn't incriminate myself.

I tried two large hotels which were full, before finding us a room in a small inn further away from the tourist area. I tucked Mimi in before I took a long shower and crawled into bed next to her. The double bed was spacious and felt luxurious after the cramped small bed at the house.

We were safe at last. I was proud of myself. I had done something really good today.

As I drifted off to sleep, I promised myself that in the morning I would seek out the police and tell them everything, but only after I had formulated a plan that would safeguard Etienne and expose the truth behind Mimi's abduction.

Chapter 29

When I woke, it was not yet light, and Mimi was still sleeping peacefully. Something had been nudging at my consciousness, something I had forgotten until now, but I was wide awake with a start as I realized it wasn't something I had dreamt. It was real.

I was remembering a conversation. That night in Paris when I met Gregory, before he had asked my name, before we talked, someone in the group had joked, "we know Gregory can get away with anything because of his connections with the police elite."

I don't remember the exact words. The guy, whose name I didn't know, had spoken in French. It sounded like he'd said *élite policière,* which to me meant high-ranking police. Gregory had shrugged, said something I can't remember, but I don't think he denied the connection, whatever it was.

I wish I'd paid more attention. At the time I thought he was attractive, but we hadn't yet spoken and most of the people there were new to me. I had no reason to pay attention, no reason to be particularly concerned that he was connected to high-ranking police officials. Now I couldn't believe I had forgotten that piece of information. How powerful were his connections? How easy would it be for him to deny any wrongdoing and to be believed? And what would that mean for me? And for Mimi?

There was more. On our road trip, when he told me about working for the children's organization, he had said there was a history of public service in his family. They were on the side of law and order. Again, I should have been more curious, asked more questions.

He had probably lied about his job. Maybe he had lied about his police connections too, but I had no way of knowing. Maybe all of it was true.

Now I was jolted awake with a shocking suspicion. What if Gregory used his family connections to find us and to accuse me of kidnapping Mimi?

The thought sent a chill down my spine. If he truly had influential connections within law enforcement, it meant that bringing Mimi directly to the authorities could put me in even greater jeopardy. It would be so easy for Gregory to deny any involvement in the kidnapping and to cast suspicion on me. I was the one who had Mimi. Was there even evidence to implicate Gregory? It would be just my word and maybe Mimi's if she remembered him. If they took a five-year-old's testimony seriously.

Too late, I realized that coming to France was not the lifesaver I had believed when we were on the boat with Etienne. The possibility of Gregory tracking us down through his connections was greater here in France.

If he thought of it, that is. If he knew we were here. But he wouldn't know unless I went to the police. Etienne wouldn't tell him and no one else had seen us leave Portugal. Etienne was in that little cove because of his boat's malfunction. I had gathered it wasn't a normal stopping off point for him.

I tried to calm myself. Gregory wouldn't think we had come to France. It would be more likely for him to believe we had made our way back to Lisbon, hitching a ride perhaps. He would believe I attempted to return Mimi to her home.

My excitement and the feeling of release I had felt yesterday diminished. I considered bringing Mimi to the door of the police station, getting her to walk in there alone and say she wanted to go home. But I would have to communicate to her what I wanted her to do. And communication was a problem. She might not understand. She might refuse, run after me. How could I disappear until I knew she was safe, even if I had a fast escape route planned out in advance?

And she could describe me. She knew my name was Lulu. She knew Etienne's name. Turning Mimi in would be dangerous.

As I lay awake in that dimly lit room, the dawn light seeping in through the window, I realized that my initial decision last night to delay involving the authorities was not only driven by fatigue and the need to protect Etienne's involvement but also by some half-conscious memory of Gregory's power. It had been wise to wait and think about it. The fear was well-founded that his reach could extend far and wide, making no place safe.

Caution was paramount and taking the time to gather more information and devise a solid plan was even more crucial. I needed to be certain that Mimi's safety wouldn't be compromised if I were to approach the police. If he was really involved in an organization which placed foster children, Gregory might even lie convincingly to the police and claim Mimi was one of his charges and had been kidnapped by me. She might be returned to him and never get back to her family.

I wished I had asked more questions about how he did things. Did he forge identification papers for the children he kidnapped? He might have a way of proving that Mimi belonged in the organization he worked for.

I needed to be cautious and strategic in my actions. I had no knowledge of the threats we faced and the best way to navigate them. Somehow, I would need to uncover the truth about Gregory's connections and find people I could trust. Until then, it might be wise not to approach the authorities.

After a very welcome shower, Mimi and I dressed in our clothes from yesterday, which were grubby, and I took her to get breakfast. I struggled, trying to explain she could go home now. Despite my fear of the consequences, I was still considering dropping her off at the police station. When I looked at her open, trusting little face, I became convinced I had no choice. I had to make sure she got back to her family.

She didn't understand what I was saying.

After breakfast I found a bookstore, thinking I would buy a book of Portuguese phrases. They only had French to Portuguese translations. I bought the book anyway. It would be of limited use since my French was not exactly fluent, but it was better than nothing.

As I paid for the book, my heart almost stopped as I glanced at a rack of newspapers and saw Mimi's little face staring back at me. Of course, there was a search for her. I grabbed the paper, folding it over to hide the picture, and hurried us out of the shop. A quick glance reassured me no one was paying us any attention.

I'd had a brainwave. I would give Mimi the paper to carry with her into the police station. Surely, they would understand this was the missing girl. Again, I hesitated. What if Gregory claimed her? The article attached to the photo simply identified her as Maria. So, her name was Maria, not Mimi. The article didn't reveal her last name or who her family was. I wondered why.

I was torn. How could I be sure the police would return her to her parents and not to Gregory? For a few moments, I even wondered if she was an abandoned child after all, just as Gregory had said. But she couldn't be. She had cried for her Mama that first night. I had to take the chance.

Chapter 30

I consulted the phrase book and found the words in Portuguese for go in, give them this.

There was a restaurant across from the police station. I could watch through the window to make sure she went inside and didn't come back out.

I walked us slowly towards the police station, then stopped on the street outside the entrance.

Bracing myself, I said haltingly, "entrar dê-lhes isto," hoping the pronunciation was close enough, and she understood I was saying, "go in, give them this."

Mimi stared at me, puzzled. She didn't understand. I repeated the words as I handed her the rolled-up paper and gestured towards the door of the police station. I leaned over to kiss her on the forehead. She reached out for my hand. And led me towards the door.

"No. You go," I said, pulling my hand away. I gestured again towards the door and started to walk away. She stood there a moment, then she ran after me.

"No, Mama," she cried.

She was crying, calling me Mama, saying something else in Portuguese, and refusing to go into the building. That—calling me Mama — was so unexpected. I stood looking at her helplessly.

People were noticing, glancing sadly at the sobbing child, and glaring judgmentally at me.

"It's okay baby," I said.

She gripped my hand, not letting go, as I hurried us quickly away from the police station.

I was at a loss. What could I do now? If I walked into the police station with her, attempted to explain who she was, would she continue clinging to me? Would she call me mama again? Would she refuse to stay with them?

And they would want information from me. Lots of details. They would probably photograph me, maybe take my fingerprints.

And what would they do to me? Would I end up in a French prison? To them, I was one of the kidnappers. That was becoming clearer to me. They would be suspicious of me, and I might not be able to change their minds.

From their point of view, I had lured Mimi into the car. I could offer no proof that I knew nothing about Gregory's intentions, only my word. What if they searched and found my record of arrests? On paper, I didn't look like an upstanding citizen. Why would they believe me?

I had changed. I had left that part of me behind. But would they believe that? I was drug free now, but my record of arrest for drug possession would not go away. And there was the complaint filed by the Nelsons about the incident involving their baby. I was not to blame, but the evidence did not support my innocence. The Nelsons believed I had been negligent, citing my history of drug-taking. I hadn't been high that night I babysat for them. The child had cried and cried. I didn't know she needed a doctor. Luckily, they had come home early, had taken her to the hospital, and she had been okay. But that complaint they filed was on my record, along with my drug arrests.

No, I couldn't walk into a French police station and identify myself as the person who was with the kidnapper in Lisbon when Mimi was kidnapped.

But now I was at a loss. How could I return her if she refused to leave my side?

She wouldn't leave me to go with strangers. If her parents, her real mama, appeared, then doubtless she would happily go to them. But they were in Lisbon, probably close to where we had found her playing. I didn't know how to find that part of the city. Even if I found it, would she know her way home from there? Would someone recognize her?

Again, I would face the same problem with the police in Portugal as in France. And Gregory might be searching in Lisbon for us. What if he found us first? I couldn't risk it.

But, meanwhile, Mimi's photo was in the newspaper. People might recognize her. I needed to change her appearance in whatever small way was possible. I took us to buy some clothes. We needed toothbrushes, underwear, tee-shirts, shorts. I bought her some hair clips and in the dressing room, tied her long hair up in a sort of loose bun. It wasn't much of a transformation, but it was better than nothing. I bought her cute sunglasses with yellow frames which she loved.

As we continued walking through the bustling streets, an idea formed. If I couldn't rely on the police, perhaps there were organizations or social services that could help us and wouldn't ask questions.

I had spotted a community center a few blocks away. I retraced our steps back and examined the sign outside. It seemed like a place where we might find help and support. Gathering my courage, I guided Mimi towards the door. They might connect us with agencies that could help.

Entering the center, I approached the reception desk. The staff looked up, two middle-aged women, their eyes filled with curiosity and warmth. In broken French, I explained our situation, emphasizing that Mimi was a missing child and needed assistance.

The receptionist listened attentively, her expression growing increasingly concerned. She made a phone call and spoke rapidly in French, relaying the details of our situation. Moments later, a woman with kind eyes, a social worker named Claire, arrived to assist us.

Claire greeted us in French with compassion and understanding. With a sinking heart, I realized she spoke no English. She spoke slowly, and I understood she was saying she had experience working with families and children in need. I struggled to explain that Mimi was from Lisbon, a missing child, and I wanted to have her returned to her family.

Claire asked for Mimi's name and that of her parents.

I looked at Mimi, who was holding my hand and looking at me trustingly.

"I think it's Maria," I said, "but I don't know her last name."

It was then that Mimi chose to tug at my hand and say, "Mama, I want home," in English.

Claire looked at both of us in surprise, then with suspicion. "You are mother?" she asked.

"No." I shook my head vigorously.

Mimi continued to cling to my hand, calling me Mama, unaware of the confusion that was brewing.

I searched for words and gestures as I tried to explain. But despite my best efforts, the woman's sympathetic gaze faded, replaced by doubt and suspicion. The miscommunication had led her to believe that I was Mimi's mother and attempting to abandon her.

Panic surged through me as I realized the gravity of the misunderstanding. In a frantic attempt to rectify the situation, I pointed at Mimi, saying, "your name," in Portuguese. She smiled and said, "Mimi," remembering our old game. I said, "No, it's Maria." She laughed and repeated, "Mimi," then pointed at me and said, "Mama."

Claire's face had become grim. Desperately, I pulled out the newspaper with Mimi's picture on it and showed it to the woman. But she hardly glanced at it.

I could see Claire had already made up her mind. Mimi's attachment to me, her calling me Mama, had convinced her. And I saw that Mimi's new hairdo altered the contours of her face sufficiently so that she looked quite different from the younger version of her that had been captured in the picture. The yellow sunglasses which she refused to remove didn't help either.

If the woman didn't think I was a mother trying to abandon her daughter, then she thought I was a sensation-seeker, even deranged, my imagination captured by the newspaper article.

Seeing the doubt etched across her face, I knew I had to make a swift decision. With a heavy heart, I recognized that the consequences of staying and trying to explain the situation could put us in even greater danger. I thanked Claire for her help. She nodded curtly and did not try to stop me as, taking Mimi's hand, I quickly walked out of the building.

Chapter 31

What to do now? My attempts to comfort Mimi in those first hours of her kidnapping had formed a bond between us. Then, on our journey to Biarritz, I had encouraged the pretense that I was her mother and had worked hard to teach her words in English, believing we would draw less unwelcome attention that way.

The child couldn't really believe I was her mother. But we were among strangers, and I was the only one she knew. It explained why she was clinging to me like a leech. I was the only thing familiar to her. When she was reunited with her parents, she would forget all about me.

Unless she didn't come from a loving family who was missing her. Maybe that was one thing Gregory got right. I could be returning her to an unhappy situation. Why had she been alone on the street?

I was puzzled about why she wouldn't say her name. Surely, she knew her name. Had I confused her by calling her Mimi? Was she trying to please me by using that name? The language barrier was such a problem. I needed to learn Portuguese so that I could understand what she was saying. She was learning words in English, but how long would it take before we could really communicate in English?

And perhaps we should leave Biarritz. If the woman at the community center had second thoughts, and realized Mimi really was the missing child from Lisbon, she might report our visit to the police. They could be looking for us. That wouldn't be a bad thing if it meant Mimi would be rescued. But it would mean trouble for me.

I realized now that the longer I kept Mimi with me, the more guilty I would look in the eyes of the authorities.

If we were in the United States, I would feel safer. I might still be found guilty, but I could find a lawyer to help. And I still had my return ticket. I could fly back from Paris to Seattle in a few days.

But I couldn't abandon Mimi. If I crept out of our hotel room while she was sleeping, I could get away. But she would wake up alone and frightened. If I wrote a long explanation in English and left it beside her, she might eventually be returned to her home.

Maybe. Or she might wander out onto the street alone, crying, looking for me, and without the long explanation I had written. She might be found by a kind person who would do the right thing. But she might not. She might just as easily be found by someone evil. I thought of how easily she had come with me and Gregory.

I couldn't bear to think of abandoning her. I would have to take her with me wherever I went. Without travel documents for her, I couldn't board a flight.

Perhaps I could get a fake ID for her, like the ones we got when we were sixteen and wanted to go to clubs. Simon had known a guy who made fake IDs. Maybe I could find someone who would do that. If I could get us to the States, I could get help there. I could decide on my next steps. I knew I wasn't thinking clearly, but right now, being in a familiar place was very appealing.

But first I wanted to leave Biarritz. I tried to remember which French cities had a large population of emigrants, thinking many of them might need forged papers in order to work in France.

Outside of Paris, there was Marseilles. I remembered reading that the city had a reputation for its vibrant underground economy and diverse communities. Marseilles offered a greater chance of finding individuals who could help me. There also might be more employment options, as I was quickly running out of money.

Of course, returning to Paris would be more logical. My flight left from there on July 15th, eleven days from now. But I didn't want to be in Paris for eleven days. I didn't want to run into Stephanie or any of the friends who knew Gregory.

I had seen a street sign pointing to the train station. We had all our belongings with us, having checked out of our room that morning. I bought a cheap canvas tote-bag and put the morning's purchases in it. We had a change of clothes, some underwear, toothbrushes, and light nightgowns, as well as the Portuguese phrase book. The newspaper with Mimi's picture I threw away.

"Let's go on a train," I said to Mimi. She nodded and smiled, but I didn't think she understood. "Choo-choo," I said, then looked up the word for train in the phrase book. I tried again. "Choo-choo. Comboio."

Mimi laughed and repeated, "choo-choo, comboio." She put her hand in mine, and we walked to the train station. It felt good to be leaving Biarritz.

At the train station, I found that the last train of the day to Marseilles was leaving in fifteen minutes. I paid for our tickets and hurried to the gate. There was no time to rethink. I settled us in our seats and saw the train was filling up fast.

A glance at the brochure I had grabbed revealed it would be a very long journey — almost twelve hours if I was reading the information correctly. I hadn't realized Marseilles was so far away. But it was too late to change my mind now. The train pulled out of the station.

As the train departed from Biarritz, I gazed out of the window, my thoughts consumed by the uncertainty that lay ahead. The rhythmic clatter of the train wheels on the tracks seemed to echo the turbulence in my mind. Mimi sat beside me, her small hand clutching her Bobbsie toy tightly. She must have sensed my unease and looked up at me with her innocent eyes, seeking reassurance.

We settled into our seats, surrounded by a mixture of locals and tourists, their conversations blending into a symphony of foreign words that only added to my feeling of isolation. I realized that the journey to Marseilles would be more than just a physical one. It would be a test of resilience, adaptability, and the courage to seek help when needed.

Chapter 32

As the train traveled through picturesque landscapes, I mulled over the challenges that awaited us in Marseilles. The language barrier loomed large, making job hunting a daunting task. My proficiency in French was limited and finding work that would support both Mimi and me would require a stroke of luck. The thought of leaving her alone while I worked gnawed at my heart. How could I ensure her safety and well-being in an unfamiliar city?

My dwindling cash reserves added to my growing anxiety. Borrowing from my credit card was a temporary solution, and I knew I needed a more sustainable plan. Desperation led me to consider cashing in my plane ticket back to Seattle, but the prospect of losing that lifeline made me hesitate. I couldn't afford to lose the chance of returning home, nor could I bear the thought of leaving Mimi behind.

Lost in my worries, I barely noticed the woman who took the seat across from us. She was middle-aged, wearing a blue dress with an exquisite silver brooch pinned to the neckline. Her hair was expertly styled. I felt shabby in my cheap tee shirt and shorts, with my hair falling untidily into my eyes.

The woman's eyes were curious and radiated warmth and interest. She smiled at Mimi and said in French, "that's a beautiful toy."

Mimi smiled back but said nothing. I looked down at her and she grabbed my hand. She was cautious around strangers. Too late, I thought sadly. If she had been less friendly to me and Gregory that day, we would not be in this situation now.

And I would never have met Mimi. I was becoming increasingly maternal towards her, responding to her need for me. And she filled my need for love and connection.

"You have a beautiful daughter," she said in French.

I said, "merci," and attempted a smile.

Perhaps that one word revealed my origins or maybe it was something else. Maybe my exhaustion was more evident than I realized, or the woman had seen the apprehension on my face.

"You seem troubled, my dear," the woman said in accented English. "Is there anything I can do to help?"

Surprised by her sudden kindness, I hesitated for a moment, unsure whether to share my struggles with a stranger. Of course, I needed to be cautious, and it was unwise to talk to strangers, but her genuine concern gave me a flicker of hope. And it had been so long since anyone asked me how I was and if they could help me. The woman was on her way to Marseilles, and she was French. Maybe she could help. It couldn't hurt to ask. She might know where I would find work.

Haltingly, I confided, "we are on our way to Marseilles where I know no one and will need a job. I am an American citizen and don't have working papers to work in France. As you can tell, my knowledge of French is limited, so it would be difficult to find work even with working papers. And if I get a job, how would I take care of Mimi while I am working?"

I tailed off, afraid I sounded pathetic, and waiting for the woman to murmur something kind before ending our conversation.

The woman had listened attentively, her expression empathetic. She didn't ask why we were traveling to Marseilles instead of to a place where there would be friends and family to help.

"I might be able to help," she said, surprising me. "I have a friend in Marseilles who runs a small language school. They often need English tutors for young children. I believe she often hires young American or English students. She has a method for arranging work permits for them. I don't know the details, but I can connect you with her, and perhaps she can offer you a job. It won't be a fortune, but it would be a start, and you might keep your daughter in the class with you."

"That would be perfect. I can't thank you enough."

Relief washed over me as I realized the implication of her offer. My foreignness, which I saw as a limitation, might turn out to be an advantage. A job teaching English would not only provide the means to support Mimi and myself over the next ten days, but might also enable me to spend more time with her. Perhaps she could be a student in my classes and would learn English. We could communicate better. Of course, it would mean that this school would have my name and passport information on file and that authorities could find me more easily. Would it mean Gregory could also find me? But I had no other option right now. I had to take the chance.

I thanked the woman profusely, as she gave me her contact information and the address and phone number of the language school. She assured me she would call her friend as soon as she reached Marseilles so that her friend, Jeanne, would expect my call.

The woman, whose name was Marie-Louise Masson, got off the train at the stop before ours. She lived in a suburb of Marseilles. As we exchanged heartfelt goodbyes, I felt a glimmer of hope for the future. Perhaps, with the help of this stranger and her connection, I could accomplish my goals in this foreign city. I could get a job, save some money, and could find someone who would create identification papers for Mimi.

It was later that I realized I would need new identification papers for myself, too. A child, after all, would need to be accompanied by the adult responsible for her.

And Gregory was probably looking for me. He was looking for someone named Lulu Ackerly. It would be wise to change my own name and have a fake ID created for me as well as for Mimi.

It would be difficult, but I could do this. I mattered to someone, and I hadn't felt I mattered for a long time. It gave me courage. With renewed determination, I glanced down at Mimi, who had fallen asleep, her little head nestled against my shoulder. As I gently stroked her hair, I whispered promises of a brighter tomorrow.

Oriana

Chapter 33

Oriana and Rob sat in silence. The worn notebook lay open on the table before them, its pages filled with fragments of Rhea's past. Oriana desperately needed to piece together the puzzle, to understand the motivations behind the kidnapping and Rhea's subsequent disappearance.

She flipped through the pages once again, searching for any missed clues or connections. Nothing stuck out, but she would take the notebook with her. At home, when she could examine it at a more leisurely pace, she might stumble across something she had missed before. But now, here in the cabin, she wondered if they should take the time to explore the surrounding area.

"We need to go back to the village," Oriana said, her voice determined. "There is no information here about who owns the cabin. If we can find the owner, we may learn more about Rhea's life and why she made the choices she did. We might even discover where she went. It's hard to believe Rhea had people in her life I knew nothing about, but then she lied to me about everything."

Oriana was aware her voice was trembling.

Rob nodded in agreement. "There must be a record of property ownership in the county offices or the library. We could search there and trace the owner of the cabin."

They locked the cabin door, and Oriana returned the key to its hiding place under the rock. The return trek to Lakeview's main street took less than ten minutes. The secluded cabin in the woods that she remembered from childhood was not deep in the forest, though it gave that impression while there.

As they approached their car in the small parking lot next to the Camden General Store, Oriana stopped and looked along the street.

Besides the general store, there was a bar and some small, weathered houses that looked like they had been built in the last century.

"I don't think we'll find answers here."

Once in the car, Rob consulted his phone. "Lakeview is a hamlet in Landen County," he read. "The county seat is the town of Arendale. There is a library there, a county office and a historical society."

Oriana glanced at the time on the car's dashboard. It was 2:30 pm. "How about going there directly? We might look at records for Lakeview."

"It's Saturday. The offices are likely closed," Rob said, "but the library or the historical society might be open."

The drive to Arendale took no more than twenty minutes. The town had a cheerful busy air, with pedestrians shopping and a stream of traffic. Lakeview seemed like a ghost town in comparison. Here, there was a pharmacy, and a hardware store and people were chatting on the street. There were several restaurants too, reminding Oriana they hadn't eaten lunch. That had to wait.

First, they walked by the county building, which housed the courthouse and the local tax office, and discovered it was indeed closed.

"Let's try the library," Rob said, pointing to the red-bricked building on the corner with the prominent sign that said *Arendale Public Library*.

As they drew close, Oriana read the sign that said it was open and would remain open until five. "We're in luck," she said.

It was quiet and empty inside. The librarian at the desk looked up curiously as they entered, hesitated, and looked around uncertainly.

"Is there something I can help you locate?" the librarian asked.

"Do you have ownership records of properties in the area?" Oriana asked.

"Yes, follow me," the woman said briskly. "What township are you interested in researching?"

"We would like to trace ownership of a cabin in the woods in Lakeview. But I don't have the address. I know exactly where it is, so I could find it on a map," Oriana replied.

"I'm sorry, but without an address or any identifying information, it'll be challenging to locate any records," the librarian explained sympathetically. "But there are some old maps of Lakeview. Perhaps you can locate the cabin on one of them and find the address that way."

She pulled out an outsized book from a shelf in a corner labeled *County History*.

"Let's see." She busily flipped pages and revealed a map labeled *Lakeview Village and Environs, circa 1950.*

Rob pored over the map eagerly. "Here is our path through the woods," he said, pointing at the small track and the words Pines Bluffs. "Only the road that forks off is not named here."

The librarian was still standing close by, obviously intrigued by their search. Now she said, "you can see a house is indicated there," she said, pointing to a small square symbol. "That is the symbol for a dwelling. It may be the address would be Pines Bluffs, or Off Pines Bluffs, something like that. But we are not the best resource on property ownership."

Oriana thanked her for her willingness to assist and asked if there were any other resources they could access to gather information on the cabin.

"The county building is the best place, if you can come back on a weekday," the librarian said.

"We were hoping to gather information today," Oriana said.

"There is another place you could check," the librarian said, thinking for a moment. "Arendale has a historical society that keeps records of local families, properties, and events. They have old newspaper clippings, photographs, and other documents. Perhaps there's a chance you might find something there. They have material for the entire county, and the building is just at the end of this street."

"Do you think it might be open now?" Oriana asked, her attention quickening.

"I believe it's open until five today. It is the white building at the end of this street on the other side."

Excited by the prospect, Oriana and Rob made their way to the Arendale Historical Society. The sign just inside the main door of the quiet building stated that they were proud to house an array of archives and artifacts dating back to 1827.

Oriana approached the reception desk and explained their purpose to a friendly elderly man who introduced himself as Lewis Jenkins. He listened intently and then directed them to a section that listed homes ownership over the years. The shelves were separated by township.

Eagerly, Oriana selected a large bound volume labeled *Lakeview Properties*.

"They are listed by street," she said disappointed, as she turned the pages.

"But look, they have houses listed for Pines Bluffs."

"Yes, but the track we took didn't have a sign. It never did, even when I was a child. It complicates things if the cabin is listed with the Pines Bluffs address, as we won't know which address is the right one, unless the address is Off Pines Bluffs, as the librarian suggested."

"This record is organized logically," Rob said. "First there are the properties on Main Street, then a street called Woodview, then Pines Bluffs, and now Lovell Lane. And there is only one house listed for Lovell Lane."

Chapter 34

"Could that be it? Lovell Lane? Maybe it used to be called Lovell Lane, and the sign fell off and was never replaced. The name sounds vaguely familiar, but I don't know why."

Rob pointed to the faded blue writing in the column under owner. "A. M. Lovell is the owner since 2006. The previous owner was James Lovell and before that, Samuel Lovell. So, the property is owned by the Lovell family and has been for a long time."

"But why was Rhea using it? Does she know A. M. Lovell?"

"We can't be sure Lovell Lane is the address of the cabin," Rob said, "but I don't see any other building close to Pines Bluffs."

There was another shelf Mr. Jenkins had suggested. It contained old copies of the local newspaper, the Landen Gazette.

"I doubt Rhea is mentioned in the newspaper," Oriana said. "She worked so hard to maintain her privacy, and now I know why. She would have been careful to keep her name out of the papers."

"The Lovells might be mentioned," Rob said. "If we learn more about them, it might help. We might even discover a connection to Rhea." He pulled out a bound copy of the paper for the year 2002 and started leafing through it.

"Let's look from 2000 to about 2012," he said, handing Oriana another bound copy.

Carefully, Oriana and Rob sifted through the newspapers, scanning each page, hoping to stumble upon a clue that would shed light on the cabin and Rhea's connection to it. The news was mainly of winter storms, store or restaurant openings, occasional petty crimes, but no mention of Lakeview or of people with Lovell as their last name.

About to give up hope of finding anything, Oriana pulled out the years 1997 to 1999. Rhea wasn't yet in New Falls then, but maybe the Lovells would be mentioned. She might as well look.

It was then that a headline caught her attention: *Local Tragedy Shocks Community - Simon's Death Leaves Town in Mourning.*

The paper mainly reported on more mundane matters. This article promised more drama, though at first Oriana didn't believe it had anything to do with Rhea or the Lovells.

She started reading. The article recounted the heartbreaking story of a young boy named Simon who had tragically lost his life in a car accident. It described the grief that had engulfed the town and the profound impact of Simon's death on his loved ones.

As Oriana delved deeper into the article, she discovered something unexpected. The last name of the grieving family was Lovell. With trembling hands, she turned the page to continue reading. Now she knew why the name Lovell had seemed so familiar.

Simon Lovell was the name of the boy Rhea had been so in love with in Idaho. But why would a small town in New York State be mourning his death? Could there be two Simon Lovells, aged twenty, who had died on the same day? That was highly unlikely.

How could this be? The connection was undeniable, and the realization sent shivers down Oriana's spine.

"Rob," she called out, her voice barely a whisper. "I think I've found something. Simon's family... Rhea's Simon - they might have a connection to the cabin. Could it be a coincidence?"

Rob pulled leaned over her shoulder, his eyes scanning the article. "It's too much of a coincidence, Oriana. It has to be the same Simon Lovell. Look." He pointed to a section later in the article that Oriana had not yet read. "Here it says the accident happened in Seattle. It *is* the same person. That's the connection Rhea has to the cabin. We need to dig deeper into this connection."

They stared at each other in shock.

Mr. Jenkins was tidying up, a discreet hint he was about to close the building for the day. Oriana glanced at the old clock over the door.

"Rob, it's after five. They're about to close."

They rose hastily and thanked Mr. Jenkins, who courteously invited them to come back on a weekday. He volunteered here on Tuesday and Thursday afternoons.

On the street, Rob said, "We can do no more here today."

"Except get some food," Oriana said. "I'm starving."

*****

"Did Rhea keep in touch with Simon's family all these years? And who is A. M. Lovell? Would that person know where Rhea is now?"

Rob shrugged. "It's all possible, I suppose. It's also possible Rhea spent time in the cabin with Simon or he told her about it. She might even have chosen New Falls because the area was familiar."

"That would have been risky. Now we know she changed her name, and my name. She wouldn't want to be recognized as Lulu. That would mean she wouldn't want the Lovells to see her and recognize her."

"She must have known that the Lovells would not show up at the cabin."

"I need to find out more about the Lovells," Oriana said.

She glanced at Rob's face, which looked weary. "But enough for today. Let's enjoy our meal."

The food was plentiful and flavorful, and they ate hungrily. When they were almost finished, Rob said, "I know you want answers about why Rhea did what she did. But do you think you are giving Rhea's disappearance all this attention because it is so overwhelming getting acquainted with the Taglias?"

As usual, Rob spoke directly, pulling no punches.

"It is overwhelming. Of course, it is. Because being a Portuguese child who was kidnapped is like a story, a fantasy. What I remember is my life with Rhea, growing up in New Falls. She was my only family for as long as I can remember. We only had each other. I need to understand what happened, why she did what she did, before I can move on."

"And why she left."

"If she thinks she will be arrested and put in jail, that would be a powerful motivation for disappearing."

"There is that. But does she ever intend returning?"

Oriana shrugged helplessly. "I don't think the Taglias will sue. While they would not object to a police investigation, I think they are so happy their search is at an end they want no further dealings with the police. But Garcia is excited about his success in solving the case. Rightly so. If I can persuade Garcia to drop the charges ......"

"Even if you could, you still have no way of letting Rhea know it would be safe for her to return to New Falls."

"I thought of another reason for Rhea's disappearance," Oriana said. "It might seem farfetched, but help me think this through. The world, or anyone who cares to look it up, would know that Rhea Stone had kidnapped Maria Taglia twenty years ago and Maria is now known as Oriana Stone, or Oriana Chalmers."

"What if there really was an evil man? What if we are wrong and Rhea did not kidnap me? When I told her I knew she had kidnapped me, she said something about rescuing me from an evil man. I assumed it was a deranged illusion or an excuse, and that she believed she had rescued me from an evil man in my family. But what if she was talking about some other man? That she was saving me from him? That man might want revenge or might fear Rhea would report him to the authorities. Rhea could be in danger."

"It still doesn't explain why she kept you from your family all these years," Rob said. "But yes, anything is possible. You had a reaction to the photo of that man, Gregory, taken in Portugal around the time you were kidnapped. Maybe he was involved. You have told Garcia about Gregory. It might lead nowhere, but who knows? Garcia might come up with something."

"I'm not ready to tell him yet that Rhea is Lulu Ackerly. I don't want the police to find her until we know more. In fact, I might not want the police to find her ever."

"She might have adopted yet another identity now. I doubt she returned to being Lulu Ackerly."

"Still, I want to know more about Lulu's early life, Simon, the cabin, and the Lovells before sharing that information with Garcia or anyone else."

Chapter 35

As soon as they returned home, Oriana opened her laptop and searched for information about the Lovells in Idaho. Immediately, news stories about Simon's tragic death popped up. Eventually, she found his family's address in Idaho.

"There is a James Lovell listed on Skyler Road, in Rogersville, Idaho," she said. "He is in his seventies, and Margaret Lovell also in her seventies lives there. They must be Simon's parents. There is a Matthew Lovell, also listed. That could be the A. M. Lovell who owns the cabin."

It was late, and Rob was stretched out in bed. It had been a long day and Oriana knew she should let him sleep. She would put away the laptop shortly and join him. But not just yet.

"See if you can find any other reference to James Lovell in the Lakeview area. The family obviously had ties to Lakeview. There might be other relatives who still live there. Samuel, who owned the cabin before James, might have lived nearby. Maybe there is a second property owned by Lovells in Arendale or close to it," Rob suggested.

"Samuel was probably James's father," Oriana mused. "I imagine he had no other children living in the area. Otherwise, why leave the cabin to James, who lives so far away?"

Oriana continued her search for the history of the Lovell family in Lakeview. She became immersed and presently noticed Rob's gentle snoring. Good. She was glad he was sleeping. She was curled up in the comfortable old armchair she had brought with her from her college digs when she and Rob married and moved to this more upscale apartment. The armchair was shabby now but comfortable and they had relegated it to a corner of the bedroom next to a small desk.

She soon became absorbed in her search. The room was quiet, with only the sound of Rob's breathing as background noise. Oriana was comfortable in the old chair, clad in her comfortable old nightgown. She could continue searching for a while longer.

After some thorough investigation, Oriana came across an obituary for Samuel Lovell. The obituary was twenty-five years old and mentioned that Samuel had a son named James Lovell, who now lived in Idaho. He also left behind a daughter named Margaret Carroll. Samuel was described as an upstanding member of the community, a well-respected lawyer and a man who had lived in Arendale all his life, a member of the historical society and the Arendale Country Club. The article stated the Lovell family had deep roots in the area, with many of their ancestors having settled there in the early 19th century.

A short time later, Oriana stumbled upon a newspaper article from the early 1900s that chronicled the life of an influential Lovell family member named Jonathan Lovell. He had been a prominent businessman in Lakeview, involved in various industries, such as timber and mining. Oriana gathered from the article in *The Landen Sun* that Lakeview had been a bigger town in 1905, when the article had been written. The article said that Jonathan Lovell was known for his philanthropic endeavors, contributing to the development of Lakeview and its surrounding communities. It wasn't clear how he was related to Samuel.

Oriana couldn't wait to share her findings with Rob and begin to piece together the history of the Lovell family in Lakeview. The Lovells had been a prominent and respected family in the area for generations, involved in various industries that helped shape the growth of Landen County. Rob would be interested in the family history and his expertise in historic preservation would be helpful.

But it would have to wait. Rob was fast asleep. Her concentration fading, Oriana eventually crawled in beside him. She thought she would be too full of questions to sleep, but it had been a long and emotional day, and soon she, too, was sleeping soundly.

Next morning, Oriana handed Rob a mug of strong coffee freshly brewed as soon as he emerged from the shower. She allowed him two sips before bursting out, "I want to reach out to Margaret and James Lovell. They were Simon's parents. They must have known Rhea well. Of course, they knew her as Lulu."

She stopped when she saw the skeptical expression on Rob's face. "I wouldn't tell them that Rhea kidnapped me and hid her identity as Lulu from me and everyone else. I would say nothing about Rhea—or Lulu. My story would be I grew up in New Falls and discovered the cabin, which led me to research who owns it. I am interested in local history, and I am curious to learn more about the Lovell family history, the history of Lakeview and the cabin."

"They are in Idaho," Rob said. "I assume you are proposing calling them. How much would they tell you, a stranger, on the phone? Or are you proposing a visit there? How do you think they would react to a stranger appearing on their doorstep asking about an old family cabin? And it's quite a journey from New York?"

"I hadn't thought of visiting there," Oriana said, her eyes brightening. "But why not? I would see the town where my mother—Rhea, that is, grew up. It would help me understand Rhea more. Maybe I could meet that teacher, Mrs. Johnson."

"In a small town, people talk to each other. Everyone knows what's going on. If you approach Mrs. Johnson and say you are the daughter of Lulu's friend, the Lovell's will hear about it. They will wonder if Lulu is now living in New Falls. Do you want to draw attention to Rhea in that way?"

Oriana's enthusiasm was dampened, but only momentarily. "I don't have to talk to Mrs. Johnson, only to the Lovells, if they will talk to me."

"But aren't you curious about Rhea's family? Why don't you want to talk to them?"

"What excuse could I give? I can use the history of the cabin and the Lovell history in Lakeview as an excuse to talk to James Lovell, but how could I explain reaching out to Lulu Ackerly's parents? I can hardly say I thought they were my grandparents, but it turns out they're not because Lulu kidnapped me in Portugal twenty years ago and I just discovered it—and by the way, she told me her name was Rhea Stone and her parents were dead."

Rob held his hand up. "I get your point, but think about whether this visit to Idaho is wise. I mean, you are working so hard to stay bonded to Rhea. You are becoming so enmeshed in her life, digging into her past like this. But you have a real, biological family who can't wait for your next visit, who really wants to know you. Why is it you don't want to pursue that heritage?"

Oriana stopped and stared at Rob, stricken. "It's so hard. My entire identity has been whipped away from me. I'm not Oriana Stone. I am Maria Taglia. I want to understand why. Why did Rhea do what she did? But you are right. I suppose it's easier to investigate Rhea's past and her identity than my own."

"I understand that this whole situation has turned your world upside down," Rob said, his tone now softer. "Discovering the truth about Rhea and your own identity as Maria Taglia is overwhelming. But remember, Oriana, your identity is not defined solely by your past. It's also shaped by the choices you make in the present and the relationships you build."

Oriana nodded, her mind clouded with conflicting emotions. "I know you're right, Rob. It's just... the idea of reaching out to Margaret and James Lovell feels like a connection to Rhea, to my past. It's like clinging to something familiar, even though it's all so twisted."

Rob put down his coffee mug and took her hand. "It's natural to seek familiarity, especially when faced with such a disorienting revelation. But you mustn't lose sight of the opportunity to forge your own path and embrace your biological family—the Taglias.

They may be strangers to you now, but they're waiting with open arms, eager to know you."

Tears welled up in Oriana's eyes as she let Rob's words sink in. She knew he was right. Her fear of embracing her biological family stemmed from a fear of loss. Losing Rhea, the woman she had believed was her mother. Trying to justify Rhea's actions was an excuse to avoid confronting her own identity.

Chapter 36

Oriana felt a wave of emotions crash over her as Rob's words sank in. She had been so preoccupied with Rhea's past and the web of secrets surrounding her she had neglected her own identity, her own roots. She had spent hours researching Rhea's history, even longer trying to piece together the puzzle of her life, and in the process, she had inadvertently neglected her own story.

Tears welled up in Oriana's eyes as she realized how much she had been avoiding the truth of her own existence. She had been using Rhea's past as a shield, an escape from grappling with her own anxieties and uncertainties. But deep down, she knew she couldn't continue running away from her own heritage forever.

"You're right, Rob," Oriana said, her voice filled with determination. "I've been so consumed by Rhea's story, trying to unravel the mysteries of her life, that I've neglected my own journey. I need to get to know the Taglias, learn about my roots, and discover who Maria Taglia truly is."

Rob stroked Oriana's hair gently. "Honey, I understand how difficult this is for you. Discovering the truth about your identity has got to be overwhelming and frightening. But remember, you are not alone in this. You have people who love you, who want to know you for who you truly are."

A surge of conflicting emotions flooded Oriana. On one hand, she yearned for a sense of belonging, a connection to her biological family that she had never known. On the other hand, the uncertainty and fear of facing her past, of potentially uncovering painful truths, made her hesitate.

Oriana looked into Rob's eyes, appreciating the unwavering support he had offered her since they first saw the picture in the newspaper of the kidnapped child.

"You're right, Rob. I've been hiding behind Rhea's story for far too long. It's time for me to confront my own identity and embrace my biological family. I need to face my fears, even if it's scary."

Rob squeezed Oriana's hand gently, his eyes filled with pride and encouragement. "I'm here for you, Oriana. Whatever you decide, I'll support you every step of the way. Just remember that your identity goes beyond a name or a past. It's the person you've become, the choices you make, and the love you share with those around you."

With Rob's reassurance, Oriana felt a renewed courage. She would reach out to her biological family. She would visit them soon and start the journey to understand her own heritage.

Over the following days, Oriana made plans to visit Lisbon in October. It would only be for a few days, but it would be a start. It would be over a long holiday weekend. She would take off an extra two days from work and get a cheap flight in October. She would travel alone, and this time would stay with the Taglias.

Carmela reported their parents were overjoyed at the news. Her mother was already fixing up a special bedroom to prepare for the return of Maria.

Oriana decided she would try to immerse herself in the family for those five days. She would try not to think so much about the past and allow new connections to be forged. She enrolled in evening classes in Portuguese and found she was absorbing the language quickly. Her knowledge of Spanish helped, but she wondered if her childhood memories were coming back, at least when it came to the language. She enjoyed the classes and got to know other students. Some of them came from Portuguese families and were motivated to learn more about their heritage.

But it was July, and the visit to Lisbon was not until October. If she could solve the mystery of Rhea before then, Oriana could commit herself more fully to her Taglia family.

After some thought, she wrote a letter to Margaret and James Lovell, explaining her genuine interest in the history of Lakeview and her discovery of the cabin. Oriana carefully crafted her words, omitting any mention of Rhea and emphasizing her interest in the history of the Lakeview area and her husband's background in preservation of historic buildings. She mentioned her own work in museum curation in Boston, but that she had grown up not far from Lakeview, hoping that her interest in the cabin would appear more professional. She added that if they were interested in talking to her on the phone or even in person, she would be delighted.

Oriana then forced herself to forget about the Lovells. She had done what she could. They might not respond. She turned her attention to her preparations for visiting the Taglias, her Portuguese studies, and the new friends she had made in the language classes.

*****

The envelope with her name printed neatly on the front had a sticker in the top left-hand corner with the name James Lovell and the Rogersville, Idaho, return address. Oriana's heart raced with a mix of excitement and nervousness as she opened the envelope and read James Lovell's response. She couldn't believe that he had written back. Even more unbelievable was he was agreeing to meet with her and discuss the cabin in Lakeview.

It was a short but courteous note. She had to go there. It was an unexpected opportunity to learn more about Rhea's past and perhaps gain some clarity about her own identity.

Rob was still uncertain about the wisdom of meeting the Lovells in person, but he offered unwavering support now that she was learning about her Portuguese culture and had planned her trip to Lisbon.

Oriana responded to James, expressing her gratitude for his willingness to meet her and suggesting possible meeting times. James responded, saying his time was flexible since he and Margaret were now retired. Oriana made plans for a quick trip to Idaho, leaving Boston on a Friday evening and returning Sunday night. James invited her to visit them on Saturday for lunch and included directions to their home.

As the day of her departure approached, Oriana's mind was a whirlwind of thoughts and emotions. She was eager to learn more about Rhea and the secrets that had been concealed for so long. Yet, she felt a sense of trepidation about what she might discover. She was trespassing into Rhea's past life as Lulu, a past Rhea, had hidden from her.

Finally, the weekend arrived. Oriana dashed out of work mid-afternoon to get the Friday evening flight to Boise, Idaho. She couldn't shake off the butterflies fluttering in her stomach as she imagined the meeting with James Lovell. Would he hold the key to the missing pieces of her identity? Would their conversation shed light on the mysteries surrounding Rhea and the cabin?

Upon arriving in Boise, Oriana rented a car at the airport. Rogersville was two hours away. She would drive there in the morning. She found a motel just outside Boise, checked in, and called Rob.

"Everything is so serene and empty here," she reported, "and yes, the motel is safe and clean and well-lit."

She woke up early, stopped at a diner and had a hearty breakfast, and set out for the two-hour drive to Rogersville. The town was smaller than she had imagined, nestled amidst picturesque mountains and tranquil forests. It exuded a sense of calm and serenity, a stark contrast to the chaos churning inside Oriana. The serenity helped calm her nerves. She had arrived too early to go directly to the Lovell's house, so she parked the car and wandered around the small down, stopping for coffee at the friendly restaurant called Linda's Place.

Finally, it was time to visit the Lovell's. Following James's directions, Oriana drove down a winding road that led to a beautiful country estate. The Lovell family's home was perched on a hill, surrounded by well-manicured gardens and tall trees that swayed gently in the breeze.

As she parked her car and made her way to the front door, Oriana's hands trembled slightly. She took a deep breath, willing herself to remain composed and open to whatever revelations awaited her. She rang the doorbell, and a few moments later, the door swung open.

Standing before her was an elderly man with kind eyes and a warm smile. James Lovell's resemblance to Simon, the boy in the photo with Rhea, was striking, and Oriana couldn't help but feel a pang of sadness at their loss.

"Hello, Oriana," James greeted her warmly. "I'm delighted to meet you finally. Please come in."

Oriana stepped into the Lovell residence, feeling a nervous anticipation. She couldn't help but notice the photos on the walls and was startled to see several of Simon and Rhea. It was a poignant reminder of the interconnectedness of her own life with the Lovell's.

"Margaret is preparing lunch," James said, "but why don't we sit and talk a little?" He led her to a couch with a view of the garden outside.

Oriana explained her interest in the history of the Lakeview and Arendale areas and Rob's work in historical preservation. She was probably repeating what she had said in her letters, but James nodded with interest.

Margaret appeared shortly, a tiny woman with a lively, curious expression. She shook Oriana's hand and said, "we don't get too many visitors from back East. Of course, our son, Matthew, lives there now and his wife is from New York. We don't see them as often as we would like."

"Let's have lunch, shall we?" James asked, and Margaret led the way to the dining table, set in a bay window overlooking a rose garden.

"How beautiful it is here," Oriana exclaimed.

"We like it," Margaret said. "Of course, with no children or grandchildren close by, we feel a bit isolated." She sighed. "Our son, Simon, died, you know."

"Yes, there was a report of it in the local Arendale paper," Oriana said. "It was such a tragedy."

The Lovells were silent for a moment, then James said brightly, "well, you are here to learn about the cabin, so let's talk about that."

The conversation then turned to a discussion of Lakeview's history and the Lovell family lineage. James shared anecdotes about his childhood, his love for the cabin, and the cherished memories they had created there.

James leaned back in his chair, his eyes brightening with nostalgia. "The cabin has been in our family for generations," he explained. "It was originally built by my great-grandfather, Samuel Lovell, back in the early 1900s. He was a visionary and saw the potential in the area. The cabin has seen many generations of Lovells, and it holds a special place in our hearts."

Chapter 37

Oriana sat across the table from James, listening to his stories and memories of Lakeview and the cabin, wondering how she could ask them about Lulu. If they talked about Simon again, she could ask more questions. If she was lucky, they might talk about Simon's girlfriend, Lulu. They must have known her well.

"You should visit our son, Matthew. I don't know if he used the cabin, but he lives not far from it."

"I would like that," Oriana said with surprise. "I didn't find any Lovells listed in the area."

"That's because their house belongs to his wife. She inherited it and it is listed in her name."

"We'll give you his phone number and the address," James promised, "and I will tell him we know you. I'm sure he will be pleased to see you."

Oriana wasn't so sure about how pleased Matthew would be, but was warmed by James' willingness to help. She thanked him and said she would definitely get in touch with him.

Margaret removed plates and returned with a coffeepot and plates of apple pie. "It's delicious," Oriana mumbled appreciatively as she tasted the cinnamon-laced apple and the flaky crust.

"Home-baked," Margaret said modestly. "I always served it with vanilla ice-cream, but we're watching our diet these days and I try not to keep ice-cream in the house."

"It's excellent on its own."

Margaret was tiny and Oriana doubted she needed to watch her diet. James was a much bigger man, and she suspected he was the one who needed to avoid the extra calories.

Margaret stood again and returned with a photo album. "There are photos here of Matthew, though mostly they are childhood photos." She cleared away the used dishes and opened the album, skimming over pages.

"Ah, here is a more recent photo." She moved the album so that Oriana could see the photo of a man and woman in their forties. They were smiling, wearing tee-shirts and shorts. Standing in front of them were a boy, and a girl aged about ten or twelve.

"That was taken about ten years ago here in our garden. Susan and Adam are now away at college, but Matthew and Alice look about the same still."

"Matthew looks like you," Oriana said to James, though she was thinking he looked like the picture of Simon she had found in Rhea's attic.

"It was Simon who looked like James," Margaret said with a sigh. "He was so like James when James was his age."

She flipped back through the album, and there it was. Oriana was staring in fascination at a photo of a teenaged Simon and Lulu, arms around each other, beaming at the camera.

"They look so happy," she said involuntarily.

"Those two were inseparable," Margaret said. "Whether that was good or bad, I don't know."

"Now, Margaret," James admonished mildly.

"They went to Seattle together. That's where he had the accident. I can't help thinking if he hadn't gone, if she hadn't encouraged him, the accident might never have happened and we might still have our Simon with us," Margaret said, tears in her eyes.

"He wanted to go, too. Maybe it was even his idea. We don't know," James said. Turning to Oriana, James explained, "Simon and Lulu were always together throughout high school. They moved to Seattle against our will, dropping out of college, though they said they would transfer to a college in Seattle. They never did."

"Then Matthew went to visit them," Margaret said. "I was worried, but Matthew came back and enrolled in college in Boise. He was two years younger than Simon."

"What happened to Lulu?" Oriana asked, holding her breath.

"We don't know. She could still be in Seattle for all we know," Margaret said with a touch of bitterness. "Oh, she was here for the funeral. She was devastated. She returned to Seattle afterwards. We didn't hear much from her after that."

"Matthew kept in touch with her," James said. "Even a couple of years later, Matthew saw her in Seattle. That's how he met Alice."

"Alice knew Lulu?" Oriana tried to conceal her excitement.

"They were friends. Lulu introduced Alice to Matthew when he visited for a weekend. Lulu had gone through a hard time after Simon's death, but she was getting over it. She told Matthew that Alice had helped her. Then, a few months later, Alice got in touch with Matthew, asking if he had heard from Lulu. It seemed she had gone on a vacation to Europe and never come back."

"Did they find out what happened to her?"

"No. She never returned. And she never contacted her parents. She just disappeared."

James sighed. "We must assume she had a dreadful accident."

"Does her family believe she is dead?" Oriana asked with a sinking feeling.

"That is the assumption," James said sadly. "Two bright shining stars gone. They should have had long, happy lives."

"Did Alice know where in Europe Lulu went?" Oriana asked. She was probably asking too many questions about Lulu, but she felt compelled to get as much information as possible.

"I believe she went to Paris and met a friend of Alice's there. After that I don't know. Alice could tell you the whole story," Margaret said.

Oriana finally took her leave, promising to stay in touch with James and Margaret. After driving a little down the quiet road, she pulled into a clearing and sat staring out the window, trying to piece together what she had learned.

Lulu - or Rhea—had been in Paris and then had disappeared. But Alice had known her, and she had married Simon's brother who owned the cabin Rhea had felt so safe visiting. It had to all be connected. Alice might know that Lulu had become Rhea. Maybe Matthew did as well. She would most definitely follow up with them.

But now she was in Rogersville, the town where Lulu grew up, where her family still lived. What else could she learn while she was here?

Her search for information about the Ackerly family had revealed that Lulu's parents had passed away a few years ago, even though an earlier search had left Oriana believing they were alive. However, she had found an address for Lulu's sister, Emily, who still lived in Rogersville and was now known as Emily Liston. Oriana's heart raced with anticipation as she contemplated reaching out to Rhea's sister.

She remembered Rob's admonition that Rogersville was a small town and people would talk. Emily might learn that Oriana Chalmers had visited the Lovells and was interested in the cabin in Lakeview. What reason would she have for reaching out to Emily?

But how long would the news of her visit to the Lovells take to reach Emily? If she acted now, today, the chances were Emily would know nothing about her? But what if news about her contact with Emily reached Alice and Matthew? Might that make them less willing to open up to her? James and Margaret had been so welcoming and so trusting. She didn't want to disappoint them or have them think she had ulterior motives. But isn't that exactly what was going on? She had kept the truth from them—used them really, if she was honest, to get information about Rhea.

Oriana sighed. Yet she knew she couldn't leave Rogersville without learning more about Emily.

As she sat there, something Margaret had said about the Ackerlys flashed into her mind and she thought, *yes, that's the answer.*

Margaret said, "they lost a child too. I heard they never heard from her. They died not knowing what happened to her. But at least they had Emily, who never moved away. In fact, she has a thriving little business right in Rogersville on Main Street."

James had said, "it is a good bookstore and adds to the appeal of Main Street."

That was it. She would visit the bookstore. Emily might not be there, but what did she have to lose? Oriana turned the car around and drove back past the Lovell's house toward the village of Rogersville.

Chapter 38

The village center was livelier now than when Oriana had stopped earlier. There was Main Street, as well as two streets leading off it. Besides Laura's Place, which she had visited earlier, there was a bustling restaurant with a bright green sign in the front that read *The Coffee Spot*. That might be a good place to stop later. She might even chat with some locals.

She headed down Main Street. There was only one bookstore. It said The Book Nook over the door. Oriana mentally thanked Margaret for mentioning Emily's bookstore. She would never have found Emily otherwise. Of course, Emily might not be here, but after another look along the length of Main Street, she was sure this was the only bookshop.

She looked at the window display, taking a moment to calm her nerves and think about what to say before stepping inside. The tinkling of the doorbell signaled her entry, and she was greeted by the comforting scent of books and the sight of Emily, engrossed in arranging shelves.

She knew right away it must be Emily. It was startling how much she resembled Rhea. But Emily's hair was an attractive brunette, short and styled, not grey and longish like Rhea's. She was dressed in a casual but smart blue blouse and black slacks. But the shape of her face and her eyes were the same as Rhea's. Oriana tried not to stare at the pointed chin, the high cheekbones.

Oriana responded to Emily's greeting with a warm smile, but was careful to maintain an air of casual interest.

"Good morning," she said pleasantly. "I couldn't help but notice your lovely bookstore. I'm a book enthusiast myself and was hoping to find some hidden gems. Do you have any recommendations?"

Emily looked up from her task, her face lighting up. "Oh, absolutely! I'd be happy to help you find something special. What genre are you interested in?"

Her voice, too, was like Rhea's. The same timbre. It was startling. If she hadn't been looking at her, Oriana would think it was Rhea speaking.

"I would be interested in anything of local interest, maybe local history," Oriana said. "I am an art historian, but very interested in the history side of that."

"You are not from around here," Emily said.

"No. I'm from New York and now live in Boston," Oriana replied.

Emily led her to a section of the bookstore which displayed books of local history, as well as some on local architecture. Oriana leafed through those as Emily tended to the other customers. She would buy a couple for Rob. He should find them interesting.

She wasn't sure how to return to their conversation, but as the shop became quieter, Emily returned.

"My husband is interested in historical preservation — in Boston. But I think he would find these interesting," Oriana said brightly.

"Boston is a good place for that," Emily commented. "We are a younger state here in Idaho, but we have our own history."

"I'm sure that's the case. And families can probably trace their history back to when Idaho became a state, even before that. Has your family been here long?"

Oriana was pleased at her skillful maneuvering of the conversation towards more personal topics.

Emily took the bait, describing the arrival of her great grandparents in Idaho and their first home, which was a simple cabin in what must have seemed like a wilderness to them at the time.

"They came from Chicago and had a small farm which their son inherited. He went into business and was quite successful, owning a hardware store and a saloon in town. He lost everything during the depression."

"That's quite an interesting story," Oriana said. "But the family recovered, I hope."

"Not that quickly. Things were rough for my father growing up."

Emily, who was obviously proud of her family's heritage, went on to share stories about her parents, John and Martha, and their influence on her life. Oriana nodded sympathetically, expressing her interest in understanding the town's history and how families like the Ackerlys had shaped its identity.

She expressed her admiration for people who had the courage to pursue their dreams, like Emily had with the bookstore. Oriana mentioned she had recently embarked on her own journey of self-discovery and was happy to connect with inspiring individuals in different towns she visited.

Of course, she should have foreseen Emily's next question.

"What brings you to Rogersville? It's quite a distance from Boston and off the beaten track."

"Actually, my husband and I were researching the history of an area in New York State and stumbled on a connection to Rogersville. I was trying to learn about an old cabin owned by people who live in Rogersville, but whose roots are in New York State."

"That would be the Lovells," Emily said, her tone neutral.

Oriana couldn't tell if she approved of them or not, but mainly she was startled and reminded that this was indeed a small town where everyone knew everything about everyone else.

"You know the Lovells?" she asked.

"Yes. I know James grew up in New York. He's lived in Rogersville all his adult life. I don't know of anyone else in Rogersville with a connection to New York. It was an easy guess,"

Emily laughed. She seemed amused. "You couldn't do that in Boston."

She continued, "Is this a school project—researching the history of the area in New York State?"

"Not exactly, but I am hoping the research will help me get accepted to a graduate program I am interested in," Oriana said vaguely. "But I am genuinely interested in the topic. I find it fascinating to learn about a town's historical roots, a town like Rogersville. And I am very interested in family history such as yours and how it parallels the development of the town."

"Most people would call Rogersville a village," Emily laughed, but Oriana could see she was intrigued by Oriana's genuine interest. Emily opened up more, sharing stories about her love for reading, her aspirations, and the challenges she faced in starting her own business. Oriana listened attentively, occasionally sharing her own anecdotes to maintain a sense of camaraderie.

They were eventually interrupted by more customers, who greeted Emily by name and wanted to pick up books Emily had ordered for them. After that, Oriana could see there would be no other opportunity to talk. She paid for her purchases, picked up a card with the shop's phone number and e-mail address.

Before leaving, Oriana thanked Emily for her time, and promised to stay in touch.

"Please do that," Emily said brightly. "I'll be interested in hearing about your research project. And I'm here every day should you ever be back this way again."

As Oriana walked out of the bookstore, she couldn't help but feel a mix of regret and excitement. She had established a connection with Emily without revealing the truth. She liked her and really wanted to know her better.

Now, armed with the knowledge of Lulu's family history and her sister's presence in Rogersville, Oriana was one step closer to unraveling the mystery surrounding Lulu's disappearance and transformation into Rhea.

Chapter 39

Oriana was impatient to contact Matthew Lovell and his wife, Alice. But it was Sunday evening when she landed at Logan airport, and she had to work all week. Besides, Rob expected a detailed account of her time in Rogersville. He agreed it was intriguing that Simon's brother Matthew, who now owned the Lakeview cabin, had also known Lulu and was married to Lulu's friend.

"It is possible they know Lulu is Rhea? Do they know Rhea has been using the cabin?"

Rob shrugged. "I don't even want to guess. But it's all possible. Coming face to face with Alice and Matthew could answer a lot of questions."

"I'll be careful," Oriana said. "I will simply say I met his parents because of our interest in local history and the Lovell's prominent role in Lakeview and the surrounding area. James suggested I contact Matthew and his wife. That sounds plausible, doesn't it?

"Yes, I suppose. What if they recognize your name?"

"There is nothing I can do about that now since James and Margaret know my name. But if they know it because Rhea told them, then I will have more information. What it will tell me exactly, I don't know," Oriana said uncertainly.

"You could try calling them during the week. If they are willing, suggest a meeting at the weekend when we can drive over."

"They don't live in Landen County," Oriana said. "In fact, their house is a good hundred miles north of there." She scrutinized the map open on her computer. "The town of Franklin will be a longer drive for us."

"Well, first things first. You will need to call since you don't have an email address for them. But give them a few days so that James has a chance to let Matthew know you will be calling."

Oriana followed Rob's advice and on Tuesday evening took a deep breath and called the number James had printed in large black letters on a page from a notepad ringed with images of wildflowers.

Oriana listened to the phone ring on the other end. Each ring felt like an eternity, amplifying her nervousness. Finally, she heard a click, and a voice filled the line.

"Hello?" a warm, friendly voice greeted.

"Hi, is this Matthew Lovell?" Oriana asked, trying to steady her voice.

"Yes, it is," Matthew replied.

"My name is Oriana. I recently met your parents, James and Margaret, in Rogersville. They suggested I get in touch with you," Oriana explained, hoping her story sounded plausible.

"Oh yes. You are doing a history of the Lakeview area," Matthew responded. "I am not sure what I can tell you. Dad is the one who really knows the history. He grew up there. I'm sure he told you that."

"Yes, and he was very helpful. I am interested in the cabin and since you are the present owner, I was curious about how it is used in the present."

"Not much, I'm afraid, but it's been in the family for generations, and doubtless we will use it more in the future."

"Thank you for your openness in discussing the history of the Lakeview area and the Lovell family," Oriana said, maintaining her guise as an enthusiast of local history. "I'm particularly interested in the cabin's significance to your family. Would you be willing to talk to me in person? I could be in Franklin this weekend, either Saturday or Sunday?"

"I think so," Matthew said. "I need to check with my wife. Is there anything else I can tell you right now?"

"As a researcher, I've been curious to learn more about how often the cabin is used and the family's connection to it. Would you mind sharing some insights?"

"Certainly," he replied. "While the cabin holds sentimental value for our family, we don't visit it as frequently as we used to. In recent years, our visits have become less frequent because of other commitments and responsibilities. However, we still attempt to go there occasionally."

Oriana mentally noted Matthew's response, trying to gauge whether Lulu could have been visiting the cabin without his knowledge. It seemed possible that Lulu could have maintained a clandestine connection to the cabin, using it without Matthew or Alice being aware. But she needed to talk to him and Alice face-to-face to steer the conversation to their past connection with Lulu.

"Given the cabin's historical significance, it's fascinating to think about the experiences and memories it holds," Oriana continued, prodding for more information. "Have you come across any peculiar occurrences or indications that the cabin has been occupied when you weren't present?"

Matthew hesitated a moment before responding. "To my knowledge, there haven't been any unusual signs of activity or indications that someone else has been using the cabin without our knowledge. However, it's possible that we might have missed something. As I mentioned earlier, we haven't been visiting as frequently as we used to."

Oriana's curiosity grew stronger, wondering if Lulu had been using the cabin for years without Matthew's awareness. She resolved to further explore this line of questioning during their meeting in Franklin.

"I appreciate your insights," Oriana said, keeping her tone neutral. "I will take detailed notes when we meet in Franklin. In the meantime, I will delve deeper into the history of the cabin."

Matthew seemed intrigued by the prospect of their meeting. "I look forward to our discussion as well," he replied. "It's always enriching to explore the history of our family and the Lakeview area."

As Oriana ended the call, she felt a sense of anticipation. She had successfully gathered some information about Matthew's connection to the cabin and learned that their visits had become less frequent. With their meeting on the horizon, she hoped that a face-to-face interaction would yield even more clues and potentially reveal Lulu's secret connection to the cabin.

Oriana and Rob set out early on Saturday morning and arrived in Franklin, close to one pm. The drive from Boston had taken longer than Oriana had expected, and she was eager not to be late. Matthew had said they would meet at the Log Cabin, a popular diner in town. Oriana felt excited and a nervous anticipation as she and Rob approached the diner. She was glad they would meet in a neutral setting. It somehow made her deception more palatable than the deception she had practiced when she visited James and Margaret Lovell.

As they entered the café, Oriana spotted the middle-aged couple gazing in anticipation at the door. It must be Matthew and Alice who were already seated at a table near the window.

With a warm smile, Oriana approached the table, followed closely by Rob. "Matthew, Alice, it's wonderful to meet you both," she greeted them, extending her hand in a friendly manner.

Matthew and Alice returned the smile and shook hands, expressing their pleasure at the meeting. They appeared genuine and welcoming, setting Oriana and Rob at ease.

As they settled into their chairs, Oriana began the conversation by expressing her appreciation for the Lovell family's historical significance in the Lakeview area. She steered the discussion towards the cabin, hoping to learn more about its recent history and its role in the Lovell family's life.

"It's truly fascinating how the cabin has been passed down through generations," Oriana remarked, her eyes subtly searching for any clues or reactions from Matthew and Alice. "I'm curious to know more about its current usage. How often do you both find the time to visit the cabin nowadays?"

Matthew exchanged a glance with Alice before responding. "To be honest, our visits have become less frequent in recent years," he admitted. "Between work and other commitments, we haven't been able to make it out there as often as we'd like. However, we still hold a deep affection for the cabin and the memories it holds."

Oriana nodded, noting their response. The information seemed consistent with what Matthew had mentioned during their phone conversation. However, she was at a loss as to how to steer the conversation towards Lulu.

It was Alice who provided the opening when she said, "I heard about the cabin even before I met Matthew. I was curious about it, since I grew up in New York State, but here in Franklin, so I'd never been in Lakeview before meeting Matthew."

Chapter 40

Oriana's eyes opened wide. "It is interesting that people in Franklin knew about the cabin. It must be a hundred miles from here."

"No, I didn't hear about it in Franklin. I was living in Seattle then. That's where I met Matthew. We met through Lulu, a mutual friend. She was the one who talked about the cabin and described it as a magical place."

"But she had never been there," Matthew said. "It was my brother Simon who wanted to go there. He is the one who would have inherited the cabin. He and Lulu were inseparable, and they planned on visiting the cabin." Matthew's voice became somber, his eyes sad.

"Your parents talked about Simon," Oriana said. "They showed me photos of him and Lulu. It was such a tragedy for your family."

Alice nodded. "Then Lulu disappeared."

"Oh, what happened?" Oriana could hardly contain her excitement.

"She went on a trip to Europe and never returned," Alice said. "She had been thinking of moving from Seattle and had been going through a rough time when I met her. I became friends with her after Simon's death, so I never knew him. The trip to Europe was meant to be healing and give her a chance to think about the next phase in her life. We were good friends before she left on her trip, so I was surprised not to hear from her. When she didn't return, I thought she had moved and hadn't told me. But eventually I started thinking she had stayed in Europe. I worried that something had happened, so I contacted Stephanie, my friend who had been living in Paris at the time. I had given Lulu her number to contact her when Lulu arrived in Paris."

"And had they met?" Oriana asked, conscious she was holding her breath.

"Yes, a couple of times. The last Stephanie heard, Lulu had changed her plans and was going on a road trip to Spain with a guy she had met, a friend of a friend of Stephanie's."

"Lulu was a lost soul back then," Matthew said. "She and Simon were inseparable all through high school and afterwards. She lost her way, got involved in drugs after he died. I visited her occasionally in Seattle, even after Simon died. But by the time she left for Europe, she was determined to make a fresh start."

"What do you think happened?" Oriana asked.

"I suppose it's possible she got pulled back into the life she was trying to escape," Alice said. "I don't want to believe that, but if she decided to stay in Europe with her new boyfriend, why not send me a note?"

"And you say Stephanie knew nothing," Oriana said, her curiosity about Stephanie growing stronger. She wanted to learn more about her, yet she also had to tread carefully, mindful of not appearing overly interested in Lulu.

"Did Stephanie say how much time she spent with Lulu in Paris or how well she knew the guy who took Lulu on the trip to Spain?"

"When Lulu didn't come back, I contacted Stephanie—oh, maybe a month after Lulu was supposed to return. She knew nothing. Someone had told her Lulu went to Spain with a guy. She said she had met Lulu a couple of times, had invited her to a party. She might have met the guy at the party."

"Are you still in contact with Stephanie?"

Alice's eyes lit up, and she laughed. "Oh yes. Stephanie and I go way back. We met during our college years and have remained close ever since. When she returned from Paris, I talked to her again about Lulu's disappearance. She assured me that Lulu had seemed well and happy when she saw her last in Paris."

Oriana nodded. At last, there might be someone who knew about Lulu/Rhea and the time she had spent in Europe. "Did

Stephanie have any additional information about Lulu? Or about the road trip to Spain or the guy who took her?"

Alice paused, her brow furrowing slightly. "I'm trying to remember. It was a long time ago. Stephanie didn't have more to add, just that Lulu and a guy—I think his name was Gregory — left Paris on a road trip to Spain. Unfortunately, that's all she knew," Alice admitted. "Stephanie didn't hear from Lulu afterwards. I could never trace the details of Lulu's journey."

"What about Gregory? Didn't Stephanie ask him?"

"She hadn't seen Gregory again. He wasn't a friend of hers, just a person at the party that night. She doesn't remember hearing anything about him again."

Oriana absorbed the information with a growing excitement, as she considered its significance to the story of her own kidnapping. Stephanie's encounter with Lulu in Europe and the road trip with Gregory provided tantalizing clues, but it seemed the trail had gone cold after that.

"I appreciate you sharing what you know," Oriana said sincerely, trying to maintain an objective demeanor. She had caught Matthew looking at her, a frown on his face. He was probably wondering why she was so interested in Lulu. She had to push for a little more information, though. She couldn't stop now.

"Stephanie's encounter with Lulu offers an intriguing glimpse into her journey, but Lulu's disappearance must be so puzzling to everyone who knew her. What happened to Stephanie?"

"She is a successful businesswoman now living in New York and married to Luis Arroyo, you know, the famous music producer." Alice laughed. "She was quite a counterculture person back then when she lived in Paris, hanging out with musicians. Now she runs a successful company selling music memorabilia. Quite a success story."

"Do you think she might talk to me?" Oriana asked without thinking.

"But she knows nothing about Lakeview or the cabin?" Alice wrinkled her nose, a puzzled look on her face.

"It's just that the story of Lulu's disappearance is intriguing, even if it is only loosely related to the story the Lakeview cabin," Oriana said, hoping the explanation was adequate.

Matthew had been silent during this exchange but now spoke, his expression tense. "I wouldn't want Simon's death to be sensationalized," he said.

"Oh, nothing like that," Oriana's shock must have shown on her face because his expression softened. "I am simply thinking of the story of the cabin being interwoven with the story of the Lovells through the years. I learned from your father about your grandfather and great grandfather. As you said, Simon would be the current owner of the cabin had he lived, and he was interested in spending time there. And since it sounds like he and Lulu would have married, she would have spent time there too."

Rob came to her rescue. "In my work on the historic preservation of old homes, the family history is interwoven with the history of the house. It's just a matter of being historically accurate. In our research, we try to be as thorough as possible."

Matthew nodded. "Of course."

After a glance at him, Alice appeared reassured and said, "Stephanie is a busy woman, but I could let her know we talked. I could give you her business email since that is public. I don't feel comfortable about sharing her private information."

"Of course. I understand," Oriana said hurriedly. "But if you could let her know who I am and if I can mention your name when I email, that would be very helpful."

Alice nodded. "We're all invested in uncovering the truth about Lulu," she said. "She was our friend. If you learn anything new, I want to know. I don't think Stephanie knows anything further, but by all means try. I did pursue it thoroughly shortly after Lulu's disappearance. Only I didn't know it was a disappearance at the time. I just thought she had extended her vacation. Then I thought she had become involved with this guy Gregory and had stayed in Europe. Maybe that's what happened. Maybe Stephanie learned more about Gregory over the years and didn't tell me."

Oriana nodded. She didn't say she had a photo of Gregory taken that year by Lulu in Portugal. Maybe that would jog Stephanie's memory. If she agreed to meet Oriana.

Chapter 41

"What do you think?" Oriana asked as she and Rob got in the car.

"They don't know Rhea has been using the cabin. And Rhea must have been very sure they wouldn't show up. She felt confident enough to leave her personal information there."

"Or she trusted them enough so that if they discovered it, they would be on her side," Oriana said.

"She left in a hurry. She didn't have time to remove her things from the cabin before leaving," Rob added. "It might not mean she trusts them, just that she panicked and ran. But they didn't find her stuff. If they did, they would know Lulu left it, and I think they would have shown that when you asked about Lulu."

"We should have taken the box," Oriana said. "In fact, I should go back and take everything Rhea left in the cabin. Now that Matthew and Alice have been reminded of Lakeview, they might pay a visit."

"Rhea's name isn't mentioned in anything in the box," Rob said.

"But they would know Lulu had been there. And if Gregory is hunting for Lulu, his attention would be drawn to the area."

"It could put you in danger - or at the very least, bring you unwanted attention."

"I have to find out Gregory's identity, learn what really happened when I was kidnapped," Oriana said with determination. "If I can get Stephanie to meet me and show her the photo of Gregory, it might jog her memory."

"Remember, Stephanie told Alice she didn't really know him. He was a friend of a friend."

"But she might remember their mutual friend."

"We are talking about people who lived in Paris twenty years ago," Rob said cautiously.

"Yes, but Garcia has resources. He wants to find Gregory. I could pass the information onto him."

"First, you have to get Stephanie to meet with you, and from Alice's description, she is a wealthy and busy businesswoman."

"I'll send her an e-mail right away."

"Think of what you want to say first."

"I'll stick to the story I told Matthew and Alice, of course."

As they continued their long drive back to Boston, Oriana drafted the email to Stephanie.

"Remember, this is going to the business email. It's more than likely an employee will open it, so nothing too personal," Rob reminded her.

Oriana read the email she had composed,

Dear Ms Arroyo, Alice Lovell suggested I contact you regarding questions I have about Lulu Ackerly. I am working on a family history of the Lovells. Alice thought your recollections of Lulu might be helpful.

"How does that sound?"

"It's the best you can do," Rob said. "It mentions Alice and Lulu, so it's clear you know people she knows."

Oriana hit send and sat back with a sigh. "Let's see what happens. If it works, I'll be taking another road trip, this time to New York."

They spent a quiet Sunday. Oriana was content to putter around their apartment. There had been too much traveling lately.

Late on Monday, Stephanie replied:

Dear Oriana, I must admit, when Alice mentioned your conversation and your interest in Lulu, I was both surprised and intrigued. It's been a while since I last heard anything about Lulu, and I'm not sure how helpful my recollections will be. But I will be glad to talk to you.

I am available to meet next week, preferably in the afternoon. I suggest we meet at Café Verdi, a little coffee shop on 53rd Street. They have a quiet ambiance that will allow us to have a meaningful conversation. Does Tuesday at 2 p.m. work for you?

Please let me know if this arrangement suits you, or if you would prefer an alternate date and time. I am open to adjusting my schedule to accommodate our meeting.

Looking forward to meeting you and sharing what I know about Lulu's time in Europe.

Best regards,

Stephanie

Oriana saw Stephanie had answered from her personal email and she responded promptly, saying she would be there. It would mean taking the day off work, but Oriana didn't think twice. This could be the breakthrough she needed in solving the mystery of her kidnapping and clearing Rhea's name.

She arrived at Café Verdi promptly at two pm the following Tuesday. She was curious about Stephanie and was hopeful she would learn something useful. As she stepped inside the upscale coffee shop, the aroma of freshly brewed coffee and the gentle hum of conversation greeted her.

A waiter came forward immediately.

"I'm meeting Ms Arroyo."

He nodded, "follow me, please." Scanning the room as she followed him, Oriana spotted an elegant woman sitting at a corner table. She exuded a sense of calm and poise. Stephanie's hazel eyes sparkled with interest as Oriana approached, and a smile formed on her lips.

"Stephanie, thank you for meeting me," Oriana said, extending her hand and returning Stephanie's smile as she shook her hand.

"I'm glad to meet you, Oriana, though I don't know how helpful I can be."

As Oriana settled into her seat, she took notice of Stephanie's appearance, thinking with surprise how sharply it contrasted with

Rhea's present appearance. They must be about the same age, but Stephanie looked years younger than Rhea. Even Alice, Rhea's former friend, with her quiet country looks, was believable as someone Rhea had known all those years ago, but not Stephanie.

Stephanie had an air of sophistication about her, with her neatly styled chestnut hair framing her face and her refined yet edgy attire hinting at a keen sense of fashion. She would have nothing in common with Rhea in the present day. Oriana wondered if they'd had anything in common in the past.

There was a quiet strength in Stephanie's demeanor, a quality that suggested she had weathered her own share of life's challenges. She remembered Alice had said Stephanie had been a barista in Paris, spending all her time with musicians and having musical ambitions of her own.

Once they had ordered their drinks, Oriana began the conversation. She had expected to have to explain her research project, but Alice must have filled Stephanie in because she had no questions and seemed prepared to talk.

"I'm eager to hear about your encounter with Lulu and any insights you might have about her time in Europe and what happened to her. Can you recall when you first met her?"

Stephanie nodded, taking a sip of her coffee before starting. "Of course, Oriana. As Alice might have mentioned, Lulu and I met in Paris, where I lived for about two years. I was in a group at the time, singing and sometimes playing guitar, intent on making it big in the music business. Lulu called. Alice had given her my number. Alice was always such a do-gooder, and I discovered Lulu had arrived in Paris the day before, alone and knowing no-one. Even on the phone, she sounded a bit lost. I met her for coffee the next day."

Stephanie leaned back, gazing into the distance. "To be honest, I wasn't enthusiastic about meeting Lulu. I had my own problems at the time and when I met her, I saw she was a scared little thing, naïve, everything I was trying not to be."

Stephanie looked back at Oriana, a regretful look on her face. "I was young and trying so hard to be hip. Lulu seemed uninteresting. I didn't know at the time about her history that her boyfriend had died so tragically. But I did invite her to a party the next day."

"Did she show up at the party?"

"Yes, and she seemed to have a good time. She spent a good deal of time talking to a dark-haired, good-looking guy. Later, I discovered his name was Gregory, and he drove her to Spain."

Oriana leaned in, her interest piqued. "Did Lulu ever mention the purpose of the road trip? Or where they planned to go after Spain?"

Stephanie furrowed her brow slightly, her gaze fixed on a distant memory. "The first day I met her, when we had coffee, Lulu told me she would be in Paris a few days and was then going by train to Madrid, making stops along the way, then returning to Paris for her flight back to Seattle. A couple of days later, when she was leaving the party, she was excited about driving to Spain. I had the impression that the road trip was Gregory's idea. He was driving to Spain and offered her a ride. She was excited about it, saw it as a spontaneous adventure, a chance to explore new places with someone who knew his way around."

Stephanie looked at Oriana ruefully. "It was a party. It was late at night. I wasn't particularly observant, but I thought there was a romance brewing, though she didn't say that. It was just the vibe I picked up. As for their plans after Spain, I'm afraid I don't have any information. It seemed like they were living in the moment. I imagine she intended returning to Paris in time for her flight back to Seattle, but I don't know that. To be honest, I didn't think about her again. It was only when Alice contacted me a month or so later that

I remembered Lulu had gone with Gregory to Spain. There was no reason she would contact me again when she returned to Paris."

Oriana nodded with surprise. From Stephanie's perspective, Lulu's journey in Europe, including the road trip with Gregory, was fueled by a sense of spontaneity and a thirst for exploration. The description of the young Lulu didn't match the person Oriana knew as Rhea. Something had changed the naïve young girl open to new experiences into the closed-off woman who shied away from the world.

"Did Lulu ever mention anything about her plans after her time in Europe?" Oriana asked, curious about Lulu's dreams at the time.

Stephanie's eyes were remorseful. "Sadly, I didn't care to get to know her. She was excited about being in Paris, mentioned a desire to continue traveling, to explore other parts of the world. But beyond that, I'm afraid I don't have any concrete information."

Oriana's mind buzzed with the revelations. The revelation that Lulu's road trip with Gregory had been a spontaneous adventure with a man she had just met, driven by a yearning for freedom and exploration, was not what she had expected.

Chapter 42

"Stephanie, I'm intrigued by this man, Gregory. Can you tell me more about him?" Oriana asked.

Stephanie's expression grew thoughtful as she considered the question. "Honestly, I didn't even remember his name until Alice started asking much later. Then I refreshed my memory by asking friends who were at the party. I didn't know Gregory myself. He was a friend of someone else who brought him to the party."

"Did that other person know him well?"

"I don't know how well they knew each other. Michel was a drummer in my band. When I asked him later about Gregory, he said they were no longer in touch."

Oriana leaned in, her interest intensifying. "Did Michel say anything about Gregory's background or his work? Anything that might identify him?"

"I got the impression he didn't like him very much. He said Gregory told a lot of tall tales. Michel began to suspect a lot of what Gregory said was lies. He told Michel his uncles were influential in the French police force. His last name was foreign, maybe Turkish, a name beginning with K. His name could have been made up, according to Michel. Michel said he had put distance between them. This was what he said when I talked to him months after Lulu had been in Paris. I pressed him about why he had grown to dislike Gregory. Michel's speculation was Gregory had ties to individuals who operated on the fringes of the law, engaging in illicit activities. Those are my words. I don't remember Michel's exact words, but that's what I thought he meant."

Oriana stared in horror at Stephanie, at a loss for words.

"I know," Stephanie nodded sadly. "He might have done something bad to Lulu. Back then, I knew nothing about her. I would have thought it possible she liked his lifestyle and was not a victim if not for Alice's concern. But even if I knew Gregory was a bad guy, I might not have been able to stop her. Remember also there is no proof. These are just Michel's suspicions."

"But since Lulu disappeared, those suspicions carry more weight."

Stephanie nodded.

Oriana was tempted to tell Stephanie what she believed a few days later in Lisbon. She was now convinced that Gregory was the one who had kidnapped her, and that Rhea had been caught up in it somehow and had taken her to safety. She wasn't sure if Rhea had gone along with Gregory's plan and the beginning and later had a change of heart, or if she had never approved of the kidnapping.

What Rhea had said on the phone the last time they talked made more sense now. She said she had not kidnapped Oriana but was rescuing her from an evil man. It was what Oriana wanted to believe, but she had to try to remain objective.

But no matter what level of involvement Rhea had in the kidnapping, Oriana thought nothing useful would result if she revealed Lulu had become Rhea? It wouldn't help find Rhea. She doubted Rhea had returned to her identity as Lulu. It would do no good to tell Stephanie about Lulu's identity as Rhea, since Stephanie didn't know how to track down Gregory or Lulu. And Stephanie would tell Alice. Oriana owed Rhea some loyalty. She had to find Rhea herself. And she had to help Garcia find Gregory.

"Your friend Michel — are you still in contact?" Oriana now asked Stephanie. "Would he talk to me?"

"I know how to reach him, yes," Stephanie said, eyes opening in surprise. "I have an email address and a phone number for him. But he is probably still in Paris."

"He might have heard more about Gregory over the years, even run into him. Don't you see? Gregory must know what happened to Lulu."

"I could try to contact him and find out," Stephanie said. "He knows I was concerned years ago about the girl who disappeared with Gregory. I felt kind of responsible. I knew I had been very blasé and unhelpful. It was a phase I was going through. Later I regretted."

"That would be great. Anything—a last name—a clue about where Gregory lives — would be helpful."

Stephanie nodded, responding to the urgency in Oriana's voice. She reached for her phone and quickly scrolled through her contacts, searching for Michel's information. After a moment, she stopped.

"I found his email address and phone number. Here," Stephanie said, handing her phone to Oriana. "This is how you can reach Michel. I'll send him a message right away, letting him know you'll be contacting him."

Oriana thanked Stephanie and quickly entered Michel's email address and phone number into her own device.

"Stephanie, how willing do you think Michel will be to help?"

Stephanie sighed, and her face filled with concern. "I honestly don't know, Oriana. Michel was always unpredictable, but he did care about what happened to Lulu. And he felt strongly that Gregory was taking advantage of people. I think he'd be willing to share whatever he knows. Just keep in mind that it might not be easy for him to recall much after all this time. Don't get your hopes up."

Oriana nodded. "I understand it will be challenging. I know it's been years, but if he has any information about Gregory or Lulu, it could make all the difference. Now that I know the story, I want to discover what happened to Lulu, maybe even help her."

"It's very generous of you. Now, I'm afraid I must run. I have appointments waiting in my office." Stephanie stood. "It was interesting to talk Oriana and let me know what you discover."

Oriana remained sitting and, when the waiter approached, ordered another cappuccino. She didn't want to waste another second before following up with Michel. She was nervous but hopeful as she composed a message to Michel, explaining her connection to Stephanie and her interest in Lulu and Gregory. Hoping his English was good enough to understand, or that he had an app on his phone that would translate what she wrote, she hit send.

After what felt like an eternity, her phone chimed with an incoming message. It was a response from Michel.

Excitement surged through Oriana as she read Michel's email. He had also received a text from Stephanie. He expressed surprise at the resurgence of interest in Lulu's disappearance. But he remembered Stephanie's concern years ago and was willing to talk to Oriana on the phone in a day or two. Thursday would be a good time as it would give him a chance to check with acquaintances and see if he could gather any updated information about Gregory.

Oriana responded, thanking him, and agreeing to call him on Thursday at six pm Boston time.

Relief washed over Oriana as she put away her phone. She might be a step closer to uncovering the truth. But Stephanie's description of Gregory, while alarming, was comforting in that now she had a reason to cling onto the hope that Rhea had herself been a victim of Gregory and had been Oriana's savior.

She sent a text to Rob to say the meeting was fruitful, finished her cappuccino and left the Café Verdi to start her long journey back to Boston.

Chapter 43

"Why not let Garcia handle things from now on? He must have contacts in Paris," Rob said that evening when Oriana recounted what she had discovered that day.

"Not yet," Oriana answered. "These people, Stephanie and Michel, are friends of friends. I'm hiding my identity from them as Lulu's sort-of daughter, or onetime daughter. I'm hiding the fact that Lulu became Rhea, and that I have been living with her all these years. It feels bad to deceive them, and I feel even worse about deceiving Matthew, his parents, and Alice. But I need to be sure Gregory is in police custody before revealing Lulu's new identity to anyone. It's safer that way, and I owe it to Rhea."

"But, yes, I want to let Garcia know Gregory is probably a shady character. I'll wait until I talk to Michel. Then I might have more information to pass on. The problem is, how do I explain how I got this information about Gregory?"

"You might have to tell him about Rhea's prior identity as Lulu," Rob said.

"I'll decide after Thursday."

On Thursday Oriana rushed home from work, so that she could talk to Michel in the privacy of the apartment. At the appointed time, she dialed Michel's number. He answered promptly. His English was good, to her relief.

"My mother is English," he said, then got down to business.

"I heard whispers and innuendos about Gregory over the years, but never heard of concrete evidence of his involvement in illegal activities. That is important for you to remember. Even though I felt suspicious about him, I never had proof he did anything illegal."

"I understand, but there were reasons for your uneasiness. Anything you can recall could be helpful."

"I never saw or heard anything that would suggest he mistreated women," Michel said. "He was a player, had lots of girlfriends, was a good-looking guy, but none of that is a crime. I lost touch with Gregory after that party," Michel said. "I regret that only because I have so little to tell you that will be helpful. But I heard rumors that Gregory was involved with a group of individuals engaged in illicit activities."

"Do you have any idea what activities they were involved in? Why were people suspicious? And could those activities be connected to Lulu's disappearance?"

"It's hard to say for certain. The rumors ranged from drug trafficking to money laundering and involvement in underground gambling. But these were just rumors, nothing concrete. And I heard nothing that hinted at treating women badly or human trafficking. I thought of that when Stephanie told me Lulu was missing. It's not to say Gregory was innocent regarding Lulu's disappearance. But I have heard nothing that would raise suspicions about him."

"The other complicating factor is Gregory had a way of exaggerating and boasting about his connections. Trying to make himself appear more important because of his connections to important people. It's hard to tell how solid those connections were. It raises more doubt about whether he got caught up in something dangerous or just wanted to appear dangerous and living on the edge. In certain circles, that would make him for attractive and respected."

"How did you meet Gregory?"

"Through a mutual friend. At first, I found him charismatic. However, before long, I got impatient with what I thought was his act. Gregory had a way of weaving intricate tales about his family's wealth and connections into conversations," Michel said, his voice tinged with bitterness. "He liked people to think he was important. He claimed his uncles were high-ranking officials in the French police force, but I could verify none of it. I didn't try at first, but later, when I grew suspicious, I tried to verify his stories. Nothing panned out. It all seemed like a web of lies."

"I began to see through his facade, and then I questioned everything he said. It was annoying, the showing off, the claims to be connected to important people in the French government. It might even have been true, though there was no proof. His mother might really have come from a wealthy and influential family, but I was a rock musician. It's not the kind of thing that impresses me even if it's true."

Oriana's eyes widened, her mind racing with possibilities. If Gregory had been fabricating his background, what else was he capable of?

"All the boasting was annoying, but not too much time passed before I suspected that there was something darker lurking beneath the surface," Michel continued.

"Over time, I started hearing hints about Gregory's involvement in money laundering," Michel continued, his voice growing quieter. "Rumors circulated about him associating with known criminals."

"Do you think he had something to do with Lulu's disappearance?" Oriana asked." Maybe she discovered he was doing something illegal, and he found that dangerous.

Michel's voice turned solemn. "I'm sorry, Oriana, but I heard nothing specific about Lulu. After she vanished, it was as if she had simply disappeared without a trace. Gregory, on the other hand, seemed to have vanished as well. It's possible he went into hiding, knowing he might be implicated in something."

Michel paused, then continued. "His last name is Kaya, or at least that's what he claimed. But like I said, he could have been lying about that too and could be using a different name now. I can also give you the name of a club in Paris where he used to hang out. This was years ago. It may not even exist anymore. But if it does, maybe someone there might know something."

"Yes, tell me the name of the club, please," Oriana urged. She had already found a notepad and had written down the name Kaya.

"It's called Le Serpent Noir," Michel said. "It's a place where known criminals gather. That was one reason for believing he socialized with a criminal element. It used to be one of their hangouts."

Heart racing, Oriana wrote down the name of the club. This information she would pass onto Garcia. Michel wasn't sure of the location but believed it was in Pigalle near Gare du Nord.

"I don't advise calling there and I certainly don't advise you go there. It's not exactly a safe haven."

Chapter 44

"It is definitely time to hand this information over to Garcia," Rob said firmly.

Oriana nodded in agreement. "Well, I'm not planning to fly to Paris to confront Gregory myself. But the chances are, Garcia or whoever he sends will not find Gregory there now."

"They might find someone who can lead them to him. It's something Garcia will want to follow up on," Rob said.

"He may want to. But this case is over twenty years old. Realistically, does Garcia's office have resources available to hunt down Gregory?"

"They may not, but it's for them to decide. You have done all you can, or all it is wise to do. You can't try to find him yourself," Rob said in alarm.

"I wouldn't even know where to start," Oriana said. "What I really want to do is find Rhea. She must have information about Gregory that could lead to his capture. But she must believe she is in danger and needs to hide from him or the police or both."

"We don't know that. We don't know why Rhea's disappeared. All we know is she left New Falls, hasn't answered your calls or reached out to you after you told her you discovered you are Maria Taglia, who was kidnapped in Lisbon twenty years ago."

"We know a lot more. We know Rhea is Lulu Ackerly who disappeared about the same time I was kidnapped and who has a photo of a man named Gregory, with the date of the photo on the back—July 1999—his name and Portugal."

"Which suggests she was in Portugal at the time you were kidnapped. We don't know how complicit she was in the kidnapping. But we know she kept you for twenty years and didn't tell you the truth, when she could have tried to find your family and reunite you. That makes her look like the kidnapper."

Oriana sighed. "You think I am desperately trying to hold on to a belief in Rhea's innocence? I don't think I am. I want to understand what she did and why she did it. The girl Stephanie describes meeting, a naïve girl newly arrived in Paris, doesn't sound like a seasoned thief or a kidnapper."

"But you know other things about her past. Alice and Matthew said she was traumatized by the death of Simon. She had a drug problem. According to Alice, she had made a new start. But maybe she relapsed. Maybe she did things she regretted in Lisbon and was afraid of being imprisoned. Maybe she did help kidnap you. And maybe she had second thoughts. And maybe she believed she was doing the right thing by running away from Gregory and taking you with her. Yes, it's possible she did that and saved you from Gregory. But she didn't continue doing the right thing and return you to your family. She is still guilty, Oriana."

"I just want to hear it from her. All of it, no matter how bad."

"Gregory didn't find her in twenty years. Maybe he wasn't even looking for her," Rob said.

"Or her new identity worked, so he couldn't find us. Now, with the news that Maria Taglia was found all over the Portuguese papers, that identity as Rhea Stone is blown. Gregory could figure out that Lulu is Rhea if he can discover who I am in the present. If he thinks Rhea knows enough to cause trouble for him, she could be in danger."

"Look, you also need to consider this. There is no actual proof Gregory did anything illegal, just the hunch of a guy who was an acquaintance of his in Paris twenty years ago—a guy you never met. Garcia may not take this information about Gregory seriously."

"Do you think I shouldn't tell Garcia what I have discovered about Gregory?"

Rob frowned. "You sent him Gregory's photo—the photo found with Rhea's things, but so far, he hasn't found a match for Gregory in any database. Gregory may be an innocent guy. But yes, I think Garcia should be kept informed. Let the police sort out what information is relevant."

"Okay. I will send the information about Gregory to Garcia right away. Maybe he can have someone check out that place in Paris, Le Serpent Noir."

"Good. How will you explain getting the information?"

"I will tell the truth, which is I talked to friends of friends of Rhea's who told me about meeting her and Gregory in Paris. I just won't say they only knew her as Lulu."

Rob nodded and sighed. He wanted this to be over, Oriana knew. She didn't blame him for that. He had never warmed to Rhea, and now he only saw her failings.

Oriana found it hard to explain her sense of loyalty and the feeling of obligation to Rhea. There was a bond between them. Rob had brothers and a father and a mother, cousins. He didn't know how it felt to have had only one person during your entire childhood. For Oriana, there had been no siblings, no cousins, no grandparents, no father. Only Rhea. Oriana thought they had known each other so well. It was profoundly shocking to discover Rhea's secret life.

"I need to go back to the Lakeview cabin and remove all of Rhea's papers," Oriana said. "I should have taken them that day. If Gregory knew Rhea as Lulu Ackerly, he could find all the information I found about Lulu in Idaho."

"But he could have discovered that years ago, when he knew her first," Rob said.

"Now that I—Maria Taglia — have been found, he could try to silence Rhea. He might renew his search. Garcia said he would protect my identity as Oriana Chalmers, but information can leak. If Gregory discovers my name, then he could discover that Rhea is really Lulu. He could connect her to the Lovells."

"But not to the cabin," Rob said. "You found the cabin because Rhea brought you there as a child."

"But if Matthew and Alice visit the cabin and find Rhea's box of memories, they will know Lulu was there. They would have no reason to hide that knowledge from anyone interested in Lulu. And because of my curiosity about the cabin, I might have prompted them to visit it."

"It looks like we'll be taking another weekend trip," Rob said with resignation. "Neither of us can afford to take any more time off from work."

"I can go alone," Oriana said.

"I'd feel better if I went with you."

"I'd like to stop off at the house in New Falls while we're there," Oriana said. "I don't expect to find Rhea has returned, but I should check for mail, maybe even check with Mallory at the shop in case she's heard from her."

"Okay, so we'll go on Saturday," Rob said.

Chapter 45

On Saturday morning, Oriana and Rob set out on their trip to the Lakeview cabin, with a stop planned at the house in New Falls on the way back. As they drove, Oriana's mind was consumed with thoughts of Rhea and the mysteries surrounding her disappearance.

They drove silently towards Lakeview with Oriana only muttering, "let's get Rhea's things from the cabin first. Then we can stop at the house."

As Oriana and Rob arrived at the Lakeview cabin, they were met with the familiar scent of pine and the tranquil stillness of the surrounding woods. The cabin stood silently, holding the secrets of its past within its walls. Everything looked the same as before.

Oriana wasted no time. She reached for the key hidden underneath the rock, opened the door, and immediately made her way to the corner where Rhea had kept her box of writings and photos. It was still there, untouched.

"I don't know why I didn't just take it when we were here last," she muttered, as Rob scanned the room for any sign that someone else had been here.

"Did you expect she would return?" he asked.

"I don't know," Oriana said uncertainly. "We didn't know then who owned the cabin and if they knew Rhea's story. Maybe I hoped that person knew about the box or could lead me to Rhea."

"I think we should take the box and leave. There will be time enough to look through the contents thoroughly at home. But since you don't want Matthew and Alice to know about Rhea, it is safer to lock up here and not return."

Oriana closed the box and Rob lifted it and carried it to the door. After one last look around, Oriana followed him, locked the door, and returned the key to its resting place underneath the rock. They trudged back through the wooded path to emerge on the side street where they had parked the car.

As Rob placed the box in the trunk, Oriana glanced at the houses across the street. They had seen no one on the street. Now she thought she saw the twitch of a curtain in a window.

"I wonder how much attention they pay to people walking into the woods," she said, nodding toward the row of houses. She was seated in the passenger seat and Rob had already started the car.

"It's a small place. They probably notice everything. I imagine someone emerging from the woods with a large carton might generate some interest," Rob replied. "But we won't be back. And Matthew and Alice, should they show up, will not interrogate the people who live in those houses. I doubt they know them."

"I wonder, is there another way in? I didn't think of this, but because Rhea and I came on the bus, we got to the cabin the way I brought you, but maybe there is another way."

"Of course, there is no place to park a car by the cabin and I didn't notice another pathway, just the one that leads to Pines Bluffs."

Rob stopped the car. They had reached the end of Main Street. "I could double back, drive to the end of this street, maybe continue a bit and make a right."

"Yes, let's do it," Oriana said. "We're not coming back, and it probably doesn't matter, but I'm curious."

Rob turned at a gas station a little outside of town and drove back through Main Street, passing the Camden general store and continuing forward until they came to a right turn. They turned onto the narrow road. A little further down, a sign pointing to the right said, "Pines Bluffs."

"Good thinking," Rob said. "Let's see where it leads."

The road narrowed and appeared to reach a dead end. To the left was a flattened grass-free patch which looked like it might serve as a parking area. To the right was a narrow track.

"We might as well get out and explore," Rob said.

In less than three minutes, they emerged into a clearing in front of an old wooden house, with a faded sign in front that said, *Pines Bluffs*. It looked unoccupied.

"There's no sign that says Private Property. The Lovell cabin could use this path too, but it's obviously much more convenient for the Pines Bluffs house."

"As I say, it's just idle curiosity on my part," Oriana said. "Rhea wouldn't have come this way, but the Lovells might. They might know the people who own Pines Bluffs."

"Let's get back to the car," Rob said. "We still have to stop at New Falls and it's a long drive home."

When they arrived at the house, Oriana felt nostalgia and sadness wash over her. This place held so many memories of her childhood, and yet it now felt like a hollow shell without Rhea's presence. They walked up the front steps, and Oriana hesitated for a moment before unlocking the door. She grabbed the mail from the box outside, not bothering to look at it. There would be some bills, which she would dutifully pay so that everything in Rhea's life would be in order should she return. *When she returns.* She had to believe she would return. That she wasn't gone forever.

Inside, the house was eerily quiet. There was a veneer of dust on the hall table. Oriana made her way to the kitchen. The note she had left for Rhea was still propped up, untouched, where she had left it. She put the small stack of mail on the kitchen table as she gazed out the window at the swing, which had been such a source of delight in her childhood.

"She hasn't been back. There is no point in checking upstairs, but I will anyway," she called out to Rob, who has looking at the half-finished necklace discarded on the living-room table.

"She left in a hurry. That's clear," he said.

Oriana was already on the stairs. A quick look into Rhea's bedroom and her own old room revealed nothing had changed. She came downstairs again quickly. The emptiness was more painful now, more final than the first time she'd come. With a sinking heart, she admitted to herself Rhea wasn't coming back.

"I'll get the bills and we can go," she said. She picked up the unopened mail from the kitchen table. As she sifted through the envelopes, her heart skipped a beat when she noticed one addressed to her. The name and address were written in block letters in black ink on the envelope. There was no return address. The letter was addressed to Oriana Stone.

With trembling hands, she tore open the envelope and unfolded the letter. It was a brief note, written in Rhea's familiar handwriting. The contents of the letter sent shivers down Oriana's spine.

My dearest Oriana,

If you're reading this letter, it means you've come back home looking for me. Maybe that means you have found it in your heart to try to understand my actions all those years ago and in time to forgive me. But knowing you as I do, I understand you want answers.

I apologize for disappearing without a word, but there were things I needed to do to keep us both safe. I cannot explain everything in this letter, but please know that I love you more than anything in this world.

There is information you can gather from various sources that, when pieced together, will help answer some questions and will lead you to the truth about our past. There is the cabin in Lakeview where we used to go. I left a box of old papers there. Take it with you. Talk to Mallory and apologize to her for my sudden disappearance. Ask her to tell you what I said about Gregory and my time in Europe. And there is one other person who can help, a man named Sebastian. Tell him you are Oriana and that I want him to tell you what he knows.

With all my love, Rhea

Chapter 46

Oriana's heart raced as she absorbed the words on the page. Rhea had left clues for her, clues that might finally unveil the secrets surrounding her kidnapping and the connection to Gregory. Mallory might hold the key to unlocking the truth.

"We have to go to the shop. Mallory might have answers for us," Oriana said, her voice tightening. "Rhea has reached out to me. She is helping me find answers."

Rob nodded, his expression mirroring Oriana's determination. "Let's go now."

They left the house and walked around the corner to the shop on Charles Street. The bell above the door jingled as they entered, and they found Mallory arranging items on a shelf in the otherwise empty shop. She looked up, her eyes widening with surprise at the sight of Oriana.

"Oriana? I'm so glad to see you," Mallory exclaimed, rushing over to embrace her tightly. "Any news about Rhea?"

Oriana pulled back slightly, her eyes searching Mallory's face for answers. "Rhea sent me a letter. She sends her apologies for leaving so suddenly, but she said nothing about coming back. She said to ask you to tell me about Gregory and her time in Europe. Please, Mallory, what is this about? I need to know the truth. About Gregory, about everything."

"It's time." Mallory sighed, went to the door, flipped the sign to closed and motioned for them to follow her into a small back office. She closed the door behind them.

Mallory took a deep breath, her eyes looking sad and concerned. She searched Oriana's face. She spoke slowly, as if she was choosing her words carefully.

"I believe Rhea was haunted by her past, Oriana," Mallory began. "When she spoke of Gregory, I could hear the fear and desperation in her voice. She was terrified that guy would find her, even years later."

"What do you know about Gregory?"

"Rhea met him in Paris and began an affair with him. It was fun and exciting at first, but later she discovered he was involved in dangerous and illicit activities. Rhea mentioned human trafficking and drug smuggling. She said she was coerced into helping him, and she found herself caught in a web of deceit and danger and feared she couldn't get away. She knew she had to escape to protect you and herself. So she changed both of your names and wouldn't even tell me her former name or yours. She said it was safer that way. She swore me to secrecy."

"I promised I would tell no one, and I kept that promise. Still, she was afraid Gregory would track her down some day and she might have to run. She made me promise to tell you, if that day should ever come, everything I have just told you. I wasn't sure the last time you came if it was the right time, but now it is."

Mallory searched Oriana's face with concern. "This must be so shocking, and I wish it hadn't come to this, but I am trying to do what Rhea wanted and tell you all I know. But there is something else, one more thing. It is something she gave me. Wait here."

Mallory left the door open, and Oriana could hear her climb the stairs to her apartment above the shop.

"Should I ask her about the kidnapping? She gave no sign she knows anything about it."

"Ask what kind of human trafficking Gregory was involved in," Rob suggested.

Mallory returned carrying a card. On it in Rhea's handwriting was the name Sebastian, a phone number, and an email address. Underneath was written *Rhea—LA*.

"Rhea said to give you this if you ever asked about Gregory and to say you can trust this person. That's all I know, my dear."

Oriana studied the name on the card. Sebastian, the person Rhea had mentioned in her letter. He was another person she could trust who would have valuable information.

"Thank you, Mallory. One last question. Do you know if Gregory's crimes involved child trafficking?"

"Rhea didn't say so, but she used the word trafficking, and she was very worried about protecting you. I could tell she feared for your safety."

If Mallory knew the truth, she hid it well. "I am telling you everything I know. Maybe this person, Sebastian, will have more answers."

Oriana would learn no more today from Mallory and had to believe Mallory was holding nothing back.

"Yes, I will contact Sebastian. Thank you, Mallory. I haven't reported Rhea missing. I will check in at the house and pay her bills until she returns."

Mallory nodded. "I will tell no one. But be prepared. She might not return. I would be sad not to see her again, but I would understand. I hope you will stay in touch, Oriana, and let me know if you hear anything from Rhea."

Oriana and Rob took their leave, and Oriana promised to visit Mallory when she came to New Falls again to check on Rhea's house.

Now it was time to call Sebastian, the man Rhea had mentioned in her letter, the man who had more clues about Rhea's and Oriana's past. Was Sebastian the one who would finally tell Oriana what role Rhea had in her kidnapping? Would he know where to find Rhea now? Or even know how to find Gregory?

Oriana's fingers were itching to punch that number into her phone, but she knew she should wait until they got home. There was a lot of traffic on I-90, and it was noisy as impatient drivers honked car horns. It would be hard to hear a voice at the other end and this call was important. She wanted to miss nothing.

Chapter 47

As soon as they arrived home, in the blessed quiet of their apartment, Oriana picked up her phone and dialed the number that Mallory had given her. After a few rings, a deep voice answered on the other end. "Hello?"

Oriana tried to keep her voice steady. "Sebastian, this is Oriana. I... I believe you knew Rhea. She mentioned you in a letter she left behind and said I should contact you."

There was a pause on the line, as if Sebastian was processing the name. "Was there a message from Rhea?"

"I just received a card with your name, this phone number and an email address," Oriana said in some confusion.

"Was there anything else on the card?"

"No. Oh, just Rhea's name and LA written after it."

"That's what I need. It's the code we agreed on," Sebastian muttered, as if talking to himself. Then in a louder, friendlier voice he said, "Oriana? Is it really you? I didn't expect to hear from you—hoped not to, in fact. This means Rhea has had to disappear."

"Yes. Anything you can tell me would be appreciated. Do you know why she disappeared?"

The surprise in Sebastian's voice, combined with apparently knowing who she was, sent a shiver of apprehension down Oriana's spine. "You... you knew about me? How much do you know?"

"Everything from the beginning."

"You know about my kidnapping?"

"Yes," Sebastian replied, his tone heavy and sorrowful. "I've known about your kidnapping since shortly after it happened. I was involved in your escape."

Oriana's heart pounded in her chest, a mix of shock, confusion, and anger coursing through her veins. Had this man helped kidnap her?

"Involved? What do you mean? How were you be involved?"

Sebastian's voice cracked with emotion. "Oriana, I know this is difficult to hear, but I need you to understand the whole truth. Rhea... she wasn't the kidnapper. She was trying to protect you from the real culprits—Gregory and his associates. She went to great lengths to keep you safe."

Conflicting emotions swirled within her—relief that this was further confirmation Rhea wasn't the villain she had believed, and an overwhelming desire to understand why Sebastian was involved and how it all fit together.

Trembling, Oriana managed to ask, her voice strained, "Why didn't Rhea ever tell me? Why did she keep the truth hidden all these years?"

Sebastian let out a sigh, his voice heavy with remorse. "Rhea believed it was the only way to ensure your safety and her own. She feared that if you were discovered, they would use you as leverage against her. It was a desperate decision. One she regretted every day. But she loved you, Oriana. That much, I can assure you."

"Just how were you involved, Sebastian?" Oriana asked.

"I met Rhea in Marseilles. Her name was Lulu then. We became friends. We trusted each other, but not at first. She grew to trust me gradually. At first, she hid from me that she had a little girl, Mimi. She told me she was running from a man who would harm her if he found her. I didn't understand. I knew she was American, and he was French. Why not return to the United States? It was then, finally, she told me about Mimi. She said Gregory had kidnapped Mimi, but she was with Gregory when it happened. She insisted she didn't know he was going to do it. He brought them to a house on the coast of Portugal. She escaped from there taking Mimi with her and made their way to Marseilles where she was hoping to get fake papers so that they could both go to the United States."

"Mimi," Oriana murmured. The name was oddly familiar, stirring up a vague memory, but it was out of reach.

"Why didn't she return Mimi to her family if she was opposed to the kidnapping?" Oriana asked, confused.

"Eventually she revealed she had a record of arrests for drug possession and there was another incident when something happened to a child she was babysitting. She was afraid the French or Portuguese police would believe she had been involved in the kidnapping of Mimi and they would detain her. She thought she would be safer in the United States. I believed she intended returning Mimi to her family then. That was her plan when she first started creating false identities."

"But something changed her mind."

"Yes. Of course, you know now that you were Mimi?"

"Yes. And she never told me about the kidnapping. I only discovered it a few weeks ago, when I was reunited with my family. But now Rhea has disappeared. I need to find her. I need answers. Where is Rhea now?" Oriana asked. Her voice, even to her ears, sounded pleading and desperate. "You must tell me if you know."

Sebastian sighed heavily. "I'm afraid I don't know. After Rhea left Marseilles, she severed all ties with me. That was twenty years ago. But she made me promise to tell you what I knew if you ever contacted me. You see, I was the one who created the new identity for the woman I knew as Lulu. I took the photos of her and you. She chose the names Rhea and Oriana Stone. I had some help in finalizing the documents, but no one else knew the true identity of Lulu or you. Only I knew. It was safer that way."

"Why didn't Rhea ever tell me?" Oriana asked, her voice quivering.

She didn't expect an answer from Sebastian, but he responded, "I know she really loved you. I believe Rhea made the tough choice to keep the truth from you, believing it was the best way to protect you.

She must have feared that knowing your true identity would only put you in greater danger. I'm sure it was a burden she carried with guilt and remorse."

"I believe she loves me," Oriana said quietly. "But now I need to find her. Do you have any hunches about where she might have gone? Even a wild guess might help. And of course, if there is anything you know that would help to find Gregory and make him pay, I could pass it on to the Portuguese police. Your name would not be mentioned."

After a moment of silence, Gregory spoke again. "There is something that might help. When I created the new identities of Rhea and Oriana Stone, Rhea or Lulu was still so worried that she had me create a second set of identities. It was for a red-haired woman named Harriet Ingersoll, and her daughter Louise. She wore a red wig for the photo. That was twenty years ago, and she wouldn't look the same, but she could be using the identity of Harriet Ingersoll."

Oriana's eyes widened at Sebastian's revelation. The mention of another set of identities sent a surge of hope through her veins. If Rhea had taken on the identity of Harriet Ingersoll, there might be a chance to find her, to uncover the truth once and for all.

"Harriet Ingersoll," Oriana repeated, getting used to the name on her tongue. "Is there anything else you can think of?"

"That is all I know. And I know nothing about Gregory except for what I told you. Honestly, I'm not sure she would want me to tell you about the Harriet identity, but you're an adult and it's been twenty years. Be careful though. If this guy, Gregory, thinks you could have him arrested, he could be dangerous."

"I will be careful. Thank you for this information."

Rhea
Chapter 48

Rhea decided not to cross the border into Canada. The passport was out of date, in any case. It would mean renewing it, providing an address, and then waiting. It was too risky. She might need the social security number to get a job, but she had a little money still, thanks to the stash of cash she had kept in the getaway suitcase. She would live frugally, stretch it out as long as possible.

The red wig was becoming irritating, physically, and visually, but she dared not remove it except at night after she had securely locked the door of whatever small hotel room she had found for the night. She also found the makeup and the conservative clothes trying, but they served a purpose as they reminded her of the role she was playing. Her name was now Harriet Ingersoll, a shop assistant from Chicago with relatives in the area. She only volunteered that information if strictly necessary. People weren't curious for the most part.

For some reason, the logic of which escaped her, she had kept the driver's license with its fake address and the picture of her in the red wig from twenty years ago. These days, people wanted to see IDs, but a quick look at a picture on a driver's license was all they wanted. No one ever scrutinized it for address or date. Probably a traffic cop might or a rental car agency, but Rhea wasn't foolish enough to rent a car. She paid for her hotel rooms in cash. At first, she only stayed one night, but as she became less anxious, she would stay two or even three nights at the same place.

She eventually stayed longer in a suburb of Rochester called Lindenhurst. She liked it because it was possible to walk places. The small inn was clean, not too expensive, and busy enough, so that no one paid any attention to her. There were other pedestrians on the surrounding streets, and her lack of a car wasn't conspicuous.

One day, she stopped for coffee in a small restaurant in the area and saw they had posted a sign for a part-time waitress for weekends. She lingered over her coffee and when the elderly waitress approached to replenish her cup, Rhea said casually, "I noticed the sign that you're hiring."

"Yeah. Are you interested?" The woman looked at Rhea, hope in her eyes.

"I might be. What hours? What's the deal?"

"Four to midnight Friday, same Saturday, but if you wanted to start at eleven, that would be great too, and eleven to nine on Sunday. It's long hours, but you can earn good tips on weekends. It gets quite busy. And he pays you in cash. I can see if Len is free to talk if you are interested in the job."

"Yes. I'm interested."

Rhea had been calculating. Payment in cash probably meant they wouldn't file tax forms. She wouldn't have an official record of her existence as Harriet Ingersoll. That suited her fine.

Len came bustling out from the kitchen, a tired-looking overweight man in his fifties with thick wavy hair dyed an improbable shade of brassy blond. He slid into the booth opposite Rhea and said, "I hear you want the weekend job."

She nodded.

"I can give you a tour if you like."

"Sure."

He didn't ask if she had worked as a waitress before. Rhea volunteered that she had worked as a shop assistant, and she paid attention to how the cash register worked. A bored young guy was stationed there now, but if it got busy at weekends, she might have to pitch in and use it.

"Any questions?"

While she was still thinking if she had, he continued, "can you start on Friday?"

It seemed she was hired. No mention was made of filling out official forms. She would be paid on Sundays in cash.

She left feeling pleased with herself. She might not make much money, but she wasn't spending much either. Her main expense was hotel rooms. She needed to find a more affordable alternative.

Her walks around the neighborhood were paying off. She came across a sign in the window of a large, quite luxurious looking red-brick house. The sign said *furnished apartment for rent*. Rhea copied down the phone number and called from the pay phone in the hotel's lobby. She was invited to come and look at the apartment. She was to ring the bell tagged Long on the ground floor.

An elderly white-haired woman with alert eyes opened the front door and ushered Rhea into a wide hall with a polished wood floor. Rhea extended her hand, which the woman took hesitantly. Rhea introduced herself as Harriet Ingersoll. The woman said, "I am Elsie Long."

"It's this way," she said, leading the way upstairs. Rhea noted the ornately carved banister. This was a beautiful house. She wondered if she could afford the rent. Before she could ask, Elsie had thrown open the door to the room at the top of the stairs to reveal a compact but quite elegant apartment with a small kitchenette area and a larger bathroom. The bedroom was tiny, but had a bed, a small bedside table with a lamp on top. The living-room area was larger and contained a couch and armchair.

"It's lovely," she said. "I would like to take it if I can afford it."

"It's $700 on the first of the month."

"$700 a month?" Rhea asked, just to be sure. That was way below what Elsie could charge for this apartment.

"There are conditions," Elsie said. "No loud parties or noise late at night. There are two other apartments besides my own, all occupied by single ladies who are quiet and respectful of other tenants. That is what I want from all my tenants."

Rhea nodded vigorously. "I certainly will not be entertaining loud guests. In fact, I will have no guests. I am new to the area, helping to care for a sick relative."

"But I do have a job locally," she added hastily, in case Elsie thought she was someone who would vanish suddenly, which of course she might.

"I would need a reference from your job," Elsie said, "and your former address."

Rhea wrote down the fake address from the driver's license bearing the name Harriet Ingersoll, making a great show of removing it from her wallet and showing it briefly, her thumb covering the date. Elsie didn't comment. Rhea wrote down Len's name and the address of the Stardust Restaurant as a reference.

"I will let him know you might call him," she said. "I'd like to move in immediately if I can."

Since it was close to the middle of the month, Elsie charged her half a month's rent and handed her two keys, one for the apartment and one for the main door. Rhea gave her $350 in cash, which she accepted without question, nodding with no hint of surprise when Rhea asked, "is cash okay?"

She wanted to ask if she could pay in cash in the future, but she would deal with that in two weeks. It might be easier to open a checking account now that she had an address and a job, but she'd rather not. It had been so long since she'd opened the checking account in New Falls, but they hadn't questioned her credentials then. She reassured herself it wouldn't be a problem.

Chapter 49

Rhea felt less like a fugitive after she had moved into the apartment. There wasn't much moving required. She checked out of the hotel with her large canvas bag containing one change of clothes. She had bought some cheap items of clothing in the past week or two. Though she would need more, she hated the dull outfits she had decided would fit her new role as Harriet and didn't want to buy more of them.

She had been living from day to day, not capable of thinking ahead. Now it seemed she would be here in one place for a little while, with a job and an apartment. She found that comforting, realizing she missed the routine of her life in New Falls, missed her house and working at the shop with Mallory.

Yet, she had been cosseted in that routine for so many years and found it liberating to work at the Stardust and exchange small talk with customers. Or maybe it was her new identity as Harriet that was liberating. But gradually she came to realize it was freeing to break out of that cocoon she had been in so long.

She even bought a newspaper occasionally, something she hadn't done in years. She was searching for anything related to the kidnapping of Maria Taglia. There was nothing.

She thought of Oriana a lot, wondering if she hated her now. One quiet night in her new apartment, she decided to write Oriana a note and mail it to their their old home rather than to Oriana's address in Boston. Rhea's reasoning was if Oriana had cut her out of her life, then she wouldn't go back to New Falls. But if she did go back, then it was a sign she missed her, or at least wanted answers from her. She would welcome communication.

In weak moments Rhea had confided in Mallory about her fear of Gregory but stopped before revealing Oriana's identity or her own. She had berated herself afterwards, fearful she had revealed too much. Now she was glad she had done so. She was glad she had given Mallory the card with Sebastian's contact information. She had done it for safekeeping only a few years ago. Now she believed Oriana would piece things together and would see that she had tried to do the right thing. She had rescued her from Gregory.

Rhea was surprised she missed her house. She missed the shop and Mallory. Most of all, she missed Oriana. Several times, she was tempted to call her. There was an old public phone outside the restaurant. But calls could be traced. She resisted the urge. Then she thought of writing Oriana a long letter telling her the whole story, but if the police searched the house, or if Oriana handed the letter over to them, they would have a confession in her handwriting. She would be condemning herself.

She thought of the cabin in Lakeview, the place where she had daydreamed of her life with Simon. She had hesitated before mentioning the cabin in her letter to Oriana. Everything she had written and saved in that box at the cabin had none of her names attached. Only someone who recognized her handwriting would associate it with her. Or someone who had been there with her. Oriana would know. Would she remember the cabin and how to get there? Rhea wondered what Oriana would make of her writings and old photos.

The cabin helped her feel close to Simon. He had described it so perfectly, even described the key hidden under the rock. He had planned on showing it to her. As a child, he had visited with his father. He loved the area. It was why Rhea looked for a house nearby after finally arriving back in the United States. She knew she couldn't go back to Seattle. She certainly couldn't go back to Idaho, nor did she want to. New Falls was close enough to Lakeview, and when she heard of the long-term rental, she felt they were meant to live there close to where Simon had been happy as a child.

At first, she had been cautious about visiting the cabin. She knew it belonged to Simon's father and that he never visited. But they might have an arrangement with someone who lived locally to check on it, even use it. But the temptation was too great. She had to see it for Simon.

The first time she visited the cabin was shortly after they arrived in New Falls. Oriana was settled in school during the day. After her anxiety had abated somewhat, now that they were safe in a small town with new identities, she started to miss her life as Lulu. She thought about Alice, her sister Emily, even Simon's parents. She wanted to reach out, tell them she was safe. But then she wouldn't be safe, and she would lose Oriana. She couldn't do it.

So, one day after Oriana was safely in school, Rhea boarded a bus to Lakeview and wandered through the woods until she found the cabin. She felt very close to Simon then when she discovered the key hidden under the rock, just where he said it would be. It was the cabin that would have been theirs, and it was serene and beautiful. It felt safe.

She visited several times that first year while Oriana was in school but could only stay an hour or two each time. She didn't bring Oriana with her until a few years later. Oriana was older then, and able to understand that this was their secret and not to be shared with anyone.

Oriana understood from a young age about keeping secrets. Rhea never told her to not talk about their time in Europe, but she didn't talk about it herself. Rhea believed that eventually Oriana forgot about it. But she never asked her. Maybe she kept it all inside.

Those were two long years in Europe, mainly spent in Marseilles. Rhea hadn't expected it to take so long to get back to the United States. But looking back, she realized it helped Oriana's transition and made her less conspicuous in New Falls..

Oriana attended the English classes Rhea taught in the little school in Marseilles. When Rhea saw that the school asked for no identification for Oriana, she named her Oriana Stone. Oriana played along, thinking this was her English name for her English class. Gradually she stopped calling herself Mimi.

The day Rhea first met Jeanne, after a cursory glance at her passport, Jeanne immediately started to tell her about the job. Later in the informal interview she asked what first name she liked people to use. Rhea thought she might have already forgotten her name, so, instead of repeating, "Lulu", she said, "people call me Rhea." Jeanne nodded in acceptance. She was known as Rhea after that. It was sometime later she added Stone.

She settled into a calm routine in Marseilles, which was odd and unexpected. She had come to the place to find someone to forge IDs for her and Oriana. Instead, she had found a decent job and lifestyle.

They could have stayed in Marseilles longer. Oriana's English was improving rapidly, though her French was not. She was becoming increasingly attached to Rhea. Of course, the other children and their parents' believed Rhea was her mother. One day Rhea realized Oriana did too, that it was no longer an act. But she didn't probe. She didn't ask Oriana what she remembered about Lisbon. Her excuse was she didn't want to blow their cover, but by then she had become attached to Oriana. She wanted Oriana to be her daughter. She had been so alone since Simon's death. Having someone who was hers was a precious thing. At times, she even fantasized that Oriana was Simon's child.

She had long since cashed in her return ticket to Seattle, not knowing when or if she would return. At first, her search to find IDs for herself and Oriana was propelled by a desire for them to have legal status as a protection against Gregory. Things were going smoothly, but she was worried that her passport declaring her to be

Lulu Ackerly was on file somewhere in the school. Or if not, she might be required to produce identification at some point.

Her search led her to Sebastian.

Chapter 50

They led a quiet life in those first months in Marseilles. They would take a little walk in the evenings, sometimes treating themselves to a dinner out, but Rhea was intent on being a good mother, so there were no late nights. After Oriana was in bed, she started making jewelry. She had learned how to do it while in Seattle and liked it. One day she saw some wooden beads she liked at an open-air stall. The young woman attending the stall had made the jewelry and told her where she bought her supplies. So Rhea visited the place one day and bought some wooden beads, string, and clasps inexpensively. She became a regular customer and her skill increased. People admired the necklaces she wore, and it gave her the idea to sell some to make extra money.

The shop also sold guitar strings and other musical supplies. One day Rhea struck up a conversation with a guy shopping there. Or he struck up the conversation with her. He was buying guitar strings and his name was Sebastian. Rhea was reticent, but she liked him. She felt protected by their new names and Oriana's increasing knowledge of English.

He was low key, didn't ask questions, didn't volunteer information about himself either. That all lowered Rhea's guard, and when he invited them to have coffee nearby, she agreed.

Their friendship developed gradually, but one day she realized Sebastian had become important in her life, providing a sense of companionship and safety in a world that had been filled with fear, distrust, and uncertainty. When he asked if she missed home, she said she hoped to return, eventually. He must have noticed her hesitation, but probably didn't understand the reason for it. Somehow, Rhea conveyed that entry into the United States would be difficult for Oriana as there was trouble with her credentials.

He assumed, of course, that Oriana was Rhea's daughter. Somewhere along the way, he understood she wasn't. Rhea was not sure what exactly revealed the truth to him. Then he had the impression Oriana's family was in the United States and Rhea didn't correct that impression. Later, she told him everything. As she opened up to him about her plight and her intentions to return Oriana to her family, Sebastian proved to be a trustworthy ally.

In the cafés of Marseilles, over cups of steaming coffee, with Oriana busily coloring in her coloring book, Rhea shared her deepest fears and concerns with Sebastian. There was no one else, and she was starved for companionship.

It was very tentative at first, saying only, "I need new credentials for Oriana, but I need to be careful."

"I know people who could help," he said.

It was a while longer before she understood he could himself create new IDs for her as well as Oriana. He could do most of the work himself, with just a little input here and there from other digital artists. He had been careful to shield that information from her. She liked that, thinking it was a sign of his discretion and ability to keep a secret.

Rhea didn't say, but he interpreted that there was a man they were trying to avoid. It was another long time before she told him about Gregory, the kidnapping, and their escape from him.

Together, they decided Rhea needed a new identity for herself too. She ended up telling him all she knew about Gregory and how she feared he would find them here in France. Sebastian listened attentively, offering his support without judgment.

Sebastian, a man of many talents, revealed his secrets, his connections, and expertise in digital artistry. When Rhea learned he possessed the skills necessary to create new identities for her and Oriana, she was elated. She had grown to trust him. His skill set would prove invaluable for their journey to the United States. With just a few discreet interactions with trusted colleagues, he could ensure that they would have a safe passage.

While they waited and planned, their friendship blossomed. They explored the vibrant streets of Marseilles together, finding solace in each other's company. Although Sebastian never pried into her past or forced her to divulge more than she was comfortable with, his silent presence offered a sense of security she had longed for.

She discovered Sebastian had his own reasons for embracing a life of solitude. His reticence and avoidance of personal topics hinted at a past filled with pain and loss. Despite the wounds they both carried, their unspoken understanding brought us closer, forming an unbreakable bond.

When the time came for Rhea and Oriana to embark on their journey to the United States, she felt sad, though she was excited to be becoming Rhea Stone officially. She knew she had to leave Sebastian behind, but the memory of his kindness and unwavering support would forever be etched in her heart.

Sebastian understood their departure was necessary, and even reassured Rhea that they would be safer in the United States.

Before parting ways, Sebastian entrusted her with his contact information, his phone number and email address. They decided on a code — her name, Rhea, followed by LA, the initials of her real name. If Oriana ever contacted him, he would tell her everything if she provided the code.

When they were finally ready to leave Marseilles for New York, she felt a pang of loss. She had grown attached to Sebastian and didn't want to leave him. But she knew they would be safer in the United States. Even though she was sad, as they boarded the plane bound for New York, the weight of the past couple of years slowly lifted from her shoulders. She felt a sense of hope and renewal. Maybe it was then she knew somewhere deep down that she would keep Oriana and raise her as her daughter, though she couldn't have put it in words.

Consciously, she was bracing to face the authorities in New York and start reuniting Oriana with her family. That never happened, of course.

When they arrived in New York, the bustling cityscape overwhelmed them. The magnitude of the metropolis was a stark contrast to the simplicity they had known in Marseilles. Rhea knew it would be a good place for them to lose themselves, but she craved a more serene life. She knew that starting a new life in a small town in upstate New York would be a safer option, away from the prying eyes and potential dangers of the city.

As time passed, Oriana grew more attached to her, convinced that Rhea was her mother. The bond between them deepened. Rhea couldn't bear the thought of separating from Oriana. She had become the family Rhea had always longed for. She was the only one who could fill the gap Simon had left behind. Rhea continued her fantasy that Oriana was his daughter. Still, she was shocked when Oriana first asked about her father, thinking she remembered her life in Lisbon, but then realizing that at school in New Falls she was making friends. The other children talked about their fathers and asked about hers. Rhea said nothing. She could separate her fantasies about Simon being Oriana's father from the reality. She would not lie to her, so she said nothing.

More practically, Rhea knew that her troubled past would complicate things if she tried to return her to her family. Her convictions for drug possession and the charge of endangering a child she had babysat would paint her as untrustworthy, raising suspicions about her intentions and causing authorities to believe she had kidnapped Oriana.

She didn't sit down one day and decide not to return Oriana to her family in Lisbon. She made the decision by creating a new life for them and postponing thoughts of the future. And then she told herself it was too late. She resolved to protect Oriana and provide her with the love and stability she deserved.

New Falls seemed like such a safe haven, a small town nestled in the picturesque landscape of upstate New York. It's accepting but not overly nosey community and a slower pace of life offered the anonymity they needed to build a new existence. Oriana was happy with her own room in the new house and the swing in the back garden. Rhea told herself she was giving her a better life than the one she'd had in Lisbon.

Rhea needed to work at a job that wouldn't require extensive background checks. Mallory's shop was a godsend. She even encouraged Rhea's jewelry-making and said she could sell some in the shop. Oriana, now enrolled in the town's elementary school, thrived, surrounded by caring teachers and new friends.

Rhea's determination to provide Oriana with a safe and loving environment never wavered. She worked tirelessly to ensure Oriana had every opportunity to grow and succeed, prioritizing her education and encouraging her talents. She was alarmed at her proficiency in Spanish, but then relaxed. If she remembered Portuguese, it would not be a cause of interest but would be considered evidence of the ease with which she learned languages. Their new life, though built on secrecy, was filled with joy and a sense of belonging, as Rhea watched Oriana blossom into a confident and compassionate young girl, unaffected by the shadows of the past.

Of course, Rhea never forgot the risks she had taken and took precautions in case the truth was discovered. While the decision not to return Oriana to her biological family carried its weight of guilt, Rhea convinced herself it was the best choice for them, for both their safety and happiness.

Oriana

Chapter 51

The message from Garcia was brief. *I have an update. Call me after 9 pm.*

Oriana assumed he must mean when it was after 9 pm in Portugal. She hoped his news was not that he had found Rhea. She found a quiet corner of the office and placed the call as soon after the specified time as she could. That was after 3 pm in Boston.

Garcia's voice crackled with excitement and urgency as he relayed the latest breakthrough in his investigation. Oriana listened intently as Garcia explained that the advanced face recognition technology they employed had identified a striking connection between the photo of the young Gregory she had provided, and a man wanted in Portugal for a kidnapping case that occurred ten years ago. The resemblance was uncanny, suggesting a potential link between Gregory and this unsolved crime.

The man in question had been suspected of abducting a young girl from Lisbon. A camera outside a store had caught an image of his face, which had been filed. Despite extensive efforts by the Portuguese authorities, the case had gone cold, leaving the girl's fate uncertain. Now, with the revelation of Gregory's involvement, a renewed hope had emerged that the truth behind that tragic event might finally be uncovered.

Garcia explained that the man in question had been operating under a different alias, successfully evading capture, and remaining under the radar of law enforcement agencies. However, with the identification made through the face recognition software, a crucial link had now been established, suggesting that the man Oriana called Gregory and the wanted kidnapper are the same person.

Perhaps even more significant was another link, still being investigated, to a man who worked for a child welfare agency. Garcia could not say more at this point but hinted that Gregory's criminal activities might expand far beyond what they had initially imagined. Garcia assured her he would keep her updated.

Oriana had promised to keep the information to herself, only sharing it with Rob. Carmela, when she called a few days later, mentioned nothing about it. But then she rarely talked about Oriana's kidnapping, only about her upcoming visit to see her family.

Oriana waited impatiently for an update from Garcia. She hoped that when Gregory was finally captured, the news would be splashed all over the news outlets. Then Rhea would know it was safe to return from wherever she was hiding. Of course, Rhea never read newspapers or watched television. Hopefully, that had changed.

The news, when it came, was alarming. It revealed Gregory's disturbing involvement in an international child welfare agency with branches in Lisbon, Madrid, and Paris. The verification had been difficult and had taken time, but now Garcia announced, "the man whose photo I submitted is the same man who works for the agency. He has been employed for over twenty years by the philanthropic organization and the photo the agency had on file for him closely matches the photo you found among Rhea's belongings."

"So, Gregory has been working on placing children in foster care for the past twenty years," Oriana said. "Surely he must have needed clearance and monitoring in that position."

"I think they did a background check when he was first interviewed for the job, but probably not after that," Garcia said. His voice was grim. "I suspect he has been exploiting his position to profit from the adoption process, charging families exorbitant sums of money for facilitating adoptions. But so far, we have no proof. Families who had adopted children in this way, paying a lot of money, would not come forward and it will be difficult to separate out the legitimate adoptions from those that involved kidnapping."

"But you are going to try?"

"Oh yes. We will persevere with this. He not only kidnaps children but also manipulates the system and preys on vulnerable families who are desperate to provide a loving home for a child in need."

Oriana gasped in horror.

"We can't prove that. Not yet," Garcia said, his tone grim. "We are still searching for the house in the picture you sent me. It is possible the house is still being used as a place to keep the kidnapped child. But in twenty years he might have moved his operation."

"If you think he works for this agency, can't you find him at work and arrest him?"

"We still need proof. He uses a different name at work. We have investigated the agency's files and so far, there is nothing to cause suspicion. All we have is a face that looks like the one in your photo. But we are watching him. We don't want him to become suspicious. Our best hope is that we can catch him in the act."

"Of course, we want to protect the children under Gregory's influence and bring him to justice before more families fall victim to his exploitation. But our focus has shifted from solely apprehending Gregory to dismantling the entire corrupt operation he has established within the child welfare agency. We need to discover if he works alone or if others are involved."

"We are attempting to interview parents who took in foster children through the agency, or who adopted children. Maybe one of them will reveal paying a large sum of money, or maybe the parents who did are nowhere to be found in the records of the agency. Or we may find agency employees who turned a blind eye to Gregory's illicit activities. If we're lucky, they will talk."

Oriana was preoccupied by the news from Garcia. She wanted to hurry along the investigation but realized there was nothing she could do. It was frustrating. She checked her phone constantly, hoping for updates from Garcia.

On her way home from work a few days later, she promised herself she would relax, try to unwind. Rob would be home a little later and they would talk about something else, maybe watch a movie. He had said she had done everything she could, and now she needed to wait for Garcia to do his job. She would try to follow Rob's advice.

As she threw off her shoes and settled down on her couch, with a thankful sigh, her phone rang. It was Garcia. He assured her that the man who worked for the child welfare agency was being watched around the clock. He wasn't going anywhere without the police knowing. "He can't travel out of the country. We have also put a tap on his phone at the agency."

"Are you sure he is Gregory?" Oriana asked, fear gnawing at her insides.

"I believe he is, but we still don't have enough proof to arrest him. Your ... mother, Rhea, could really help her case if she could come forward and identify him," Garcia said.

"Could it mean she would be exonerated?" Oriana asked.

"I believe so."

"I wish I could ask her, but I don't know how to find her. If she contacts me, I will do everything I can to persuade her to come forward," Oriana promised.

Chapter 52

Oriana felt helpless and frustrated at not being able to find Rhea. If only Rhea would check in with her and leave a number or some other way for Oriana to reach her. She could identify Gregory and perhaps play a major role in capturing him. There would no longer be a need to hide. She would be exonerated.

Thanks to Sebastian, Oriana believed Rhea was using the alias Harriet Ingersoll, but a search of that name had led nowhere. If Rhea was sticking to her old habits, it meant she didn't have a cell phone, didn't have any online accounts, and probably didn't even read newspapers.

"What places would she avoid?" Rob asked. "At least there might be places you could rule out."

"Obviously she is not in New Falls or Lakeview. She is no longer in this area. I'm sure of that. She wouldn't want to risk being recognized. Maybe that means she is no longer in New York."

"Would she have gone to a city—New York City — or another big city where she could more easily be anonymous?"

"She doesn't like cities, finds them too noisy and crowded. Remember how she refused to visit us in Boston?"

"She could have gone to Seattle. In her old life as Lulu, she lived there."

"That would be a reason to stay away. She doesn't want to be recognized. Oh, it's so frustrating," Oriana sighed. "She could be anywhere."

"Could she have left the country?" Rob asked.

"No. That would mean showing a passport. If she ever had a passport under the name of Harriet Ingersoll, it would be out of date now, assuming she did nothing to update it since Sebastian created it. And I imagine she would want to avoid using her identity as Harriet Ingersoll unless absolutely necessary."

Oriana brightened. "Yes, that's something. She hasn't left the country. She probably needs to earn some money. I can't imagine she took much extra cash with her. She might try to get a job where she doesn't have to file taxes—again wanting to fly under the radar."

Oriana snapped her fingers. "Her jewelry-making. She might continue doing that and might try to sell it. She would need to buy supplies."

"I don't see how that helps in finding her."

"I have an idea. It may be a waste of time, but there is nothing else. Rhea used to buy a magazine about jewelry-making. It's called *Stringing Along*. She said she would get ideas from it about designs. There would be ads for sales of beads and other materials. She sometimes ordered supplies in bulk from them or from a merchant who advertised on their pages."

"How would that help?" Rob asked. "Do you think she had an account with them?"

"I don't know. That is another question. How did she pay them? But she wouldn't use an account with the name Rhea Stone now. That's not what I was thinking."

"I remember there was a section with personal ads and messages at the back — people offering their services or wanting to exchange design ideas. That sort of thing. She would read the ads sometimes."

"I could take out an ad. She may never read those ads, may not even have access to the magazine. But if she does and I make it large and unusual enough, she might see it and respond. It's not much, but it's all I've got. Traditional searches are not yielding any results. It's time to think outside the box."

Oriana was already searching for information about the magazine online. "Here it is. It is a magazine with ideas for crafting designs using wooden beads and metal."

Oriana clicked on a link for placing ads. "They are providing a choice—personal or commercial ads. This is perfect. It might just work."

Oriana made many changes to the message before she pronounced herself satisfied.

Mom, Rhea, Harriet, or Lulu, please respond. Your knowledge is needed to place G where it belongs. The reward for helping will free you to live the life you want. Ori-Mar.

She read the message out to Rob. "Is it too weird? Too cryptic?"

"It is weird, but I like the use of all Rhea's names. That should get her attention, as well as the abbreviation of your two names. And no one else will make any sense of it. You may get some oddball responses, but Gregory will not be reading it."

"Rhea may not read it, but I can think of nothing better right now."

Oriana tapped in her credit card number to pay for the ad and hit send. "Well, it's done. Now we wait," she said with a sigh. "We might have to wait a while—weeks, even months, until the next issue appears on newsstands. There is an online version, and the ad will appear on it almost instantly, but I don't expect Rhea to read that. I don't even think she knows how to use a computer."

"Even though Rhea stayed away from newspapers and television news, now that she is hiding, she might search for news about Gregory and the kidnapping. She might want to search to see if there are any reports of her disappearance," Rob said.

"*The New Falls Gazette*—she might read it for local news," Oriana said.

"It's a small local paper, not available once you get away from the area," Rob pointed out. "But a larger local paper might be more widely available."

Oriana pondered Rob's suggestion and explored the idea further. She conducted an online search for larger local newspapers that covered the broader region beyond New Falls. After some digging, she found a newspaper called *The Metropolitan Herald,* known for its extensive coverage of various cities and towns in the vicinity.

Excited by the possibility, Oriana placed the ad she had composed in the personal ads section of *The Metropolitan Herald.* She knew it was a long shot, but she hoped that Rhea might have resorted to reading such newspapers in her quest for information while staying hidden. The ad in *The Metropolitan Herald* would appear much sooner than the ad in the craft magazine.

But weeks passed with no contact from Rhea. Finally, the next issue of *Stringing Along* was published. Oriana anxiously waited to see if Rhea would respond to her ad. She monitored the magazine's online platform as well, in case Rhea had somehow gained access to the internet.

It was late September, and Oriana had almost given up. It had been a slim chance that Rhea would find a copy of *Stringing Along* or would even be interested in reading it. She only hoped that Garcia would accumulate enough evidence to arrest Gregory.

Chapter 53

It had been an uneventful day at work and Oriana was preparing dinner at home when her phone rang. Hoping it wasn't Rob to say he would be late, she hardly looked at the caller ID, which displayed an unfamiliar number. She had accepted the call before she realized it might be Gregory or someone working for him with another unpleasant message.

Her heart pounding in her chest, she held the phone to her ear and didn't speak.

"Hello?" The voice on the other end was soft and hesitant, but undeniably familiar. "Oriana... it's me, Rhea."

Tears welled up in Oriana's eyes as she realizes her mother was finally reaching out to her after all this time. She struggled to compose herself, overwhelmed by a flood of emotions. "Rhea, is it really you? Are you safe?"

There was a slight pause before Rhea responded. "Yes, Oriana, I'm safe. I've been hiding, trying to keep one step ahead of Gregory. I saw your ad in the magazine. It was you, wasn't it? I knew it had to be from you. I've missed you so much."

Oriana's voice trembled with a mix of relief and longing. "Oh, Mom, I've missed you too. I want you to know that I believe in your innocence. We can prove it together, but first, I need to make sure you're safe. Where are you?"

Rhea hesitated for a moment before saying, "It's better if I don't reveal my exact location over the phone, but I'm far away from New Falls and taking every precaution to remain hidden. Of course, I trust you, but we must proceed with caution."

"I understand. We'll take steps to ensure your safety. I am in touch with the detective in Portugal who worked on the case. He has been working tirelessly to gather evidence against Gregory. He believes he has found him. We can clear your name and bring him to justice, but the evidence you could provide would make the difference."

Rhea's voice was gentle as she responded. "Thank you, Oriana. I never wanted you to go through any of this. I'll do whatever it takes to help you, but please promise me you'll be careful. Gregory is dangerous."

"I promise, Mom. We'll be careful and strategic. Together, we'll put an end to this nightmare. You won't have to live in fear anymore, but your cooperation with the Portuguese police is crucial. If you talk to Garcia and tell him what you know, you could help in Gregory's capture. You could identify him. I found that photo you took of him. If you help to put him behind bars you would be exonerated, and Gregory would be locked up and unable to hurt anyone. You could do it on the phone and remain hidden. Call Garcia," Oriana pleaded.

When Rhea hesitated, Oriana continued, emphasizing the importance of Rhea's cooperation in bringing Gregory to justice. "I understand the risks involved in reaching out to Detective Garcia directly, but it is very important to show you will cooperate. I believe it is a crucial step also in ensuring our safety by providing the evidence needed to exonerate you from all blame."

When Rhea remained silent, Oriana continued, "Please believe me. Detective Garcia is the key to exposing Gregory's crimes. He's been tirelessly working on the case and gathering evidence against him. If you speak with him, tell him everything you know. It could be the breakthrough we need to capture Gregory and ensure our safety."

Rhea finally spoke, her voice high and uncertain. "But Oriana, I've been hiding for so long. I'm afraid of what might happen if I make contact. What if Gregory finds out? What if he has contacts within the police department?"

Oriana took a deep breath, her determination unwavering. "Rhea, I understand your fear, but we can't let fear control our lives any longer. With Detective Garcia's involvement, we can ensure that your identity remains protected. He has the resources and expertise to keep you safe. We need to trust in his ability to handle this situation. I have his private cell phone number. I have been communicating with him that way. I really believe it is safe."

After a moment of silence, Rhea's spoke again. This time, her voice was strong and clear. "You're right, Oriana. I can't let fear dictate my actions. I've lived too long in fear. It's time to end it. I'll reach out to Detective Garcia on the phone."

Oriana quickly provided Garcia's number and offered to send him a message, letting him know to expect her call. "I will tell him to expect your call after ten pm tonight." She hesitated. "That is Portuguese time. You need to subtract five or six hours or even seven, depending on where you are in the United States."

She badly wanted to know where Rhea was, but didn't want to pressure her to reveal her whereabouts.

Rhea simply said, "I will call tonight."

She also didn't say that when Gregory was prosecuted, Rhea's physical presence would probably be required. One step at a time. She wasn't sure how Garcia would handle information-gathering over the phone. Rhea was probably calling from a public phone unless she had become more enterprising and bought a cell phone. Did she even know about those?

"Mom, you know you could buy a prepaid cell phone. It can't be traced to you. You could call Garcia and ask him to call you back. Or you could give me the number and I could give it to him."

"I've heard of those," Rhea said. "I might do that."

Oriana laughed. This was progress.

"I promise I will be in touch again soon," Rhea said, before hanging up.

Oriana immediately called Garcia's private cell phone and left him a message to expect Rhea's call after ten pm. "She is reluctant to reveal her location but will talk to you on the phone. It's the best I could do."

Garcia responded shortly afterwards with, "excellent work. We are closing in."

Rhea, true to her word, contacted Detective Garcia, and reported the next day to Oriana that in the lengthy phone call with Garcia, she shared everything she knew about Gregory. When Rhea called Oriana the next day, her voice was light and triumphant. "He said I had provided crucial details about the house in Portugal where Gregory kept us captive. His men are watching Gregory at his place of work, and they will arrest him sometime today."

Rhea added, a note of wonder in her voice, "I never thought this day would come."

"Rob and I can go and get you, wherever you are, and bring you home," Oriana said.

"I want to wait until I get the word from Garcia that Gregory is behind bars. Then I will return home to New Falls. And we will have a long talk then. I promise you that. I will tell you everything."

Oriana had to be content with that.

Chapter 54

It turned out Gregory had been working alone on the child abductions, but he sometimes used unsuspecting women like Lulu had been, to lure the child. Many of the women were tourists in France, Spain, and Portugal, traveling alone and delighted to have an attractive man who knew those countries drive them around on a sightseeing trip.

The receivers of the abducted children were couples who had approached the agency where Gregory worked. They were willing to be foster parents but were desperate to adopt. Gregory had been good at deciphering who was willing to pay for a private adoption without questioning the details. The couples believed they were signing official adoption papers drafted by another agency Gregory represented. He led them to believe that the other agency was a separate service, and he would get into trouble at his job if they knew he was representing another agency. The families remained silent.

Much of this Garcia discovered when a search warrant yielded records kept in Gregory's office. In a file at the back of his desk were details of families' names, addresses, phone numbers, and money paid in euros. At the bottom of the page there was typically a single name and an age with a question mark after it, as well as a location such as Plaza de la Reya, Salamanca. Sometimes a female name was entered in parentheses, never the same name twice.

"How arrogant to keep the records at his place of work," Oriana said in astonishment when she heard. She was hungry for details but Garcia, after letting her and Rhea know Garcia was in custody, said he could not share more details of the police investigation, but could say Gregory was wanted for other crimes where he had accomplices. It would all take months, but Rhea's official written testimony would be required, though Garcia believed it was no longer necessary for

Gregory's conviction. The records in his office provided abundant proof.

Oriana could piece together enough information to gather that the people Gregory had listed in his records were contacted and admitted to the private adoptions. Photos of their son or daughter taken shortly after the adoption were matched with those of missing children over the years in several countries, mostly in northern Spain, southwestern regions of France and Portugal. The families who adopted generally lived in other countries, in Scandinavia, Germany, the United States, even a couple in Australia.

Rhea returned home to New Falls on the bus and when Oriana arrived on the following Saturday, she had been back several days. Oriana rang the front doorbell as she usually did, before using her key to open the door. Rhea appeared in the hallway, standing tentatively in the doorway to the kitchen.

Oriana hurried towards her and hugged her tightly. "It's so good to have you back."

"I'm so sorry for all of it," Rhea gasped. She was wearing one of her usual long dresses with flower patterns in turquoise and pink, but her hair was different. It was now a light brown instead of gray and styled attractively.

"Your hair. I like it."

Rhea patted her hair, pleased. "I got it done yesterday. My time as Harriet taught me to be flexible. While I don't want red hair, I decided I no long want gray hair either. I may update my clothes, too."

"You seem more relaxed than I've ever known you. What a burden you carried all these years."

They sat at the kitchen table and talked for hours. Oriana had made the right decision to come alone, without Rob. He had insisted, and she was glad she did.

Rhea was amazed to learn of Oriana's visit to Rogersville and her meeting with Emily, and Simon's parents, and even more amazed to learn that her old friend Alice had married Simon's brother Matthew.

"They would all love to see you and talk to you. Even Mrs. Johnson, your old teacher."

Rhea gazed at her, a faraway look in her eyes. "I've been so alone all this time. Of course, I had you, but I had lost my past."

"But you haven't. It's all there. Of course, they will all discover I lied to them, but so be it."

"Your family—the Taglias — what do they think?"

"They are overjoyed that Gregory has been captured. They are thankful to you for taking care of me."

"They must be angry that I kept you from them all these years," Rhea sighed.

"I think they understand why. But I will see them next week. I am going for a brief visit. Then I will know for sure how they feel. Maybe you can even meet them sometime."

Rhea shook her head distractedly. "That might be bizarre. But Garcia would be pleased if I went to Lisbon to provide testimony against Gregory."

"Perhaps you and I can go together."

Rhea made no comment.

"When you are ready, you might want to meet Matthew and Alice."

"I still need a little time to recover. I went to see Mallory at the shop, and I had to explain things to her. She is glad to have me back working at the shop, but now that I don't have to be in hiding any more, I am ready to explore other options. I might even get a cell phone and a computer."

"Wonderful."

"You know, I was always so scared to have my name on file anywhere. I lived in the shadows all these years."

"Do you want to stop being Rhea Stone and go back to being Lulu Ackerly?"

Rhea hesitated. "Would it be strange to be both? People in New Falls know me as Rhea. I might remain Rhea to them. But people in Idaho only know Lulu."

"I think it would be fine to do it that way. I also think it would be a good thing to build up your identity as Lulu—get a checking account, a credit card, a cell phone using your identity as Lulu. Renew your passport. Anything official should be Lulu, because if you do those things as Rhea, it probably would be considered as fraud or whatever the proper term is."

Chapter 55

It was October and time for Oriana's visit to Portugal. She was met at the airport by Carmela and Manuel. They both hugged her excitedly. Manual had overcome his shyness. They had exchanged texts and emails in the past months as Oriana's Portuguese had rapidly improved. Now they only spoke to her in Portuguese. They asked about Rob but were clearly delighted to have her visit alone.

The story of Gregory's arrest was big news, as was the daring escape of Rhea with the young Maria Taglia. Only Rhea's name had not been released by the police. The Taglias regarded Rhea as a heroine who had saved Maria.

Oriana listened, astonished. She hadn't expected this. They believed Rhea had kept the secret out of fear that Gregory would hurt their Maria even when she was an adult. Obviously, they hadn't learned of Rhea's fears of being accused of being a kidnapper.

They wanted to hear about Oriana's search for Rhea and the story Rhea had told her about how astonished she was the day she was kidnapped when Gregory approached little Maria and her Bobbsie doll.

"Yes, you always played with that doll. You took it everywhere," Maria's mother said tearfully.

Oriana told the story of the escape in the boat to France and hiding from Gregory. She didn't say that she had started calling Rhea Mama then, or that she refused to go into the police station in Biarritz by herself. During one of their long talks, Rhea described how the young Oriana, who she had called Mimi, refused to leave her and how she couldn't bear to walk away and leave the young Oriana alone.

"Rhea might have to come to Lisbon to see Garcia and make a formal statement. She might have to come for the trial," Oriana said.

"She must come and see us," Oriana's mother said. Her father nodded vigorously in agreement.

"I think she fears you will be angry with her for hiding the truth from me for so long and for keeping us apart," Oriana said.

"We understand she was afraid and tried to protect you," her parents protested.

Oriana felt a burst of love for their generous and forgiving spirit. "I will tell her," she promised. "And if she comes, I will come too."

It seemed surreal, but it was what she needed, to weave together her two families.

Early on Sunday morning, they all drove to the countryside to visit Maria's grandparents and various cousins, including the cousin, Anna, who was her childhood friend. Oriana didn't remember her, but had been told that they used to play together. Anna was almost two years older than Maria, and on the day she was kidnapped, her mother thought the two children were playing together. Anna hugged her tearfully and explained she had gone home, two blocks away, to bring back a toy. When she returned a few minutes later, she couldn't find Maria. She had been blamed and had suffered years of guilt for having abandoned her young cousin. They promised to stay in touch.

By the end of the visit, Oriana felt a sense of belonging she hadn't felt up till now. Things felt familiar somehow. She had been speaking and listening to Portuguese only over the past five days, except for when she talked on the phone to Rob and to Rhea. She was excited that she understood almost everything she heard. When she missed words or meanings, they good-humoredly explained.

She met Garcia once. He thanked her for her help and assured her yet again that Rhea would suffer no legal consequences. "I can only speak about my investigation here in Portugal. Since she has been using a false identity in the United States, there may be some problems related to that for her to tackle there," he said soberly.

"She is consulting a lawyer," Oriana said.

This was true, to Oriana's great relief. Now that Rhea knew she was safe, she was agreeable to reclaiming her identity as Lulu and had set up an appointment with the lawyer Rob had found for Oriana.

Oriana had located copies of her birth certificate in Lisbon so that she could apply for a passport as Maria Taglia. But it was complicated as she had married Rob using the name of Oriana Stone, using a birth certificate that stated she had been born in Framingham, Massachusetts. The lawyer was straightening out the legalities of the marriage certificate. He had advised her not to change her education or work record, explaining that since she was continuing to use Oriana as her first name, it was legitimate.

His preliminary opinion about Rhea's legal status was that it was less complicated, since Rhea had kept under the radar. She hadn't bought property or filed taxes as Rhea Stone. She had only used the Rhea Stone passport once, when she and Oriana had returned from Europe twenty years ago. There had been no crime committed using the false identity. His advice so far was that she reclaim her identity as Lulu Ackerly. Again, there was nothing to stop her using the name Rhea for work purposes or among friends.

Oriana left Lisbon with promises to return for a visit soon. On the flight back, she felt a sense of peace she hadn't experienced since that first morning in Lisbon when she had seen her photo in the newspaper. The two parts of her life were weaving together.

There was one more thing that needed to happen.

Chapter 56

"You need to reach out to Alice and Matthew."

Rhea looked at Oriana uncertainly.

"That seems like the easiest first step since they are in New York," Oriana continued. "Though perhaps a better first step would be to contact your sister. Yes, that would be better. She is your family. She has a right to know first."

"She might hate me."

"Even the Taglias don't hate you. You should go there, to Rogersville, see Emily and then visit the Lovells. I will go with you if you like. They have more reason to hate me. I'm the one who lied to them, hid what I knew from them."

"I'd like to see Emily," Rhea said quietly.

"Call her," Oriana commanded. "The news of Gregory's arrest and his kidnapping operation is spreading. Your name has been kept out of the reports so far, but it may seep in. You don't want Emily or the Lovells to find out that way.

Rhea called Emily. It was a long conversation. Emily wanted her to visit. Rhea promised she would.

"I think you should be the one to call James Lovell," Rhea announced. "You saw him and Margaret recently. They haven't seen me for twenty-two years."

"I will, if you call Alice," Oriana announced.

Rhea agreed, and Oriana picked up the phone. She stumbled over her words as she tried to explain to James that Rhea was Lulu and the woman she had believed was her mother. There was a silence at James' end of the line, so that Oriana thought he had hung up. He then announced that he was glad Lulu had done something so helpful. Oriana didn't mention Lulu's use of the cabin. That could come later. Rhea could decide what she wanted to say.

Rhea's conversation with Alice was more jubilant. Again, no mention was made of the cabin. Alice seemed to believe Oriana had contacted the Lovells because she had discovered the connection between Lulu and Simon and was trying to find Lulu. Arrangements were made to get together.

Rhea was already looking more relaxed. She was friendly with Rob. Her suspicious demeanor had disappeared, and Oriana noted with interest that they chatted more easily. Rhea didn't seem so eccentric anymore, but more open, more modern somehow. Her secrets had taken their toll, but she was freer now that she no longer needed to hide herself away. She was blossoming into a happy and carefree woman.

And Oriana realized with a delighted wonder that she now had lots of relatives. There were the Taglias of course, who were blood relatives, but the Lovells claimed her as family, as well as Emily who insisted she always wanted a niece.

Rhea had not met the Taglias yet, but Oriana expected that would happen too.

END

From the Author

Readers, thank you for reading my book. You can find me on Facebook.

(https://www.facebook.com/writingingisfun)

and Instagram .

(https://www.instagram.com/bailielawsonauthor)

Or join my seasonal mailing list for book news and more.

bailielawson.wordpress.com/contact/

Reader reviews and recommendations are a big boost to authors.

If you enjoyed my books, please tell your friends in person and online.

Thank you.

Also available by Bailie Lawson

Finding Juniper, Fanfare, The Imaginary Husband,
Uncovering Julien's Past, Una's Journey,
A Fortune in the Roof,
Glued Back Stronger, The Other Breda Gulley,
The Jealousy Factor, and Who Is Gigi?

The Lia Bracken series. (can be read in any order)
Well-Travelled Ancient Artifacts (Book 1)
Pixie Dust: Enchantment and Its Consequences (Book 2)
The Ravensworth Affair (Book 3)

About the Author

Bailie Lawson was born in Ireland and has lived in New York and the Northeastern United States. Before becoming a full-time author, she had a career in psychology as a psychotherapist and professor.

Following is an excerpt from
The Jealousy Factor

NOW
Chapter 1

I was looking at the painting created by my lover's murderer. She had captured his profile so perfectly. I gazed in horrified fascination, pulled into the painting, reminded of a different time and place.

It was him. It had to be. The likeness was uncanny. But how had this painting—these paintings — made their way here to this tiny gallery in this small town in Massachusetts?

Was she here? I looked around fearfully. My heart pounded sickeningly in my chest.

The gallery was quiet, almost empty. Serene. In the front there was the young pony-tailed attendant behind a desk. I could see an elderly couple wandering around in the next room. And my husband, of course, who had gone off to look at a large painting a few feet from me.

I stared at the printed information on the card next to the painting. The artist's name was printed in clear bold letters. It said *Leigh Nevie, a local artist.*

It could be a different Leigh Nevie, of course–another artist with the same name. But as I looked at the painting of the man with the blue eyes and troubled face, it reminded me too much of him. It was her — his murderer. And she could be close by. She wasn't behind bars anymore. And she was audaciously painting pictures of him. The painting was called *Indecision.*

I felt a surge of anger. How dare she? Why draw attention to herself in this way? Why not skulk away and hide in the shadows?

Erik called softly. I composed my face carefully and walked over to where he was standing, gazing with rapt attention. The large painting hit me viscerally in the stomach. I recoiled. Ian's eyes, his face, smiled at me from the canvas, larger than life.

"Interesting, isn't it?" Erik commented. "I like the unusual use of colors. These are by far the best paintings here."

He left me standing there, unable to tear my eyes away as he walked over to the desk and picked up a card with more information about Leigh Nevie.

"Yes, she's remarkable," I heard the pony-tailed man say. He had seemed oblivious, but must have heard Erik's comments. "In fact, there will be a reception on Friday at five to meet the artists. You might want to attend. Leigh will be here."

I jerked my head around. "She'll be here? In person?"

My surprise seemed to be interpreted as delight at the prospect of meeting the artist.

"We'll try to make it," Erik said.

Inwardly, I groaned. This is not what I wanted to happen. I never wanted to see that woman again. It had been eight years since I had been back in the United States, twelve years since Ian's murder. She had been arrested fairly quickly, and I had already left New York by the time her trial commenced. Later, I heard she had been found guilty. I couldn't stop myself from checking up on the news about the trial. I also knew she had been released on a technicality after nine years. After that, she had disappeared from the news reports.

So, what was she doing now in this small university town of Alcott exhibiting paintings—startling likenesses of the man she had killed?

As Friday approached, I thought of ways to distract Erik. But there was nothing scheduled at the university, and he didn't want to take a long sightseeing drive anywhere. He wanted to work on the following week's lectures on Friday morning. He reminded me we had "things to do" the rest of the weekend, and that the gallery reception would be the perfect thing for late in the day on Friday. We had nothing else scheduled then.

I knew I couldn't get out of it without a long explanation and an even longer discussion. And I didn't want to drag up the past, not even with Erik. He was kind and understanding, and I wasn't in the habit of hiding things from him. But I really wanted to leave that part of my life in the past. I didn't want to answer questions about it, however kind and well-meaning.

I had said nothing to Erik about knowing Leigh, or that the paintings were of Ian. Of course, I could have told him and explained why I didn't want to go to the reception and why I didn't want to meet Leigh. He would have understood, and we would not have gone. But he would have been curious, and I would have felt compelled to explain. And I was unsettled. My mind flooded with Ian's face, memories floating back of things he'd said, things we'd done. I didn't want to talk about it.

Years ago, when we were getting to know each other, I had told Erik about a painful relationship in my past. He knew that a former boyfriend, Ian Redman, had been poisoned onstage. I had talked as if there were two different men and that the painful relationship had not been with Ian. The case had been all over the news for quite a while. I gave the impression that Ian and I had dated long before his dramatic onstage poisoning.

I couldn't say why I had played down the relationship. Maybe because the memory of it still hurt when I met Erik. Maybe because Ian's death was still so shocking. Probably it was both, and I wanted to escape into an entirely new life and a healthier relationship. My time with Ian had been exciting, but obsessive and toxic. I wanted to leave all that behind and live in Europe with Erik.

Now, as I got ready to go to the gallery reception, I hoped my appearance had changed sufficiently over the years, so that Leigh wouldn't recognize me.

Not that much, though. I am still recognizable.

Of course, I looked older. My hair was-short and stylish, not long and wild. My clothes were more expensive, classic rather than bohemian, less experimental. I wore more muted colors now. Maybe she wouldn't recognize me.

Leigh and I had never seen much of each other in those days, and why would she remember me out of all the women Ian knew all those years ago? There had been so many women. I realize that now. She had never paid me much attention. I hadn't mattered to her back then. I wouldn't have stood out.

Of course, I didn't know any of that at the beginning. I didn't know about the other women or his history of being unfaithful, or his belief in open relationships. And I didn't know about Leigh. I discovered all that and other unsavory details about his life gradually as our relationship unraveled. After I was already hooked.

Chapter 2

I was resigned by the time Friday arrived. I contemplated wearing sunglasses in an attempt to disguise myself and decided it would look odd and draw the very attention I wanted to avoid. Who would wear sunglasses indoors at an art exhibition? I also decided to forego the large straw hat I held uncertainly in my hands. After the gallery reception, we had dinner plans with colleagues of Erik from the university and a large straw hat would look odd.

There was a crowd in the gallery when we arrived. That was promising. We could get lost in the crowd. Correction-*I* could get lost. Erik, with his mane of silver-gray hair and his height, always stood out. And he was friendly and charming. He was already talking to a group of what appeared to be students. I edged further away from him.

Then she was there, standing next to the pony-tailed guy, whose nametag said Osborn. She had a nametag too, but I didn't need to read it. She hadn't changed.

It shocked me she looked the same. Oh, maybe her face had aged a little, but she was still beautiful. She had the same long wavy dark hair now streaked with gray, looked effortlessly elegant, even in the shapeless black smock and leggings.

And she was staring directly at me, a puzzled look on her face.

Does she know exactly who I am or is she struggling to remember?

I looked away, tried to move, but the crowd blocked me. When I looked back, she was still looking at me, but now she looked annoyed, even angry. That was confusing. I'm the one who should be angry. She had no right.

Then Erik was at her side, charming, introducing himself, saying he loved her paintings. I tried again to disappear into the crowd. Too late. Erik was calling me, and as he called my name, I could see the flash of recognition on her face.

He was saying, "this is my wife, Rachel". He reached out an arm as if to pull me closer, even though I was too far away. I found myself jostled closer by someone behind me.

Erik was saying, "we both really like your work."

"Rachel!" Leigh said, looking at me wide-eyed. Without looking at Erik, she said, "we know each other. We used to know each other."

Her expression was hard to read. Her eyes were sad, but also questioning, and puzzled. She studied my face as if trying to read something in it.

I had to say something. "Yes, of course, in New York, all those years ago. And yes, your work is wonderful."

"It haunts me still. I had to paint him. Not that it helps, but I feel compelled. Of course, I didn't do it. But someone did." Her voice had dropped. She was almost whispering, leaning towards me. Erik was straining to hear and looking puzzled.

As if remembering that he was standing there too, she raised her voice and looked at him.

"Our friend died. He is the one in my paintings."

Erik nodded and remained silent. I could tell he was still puzzled, but he knew when to listen. That was one of the things I liked about him.

We talked inconsequentially for a little after that. A colleague of Erik's from the university appeared and monopolized him. The crowd had thinned out. I wanted to leave but saw that Erik was deeply engrossed in his conversation.

I was drawn to the small painting again, the one she had called *Indecision,* and stood studying it sadly. She had captured so perfectly his facial expression. It brought back such memories.

Suddenly, she was standing next to me again.

"He did love you, you know."

I was surprised—surprised she was saying it, surprised she even knew. And of course, I was surprised she remembered me and wanted to talk to me. My animosity towards her was evaporating.

I sighed. "We loved each other once. But then there was all the craziness."

I didn't add *you didn't help with that*, but I was thinking it.

"I didn't do it. You must believe me."

"You were released. That's what I heard. I was out of the country by then."

Trying to forget, to block it all out.

"I served nine long years before the appeal overturned my conviction. It was dreadful. But the worst thing was, I knew the actual murderer was out there still. I want to track that person down. I owe that to him."

I looked at her then. "There was evidence that implicated you, wasn't there?"

"It was circumstantial. That's what my lawyers said."

Her eyes were imploring as she repeated, "I didn't do it."

She seemed so earnest, so sincere. Years ago, I had accepted that she had done it. Her conviction had helped me move on. Now, looking at her imploring eyes, I didn't know what to believe.

"Do you suspect someone?" I asked, for want to something to say. I wasn't sure I wanted to hear the answer.

"There are a few people–all women. I must admit you were on the list for a long time, but I've decided it couldn't be you."

"How can you be sure?" I asked and then was sorry when her face changed, and she looked at me with fear.

"I mean, what is the logical process you are following? On what basis are you suspecting people and ruling out others?"

"I always thought you were sane, even if volatile. You wore your heart on your sleeve. It was painful to watch sometimes. I knew so much about what he was doing. He was so flawed, but I knew he loved you and was terrified of loving you. But you were sane. There were others who were not - crazy women. There was that part of him that was so drawn to the crazy, wild, and destructive."

I nodded in agreement as fragments of submerged memories resurfaced, still painful, after twelve years. Her calm, even voice was oddly familiar. That too had not changed.

"It surprised me when you were convicted," I admitted. "You had seemed so remote, so emotionally in control, so incredibly sophisticated, not jealous and possessive like me. You seemed so comfortable with open relationships. I didn't think you cared enough to kill him."

I surprised myself with my openness. When had I processed all this? In the past, I would never have revealed my true opinion of her to her face. But then, had we ever had such an emotionally honest conversation? I knew we hadn't.

"I loved him in my own way, but you are right that I wasn't jealous. I knew I would never lose him, that we would always be friends. We had known each other for such a long time, since we were kids in Boston."

I stared at her, remembering how I was surprised when I heard she was convicted, but then had accepted it. They had proof and there were no other suspects as far as I knew. Her arrest had provided closure. I had wanted to get far away by then. To forget everything. To forget I ever knew him.

Now she looked at me imploringly, her eyes sad. "I really didn't do it. It haunts me. I want to find out who did. Will you help me?"

Milton Keynes UK
Ingram Content Group UK Ltd.
UKHW010159230823
427286UK00001B/79